KAT DRUMMOND — BOOK

PART-TIME MONSTER HUNTER

NICHOLAS WOODE-SMITH

1

Copyright © 2019

Kat Drummond

All rights reserved

This is a work of fiction. Any similarity to real persons, living or dead, is coincidental and not intended by the author.

ISBN: 9781690981572

Contents

Chapter 1. Corpses

You should never get used to the smell of rotting corpses. It's bad for your health. They carry all sorts of diseases. Typhoid, cholera, the plague. And even necro-sick. They aren't a pretty sight and, by the Rifts, do they smell. And if you aren't fast enough, they'll take a nice big chunk out of you.

Me? I'm used to the smell of corpses. I spend a lot of time around them. They smell as you'd expect, but I got used to it pretty fast. What I never got used to were their sounds. Corpses never shut up! They're always moaning, groaning, growling and howling. Sometimes, they hiss like a cat, or gurgle like they're trying out some mouthwash (trust me, they aren't). That's the thing about the undead, though - they've got patterns. They're consistent. You find out what type of necro-species or whatchamacallit they are, and then you can understand a lot about them.

If they walk upright, have misty eyes, smell like year-old meat, walk slowly and won't stop groaning, then it's probably a zombie on your hands. If they are hunched, have fangs, blackened skin like ash and red eyes, they're a ghoul. And if they're running around on all fours, covered in debris, quills and scabs – then you're probably not fast enough to run away, 'cause then you've got a gül.

I'm definitely not fast enough to outrun a gül. Lucky for me, I'm not trying to. Also, lucky for me, this gül was as noisy as any other corpse I've faced in my short career, making it easy to find. This was one of the gurgle/hiss variety. It was spitting up a storm, hissing, gurgling and banging its fists on the ground like an angry gorilla. From my hiding spot on the floor above it, I could see the cause of its frustration. A padlocked meat locker. The gül's grotesque elongated fingers were flayed, smearing black-red blood on the already dirty locker.

I shook my head. The monster was hungry.

That's a stupid thing to think. The undead were always hungry! Except for skeletons, of course. They were content...most of the time.

But this gül was particularly hungry. It had been working all night at this locker full of rotting meat to no avail. Only a few scratches and black-red bloodstains on the yellowed white exterior to show for its troubles.

"Probably just got out of a rift," the voice in my head said.

I didn't respond. I was the only one who could hear the voice, but it could only hear me if I spoke aloud. That was not the most prudent thing to do under the circumstances.

"They're very antsy when they just arrive, Kat," the voice continued. "Be careful."

"And they're also very groggy and not used to a human who can defend herself." I wanted to say. Instead, I remained quiet.

I had done this before. Plenty of times before. Avoid the quills. Avoid the claws. Avoid the teeth. Slice a tendon on its back leg to incapacitate it. End it with a clean beheading or stab through the skull. Güls had weak bones. Biproduct of the stretching and deformations.

Yeah, I had done this plenty of times before. I knew the patterns. I had my own. The undead never survived long enough to learn mine.

But despite all the times I'd done this before, my heart still beat like a war-drum.

You can do this, Kat, I told myself.

My short swords' blades caught some light from the street. The steel glinted in the musty dark. They were new blades. Slightly curved. Stainless steel. Cheap. I hoped they would last.

I took a quiet breath.

The gül had mounted the meat-locker and was trying to pull the door off. From the hole in the floor of this dilapidated apartment building, I had a clear drop to the gül's neck. A clean stab. A clean plunge.

I nodded, as if I had just won an argument with myself.

And then I jumped.

I held my twin blades together, facing down. They'd find their mark…

The gül disappeared in a sickly flesh coloured blur. I hit the ground with a thud. A gargling roar filled my ears. I ducked. A clawed hand the size of a tennis racket strafed the air where I had just been. I stabbed behind me from a crouch, hit nothing…

"Sloppy footwork," the voice said.

"Shut up, Treth!" I yelled. No need to be quiet anymore.

I turned just in time to roll away from the gül lunging at me. It had taken a running start and stopped just before battering into the locker. It turned to me and arched its back. Bones and blades protruded from its flesh like a grotesque porcupine. It growled, deep and menacing. Güls were like wild animals. Always trying to intimidate their opponents.

"Trying to scare me off, bub?" I said. I clanged my swords together, sending out a metal ring that seemed to unnerve the undead beast before me. "You ain't scarier than a nightkin and I eat them for breakfast."

"You never eat breakfast," Treth commented.

"It doesn't know that."

"And neither does it understand or care what you are saying."

The gül started to circle, slowly. I took a defensive stance. Off-hand sword in front with my right-hand blade pulled back, ready to strike.

The gül bit the air in front of it with an audible chomp. Drool, filled with its own corrupt blood, pooled below it. I charged, holding my dual-blades in an X across my chest. The gül hissed and jumped towards me, leaping through the air with its rabbit-like hindlegs.

I couldn't help but smirk.

Mid-charge, I dropped to my knees and slid. The underbelly of the beast passed right over me, revealing its outstretched legs. I cut out in a wide arc and was rewarded with a spray of black-red blood. I was glad for my goggles and doctor's mask then. Didn't want to get necro-blood in my mouth.

I stood up. Blood and dirt covered my kneepads. I rubbed some black off my goggles with my sleeve. The gül had collided with the floor. Its hind-legs were limp, held on by thin fleshy tendrils. It was dragging itself towards me, leaving a trail of blood on the decaying hard-wood floors. Its gurgles sounded like a whine. Like a hurt dog crossed with a kettle that really needed to be thrown away.

"Don't underestimate it," Treth, the voice in my head, said.

"I know, I know. I won't make the same mistake that I did with that wandering zom last month."

Treth seemed to grumble. He didn't take my claim seriously.

I walked to the pathetic creature. It slashed towards my legs. Long arms still made it dangerous. I feinted going forward and when it lunged with its one hand, I chopped it off. It howled and then swiped with its other hand. I raised my other sword to block.

Clang and snap.

Shit.

I jumped away just in time, still holding the now half-blade hilt of my off-hand short sword.

"Cheap garbage," I hissed through gritted teeth, sheathing the half-blade. Hopefully, I could sell it for scrap.

"That's what I told you when you bought it on that glowing box," Treth said.

"The computer. I bought it on the computer..."

I stepped back quickly as the gül crawled one-handed to my position, and then continued.

"And I gotta eat. Sorry that no Lady of the Lake has bequeathed me some holy sword like you palis probably got. This is Earth and I'm eating ramen for dinner. We're using $8 swords if they snap or not."

"False economy…"

The gül stopped and tried to swipe again. I jumped up onto the meat locker and then strolled to the other side of the room.

"Didn't know they had economics in Land of the Knightly Things."

'Ava…' Treth grumbled under his disembodied breath. Then spoke properly.

"Put this thing down. It's pathetic to look at."

"Right-o, boss paladin sir."

I walked towards the gül. Its sickly yellow eyes followed me, and it began scratching the air in front of it.

I frowned. It really was pathetic. And yet, it had the ability to do so much harm.

I side-stepped its claw and plunged my sword deep into its skull.

It stopped hissing and gurgling, and its arm collapsed, limp.

Suck and squelch. I withdrew the sword and flicked it, splattering blood and grey skin flakes across the room. I cleaned off the excess blood with a cloth before sheathing. This sword survived its first night. It deserved a little care.

"Another day, another dollar," I said, stretching my arms and legs. That fall really did a number on my knees.

"That all you care about, Kat?"

"Course not," I said, retrieving a sawblade from my bag. "Slaying these things is its own reward, but gotta eat. And gotta get new gear."

I began sawing at the limbs of the gül. The pieces separated easily, if not cleanly, from their host. The bones were brittle and were cut effortlessly. Its blood had stopped flowing instantly after whatever necromantic aura infesting it had been destroyed. It was just the flesh that was difficult to stomach. It pulled apart like wet paper. I resisted gagging and turned my attention away from the discoloured gooey sight.

"Long specimen," I observed, examining the now genuinely lifeless corpse. Its torso stretched around two metres long. It was thin. Its flaky skin hugged close to its brittle skeleton. Güls always relied on speed over brawn.

"I faced beasts like this twice the size in my world."

"Hopefully, I won't have to."

I stood and cracked my back. Segments of the gül's arms and legs had been deposited in plastic bags. I knelt and sawed off its head. That also went in a bag.

"Grotesque work. You should just burn them," Treth said, his voice filled with an all too common tinge of disappointment. I imagined him shaking his head, hands on his hips.

"And miss out on most of my payday? The landlady over yonder is paying me enough for a week's worth of ramen. Half a week if I want stir-fry. The bits are where the money's at."

Treth was probably rolling his invisible eyes round about now.

Every piece of the gül was eventually placed in one of four plastic shopping bags. I hoisted two in each hand and left the room and the stench of rotting beef. I'd have to make sure to remember to report the locker to Sanitation. It was a big necro-risk.

I sighed. Abandoned buildings like this were common in this part of the state of Hope City. They attracted all types of malcontents. Not just rogue sorcerers, but all manner of imps and the undead. They were attracted to the decay. And as the decay attracted them, the area continued to darken as its weyline was corrupted with dark magic.

"Any critiques, Treth?" I asked. He had been unusually quiet during the surgery. I didn't like him spouting criticism when I was in the middle of a fight, but I did value his input. As I had begrudgingly accepted a year before – he was much better at this than I. A lot of what I now knew, I owed to him.

"The slide was flashy," Treth replied, matter of factly.

"Thank you."

"Wasn't a compliment."

I snorted in amusement. The bits in my bags squelched as I mounted the steps and began to descend the concrete stairway. Old flyers, covered in dirt, were stuck to the steps and the walls. They were old "The End is Nigh!" posters. Decades old. Practically artefacts. Of course, they had been wrong, but couldn't blame doomsayers when magical portals were opening up all around, spilling out dragons, nymphs and the gods of human myth.

"So, how would you have fought that?"

Treth took a breath. He loved talking about this.

"I would have come through the doorway. Shield first. Planted it before me, sword pointed straight out by its side. I'd have made an oath to Bel and then shouted taunts at the beast. With its small, twisted mind, the undead would have charged into my kill zone, where I would have thrust with my sword – ending its miserable unlife in one stab."

"There's a problem with me doing that…"

"Not flashy enough?"

"I don't own a shield."

The night air was cool on my face. A gust of wind carried the smell of salt. It was refreshing, if a bit chilly. I hoped that the salty sea smell would overcome the rotting stench of necro-blood and guts covering my clothes. The night was dark. No stars out. Just a lonely streetlight lit the entire street, providing a golden pool on the tarmac. It was quiet. No wonder the landlady from a block away had wanted me to check it out. The noise of a corpse smacking at a fridge was the only thing that would have been heard for hundreds of metres. The wind would have carried the gurgles and inhuman screeches even further.

I put down the squelchy bloody bags and took out my phone.

"Shit," I swore. I had tried to swipe the phone open without taking off my gloves. "Blood all over my damn screen."

"This is why you should use falcons. They're reliable and don't balk at a bit of blood."

"They also can't take apps."

I wiped away the blood with my almost fully bloodied sleeve and took off my glove. My phone wallpaper was some study notes for an upcoming history test. I frowned.

When was the test again?

I hadn't managed to study at all this week. Too much work for too little pay. First, there was that rogue zombie eating someone's trash, then a wight who decided to camp out in someone's treehouse. That wasn't to mention the lesser vampire squirrel that had killed my neighbour's dog.

Yeah, it had been a busy week.

I logged into the MonsterSlayer app on my smartphone and checked the ongoing jobs tab. I selected this particular job and took a photo of the bags and sent it through. A few minutes later, I received a message:

"I can finally get some sleep but didn't need to see that!"

A notification popped up. $50 had been sent to my account. I grinned. That would keep me nice and fed for a little bit. But that wasn't where the money was. I changed to a different app: MonsterMarket.

While eliminating monsters was good and all, it wasn't that rewarding. Any dolt with a blunt instrument could swat an imp. The real money in hunting came from butchering the prey and then selling the parts to alchemists, mages and corporations for a quick buck. Even decades after the Vortex Rift opened and magic came into the world, people were still needing fantastical beasts to dissect.

"Anyone looking for goolie bits?" I said, in a sing song voice, to myself as I selected the search filters, looking for a buyer. "Ugh, Rifts…"

There was a buyer. Looking for a full dismembered gül. They were offering $100 for the body. But…it was

Drakenbane. A top-notch executive level monster hunting agency. And one that I really didn't like.

I quickly checked to see if there were any other eligible buyers. None. I clenched my fist and with my other hand, pressed the sales button. My location was sent to Drakenbane's courier. I really hoped it wasn't Brett…

And it was Brett.

He arrived half an hour later. I had just settled into some studying for my history test on the establishment of the first elf colony in New Zealand, when an armoured car blaring scream metal almost knocked over a corner bin and screeched to a halt in front of me.

"Would you consider him flashy?" Treth asked.

"No," I whispered, as Brett got out of the armoured car. He was the typical agency muscle-head. Arms the size of tree trunks. Black hair in a lengthening buzz cut. Stubble meticulously kept light, like a movie-star or male model. He wore a black Kevlar vest, with combat pads on his shoulders and arms. Slung over his shoulder was a pump-action shotgun. Emblazoned on his dark grey-clad chest was a stylistic symbol of a crimson dragon in flight.

"Oi, Katty!" he called with a grin, immediately lighting a cigarette. I hoped that didn't mean he meant to stay around longer than necessary. The dark was subsiding. He took a drag of the cigarette and then exhaled, generating an acrid smog. I only just stopped myself from coughing.

"Brett," I said, simply, and then indicated to the packets behind me with my thumb. He ignored the gesture, eyeing me up and down. His eyes rested on the hilt of my sword.

"Still using blades, Katty? You aren't going to get anywhere if you don't get a gun."

"Alas, Brett. Easier said than done. I don't have a license and don't have an agency backing me to pull the strings."

Brett took another drag and blew another cloud in my face. "Drakenbane could change that, Katty."

"You know that Drakenbane rejected my application."

Brett snorted derisively. "Ah, right. 'Cause of your hang ups on killing non-undead. Stabbing drakes give you a stomach-ache?"

"Undead are more a threat than some overgrown geckos."

"Tell that to the executives shitting themselves whenever the little shits do fly-bys on their high rises."

I rolled my eyes. That's just what I wanted to tell them. But they paid the bills, even if it was the undead tearing the slums apart.

"So…got my money?" I asked, tapping my foot impatiently. I made sure he heard the tap-tap-tap on the tarmac.

"Relax, Katty." Brett took a final drag and then tossed the still lit cigarette onto the street. He sauntered over to the bags and opened one. A waft must have hit him as his face went white and he recoiled.

"Some rank zombie bits you got there."

"Gül bits."

"What's the difference?"

I sighed. "Zombies are the slaves of necromancers. Ghouls are the slaves of vampires. Güls are feral. They act like wild animals. This one looked like it was straight outta a rift."

"Know it all," Brett chided, picking up the bags and carrying them over to the truck. "Will make fine dragon bait all the same."

"A dragon would never fall for that," Treth laughed. I did not give Brett the benefit of a response. I only asked:

"My money?"

"Sure, sure."

Brett rubbed his hands on his black-camo jeans and took out a wallet. He drew out three blue and red notes. I quickly counted them and was relieved to see that Brett hadn't short-changed me.

"Thanks. Now cheers."

I began running down the street. The sun was rising.

"Hey! Not wanting to hang out?"

"Our relationship is strictly professional, Brett."

I was around the street corner before he could respond.

Chapter 2. Early Riser

The sun was firmly in the sky, flooding the land with a merciful golden tinge when I finally reached my apartment. The vampires would be going into hiding now, along with the rest of the dregs of this magical society.

My apartment building was a small, dingy little place, right in the shadow of a magicorp skyscraper. Its rent had plummeted after repeated wraith sightings. While that normally would be cause for alarm, as wraiths were quite partial to eviscerating the living, I hadn't seen a wraith for the year and a half I had been living here.

I fiddled with the lock to my door, my vision bleary from exhaustion. It was jammed again. There were downsides to cheap rent. I heard mewling on the other side.

"Yes, I'm home, Alex. Just...be...patient."

I fell flat on my face as the door opened under my weight. Alex, my black and white tuxedo cat, came up to me and licked my nose. The cat's sandpaper tongue tickled me, and I couldn't help but chuckle.

"Thanks, Alex."

I lifted myself up and surveyed my apartment. Messy as I had left it. The rubbish bin was overflowing with polystyrene ramen cups, study-notes adorned tables, floor and windowsill, and the curtains hadn't been dusted in a year. I shook my head at my own untidiness.

"First out of these clothes, and then…sleep."

Alex meowed.

I rubbed my head. My eyes were heavy. "How could I forget my favourite little guy?"

I closed my door behind me and shambled further into the apartment to the small kitchen adjoined to the lounge/bedroom. I cracked open a can of cat food and let Alex eat straight out of the can.

I sniffed. I reeked of sweat and blood. I needed a wash. The bathroom thankfully had a shower, but I was too tired for that. Too tired…

My vision blurred, and I swayed. My sword clinked on the coffee table. When did I get to the coffee table? I reached to unbuckle my sword belt and felt nothing.

***

"Kat…Kat?" Treth whispered.

"Let me sleep," I mumbled, eyes closed.

"You're going to get sick, Kat…"

"You're not my mom."

"And you're going to be late for class…"

23

I jumped up with a start. I had been keeled over in my living room. A wet puddle of drool had soaked into the carpet. I quickly checked my smartphone.

Forty minutes till class…and I'd been only asleep for ten minutes.

"Rift-damn Brett."

I brought my hand to my eyes to rub out the sleep but then noticed my sleeves. They were still covered in necro-blood.

"Shit."

I realised *I* was still covered in necro-blood.

"Get dressed. I'll close my eyes."

"Do you even have eyes?"

"You know what I mean."

I let out a small chuckle. Treth, always the chivalrous and innocent knight-paladin.

I peeled off the layers of monster-hunting gear and discarded them in a wash basket. At least I had money to pay for a full purification now over and above a cosmetic clean. Must've picked up some curse in the last few weeks with all the necro-blood that had been touching it. Not to mention the wight incantations! Detergent didn't get out magical stains, so I'd need to splurge on a bit of exorcism.

To replace my currently filthy clothes, I put on some denim jeans and a black t-shirt with the logo of the band *Rage*.

"Always the goth," my friend Trudie would say. She was one to talk! She wore a spiked collar. And *Rage* wasn't goth. It was punk. Big difference.

I made my way to the bathroom to wash my face and put on all manner of chemicals to mask the stench of my late night. I would shower when I got home. The necro-blood didn't touch my skin and I had mistakenly ingested so much of it already I must've become at least a little bit immune.

In the mirror, I was greeted by a girl of nineteen years with dark-chestnut hair tied into a messy bun with a black hair tie, caked in dirt. She had heavy bags under her eyes. They weren't just from a single night of sleeplessness, but a saga of restless nights and hunts.

Done with the necessities of civilised life, I petted Alex and left.

"The buses better be running on time."

"They never are," Treth replied. "You should get a horse."

"With all the money I have, yeah. And I'd much rather be in a bus or car when zombies are roaming around than on horseback."

"Not if it was my master's horse." Treth's voice started sounding distant, happy. He was lost in memory. "Gallant was the finest steed in the duchy. Even wraiths couldn't spook him. My master rode him into battle and never once did he balk or flinch. A brave, wonderful stallion."

Treth's tone saddened. "Haven't seen any like him here."

"We can go to the countryside sometime, Treth. I'm sure there'll be some decent horses out in the farmlands."

I couldn't really tell for sure, but I felt Treth give me an appreciative smile.

The bus was on time, but so was traffic. Just as the bus started moving, with me and one other head-phoned passenger inside, it stopped, and then started again. Bumper to bumper. Probably a damn griffin holding up traffic. If one had made its nest in an intersection, traffic would be at a standstill for hours until the City could decide which agency to hire to eliminate it.

I took out my phone and opened the news.

"Russian MagiPol have detained three sorcerers attempting to tap into the weylines near the Vortex Rift in Siberia."

"Why do they even guard it? The frost wyrms will get anyone strong enough to survive the spark pulses," Treth said.

"They thought they needed to guard it back then and never stopped. Nothing as permanent as a temporary government programme."

I glanced at the next headline: Necromancer Warlords increase hold on Central Africa.

"And nothing they hate more than doing what they are supposed to do."

I closed my phone and the less than stellar news headlines and looked out the window. The sun had risen only slightly more in the minutes that I had been in my apartment, bathing Hope City and the Cape in a magical golden haze. From the bus window, I could clearly see Table Mountain, in all its glory. The flat-topped mountain had a table-cloth of clouds, casting a slight shadow where its rock-grey was not painted gold in the morning light. Rising above the pale grey cloud was an obsidian tower, tinted yellow in the dawn sun. The Titan Citadel.

No matter how bad this city gets, I thought, *that damn mountain makes it all worth it.*

It was just so unfortunate that it was usually closed to the public to allow for pilgrimages to the citadel and the peaks. I was not an acolyte of the Titan under the Mountain, nor one of the mages that kept it asleep, so I had never managed to reach Table Mountain's flat top. The closest I came was my university, constructed over two centuries before and still named after the old city of yore: The University of Cape Town.

I sometimes wondered why the city was renamed after the Cataclysm, when the Vortex Rift opened and unlocked magic and released monsters on our world. As the city was consumed by dark magic, refugees and monsters, the weak bureaucrat who found himself unfortunate enough to be in charge must've thought renaming the city after the 'Cape of Good Hope' historical nomenclature was a swell idea.

It didn't really bring much hope.

Hope City was an urban sprawl. The old city was either kept afloat by magic corporations, a local monster hunting agency or sheer stubborn tenacity. Everywhere else was decaying. A husk of a city ruled by sorcerous crime bosses, vampire cartels and cabals of necromancers seeking to turn the last bastion of freedom on the African continent into another undead wasteland.

I clenched my fist.

And the damn Council does nothing about it.

I released my fist and looked again at that damn mountain. Maybe it was for the best that they didn't do anything. The Council government tended to make a mess of things. The better the intentions, the worse the mess. Just like when I phoned Sanitation to clean up some discarded zombies after a gangster popped their necromancer. Guys arrived all prim and proper and picked up the zombie bits, no sweat. I soon found out they'd thrown it in the bay, choking countless seals on necro-blood and rotting corpses.

That was the last time I trusted Sanitation to do a job unmonitored. I might have hated Drakenbane, but they never did stuff like that. The big agencies might ignore the little guys and chase the big fancy monsters instead of the gruesome and much more sinister ones, but at least they were competent.

The engine on the bus renewed its huff and I jolted as the traffic started its melancholic crawl again. Then it stopped. I tapped my foot, impatiently, and checked the time on my cell. I was going to be late.

I peered out the other window. This part of town was a much better sight than the decaying suburb I had been hunting in last night. Shops were opening, displaying wares ranging from computer hardware to good-luck charms. Banners with old-timey fonts contrasted with neon-signs and computer displays. If one didn't travel out of these parts of Hope City, one'd forget all the problems the city was facing. Their biggest concern would just be rising taxes to pay for the Titan Magi and the occasional interruption by a monster. These were petty problems that Hope City denizens were adept at complaining about but problems that remained comparatively petty nonetheless. The richer residents of this too-large city didn't understand the real dangers facing their home. No wall separated the city-centre and new weyline locales from the undead and crime-infested slums. Only hunters did. Hunters like me.

The bus wrenched forward and continued at a healthy, walking pace. I checked the time again. It would be almost quicker to walk! I sighed. I hoped this lecture wouldn't be too important, but this close to test season, it was likely to be. I opened some notes on my phone. I could at least use this time to study.

"Kat," Treth said.

"What?" I whispered back, my eyes scanning across a passage about the establishment of the first weyline business district in Hope City.

"Look out the window."

I rolled my eyes but did so. Just outside, in an alley between shops, were three men. Two wore red jackets, stitched with rune-enhancers. The symbols would enhance latent magical energy and help its incantation. Behind the two jacket wearers was a boy around my age, cowering. He was clutching a leather bag as the jacket wearers shoved into him. A spark. The one now held a flame in his palm.

"Not my problem."

I turned back to my notes. Treth did not respond. I itched. My heart beat fast. Faster. I pocketed my phone and jumped out the bus window.

What are you doing, Kat? I asked myself. I did not reply. I withdrew a paper sachet out of my pocket and started shaking it, feeling the sands within swoosh from side to side.

Closer to the three, I heard them speak.

"These are just books. They are useless to you," the victim panted, anxiously.

"You assuming we don't read?!" one of the assailants retorted. He held the flame in his hand closer. The boy's face paled.

"We've got the Spark, and you don't. All the books that matter don't matter to a husk like you. Give us the bag."

"Hey!" I called, arriving at the scene, only a few metres from the three.

The jacket-wearers turned, irritation and anger turning to bemusement.

"Scram, chick, we got no beef with you."

"That's unfortunate," I said, still shaking the paper sachet. It was getting warmer. "I've got beef with you."

Before the jacket-wearing mages could react, I tore open the sachet and threw its contents over them. As I had hoped, not only did the one not extinguish his flame, the other attempted to cast as well. Their magic backfired as the powdered demanzite hit them. The anti-magical mineral not only dispelled active casting, but temporarily burnt out magic-users spark. The powder hit the mages and there was a flash. Screaming followed as the mages covered their eyes and ears. Apparently, demanzite caused extreme sensory overload in its victims. The Mages Union had lobbied to get it outlawed. Lucky for "husks" like me, the usually harmless mineral was still available at alchemists around the city.

The flash abated, and I followed through by kicking both men in the stomach, doubling them over. They keeled over onto the floor, their babbled speech sounding a tad like incantations. The powder wouldn't last much longer, and it was my last sachet.

My last sachet...

Shit.

I shook my head in frustration. Demanzite wasn't cheap and I needed it against wights, and if I ever found one of the necromancers behind a zombie horde.

Too late now, though. I looked around. The victim was gone. No sign of him.

"Ungrateful..."

"Heroes don't need gratitude to do what they do, Kat," Treth quoted. I didn't exactly know who he was quoting but Treth's tone always changed when he was sharing the wisdom of his long-lost masters and comrades.

I grunted. Gratitude and reward were things Treth claimed to not need, but I was quite partial to both.

The mages at my feet were beginning to rise. I bolted.

***

I arrived on campus somehow minutes before my lecture was to begin. Despite all the curses that were doubtlessly clinging to me, it seemed my luck was still healthy. I looked up at the stairway to the main avenue of the campus, where my class was located. When I first became a student, the stairs were daunting. Every morning was a huff bringing searing pain across my body. With my new part-time work, however, it was a breeze.

I effortlessly ascended the stairs to the sound of protest chanting and shouts.

"You are the monster!"

"No to flaying fairies!"

"Down with the Agencies!"

Another one! I thought the protesters got their fill of demonstrating last week. They were protesting the general treatment of what society deemed monsters by picketing on campus, being a nuisance and disrupting foot traffic. I don't know why they thought campus was the appropriate place to protest. Most of the university administration were sympathetic to them and had no power over what society called things. My Undead Studies lecturer even refused to refer to the undead as monsters, much to my chagrin. If anything, the protesters should be protesting the likes of Drakenbane – but that'd require them to go into a dangerous neighbourhood, where they'd see what their precious "non-monsters" were really like.

I didn't always look upon the protests disparagingly. Pixies and fairies were, for the most part, harmless, but were often slain and collected by alchemists to be used in product development and magical rituals. But, when the protesters started arguing for the rights of zombies, my sympathy for them stopped.

I clenched my fists, took a deep breath, and waded into the morass. I hoped that the barely coated stench of necro-blood on my hair would cause the protesters to give me a wide-berth. It did not. And by the time I had forced my way through the horde of people stinking worse than I, I was thoroughly late for class. I lost all sympathy I might have had for the protesters.

I opened the doors to the lecture theatre. Mercifully, people were still filing in halfway through the class. Despite Undead Studies being quite a hardcore subject, this could not change the apathy of the typical university student.

I took a seat at the back and began scribbling down notes by pen, despite my exhaustion and bleary vision. I used my phone to study, but I preferred taking down the initial notes by hand. My friend, Trudie, always tried to convince me to just type straight onto my cell, or get a laptop, but old habits die hard.

"All undead corrupt weyline purity," the lecturer said, as I scribbled down what she said and the notes on the board.

"Not wights, or masterless undead," Treth said.

I ignored him and continued note-taking.

"Corrupted weylines attract more undead, creating a self-driven cycle," the lecturer continued, drawing a circle on the whiteboard with a marker.

"Unicorn waste!" Treth swore, a rare occurrence for him. "Undead are created by intentional necromantic incantation…"

"Sssshhh," I whispered, covering my mouth so that nobody could see me speak.

"She doesn't know the first thing about undead, Kat."

"Shut up…"

"Problem, Ms Drummond?" the lecturer asked, stopping her note-taking. The entire class looked back at me. My face heated up.

"Nope, sorry."

The lecturer nodded and continued. Mercifully, Treth did not speak again.

***

I almost dozed off twice during the class. When the cacophony of shuffling people and papers signalled the end of class, I was glad to be able to leave. Unfortunately, I still had history later in the day.

Outside the lecture theatre, I was greeted by the sight of a short girl wearing a spiked collar and black leather jacket. She had short black hair with a blue-highlighted fringe. Her lipstick was black.

I smiled as I approached my friend, bustling past some students also eager to leave the class.

I greeted Trudie with a hug, hoping she didn't notice the smell. Well, she should be used to it. I'd been in the game for over a year now.

"How is my big man?" she immediately asked.

"Alex is fine, Trudie."

Sometimes, I was sure that Trudie liked Alex more than she liked me. I was fine with that. Alex was worth liking. He'd been a little black ball of sunshine in my life since I'd saved him from a pack of undead dogs. I didn't know anything about his life before he was cornered by the beasts, but since that point, we were inseparable – and Trudie loved him.

We walked off towards the cafeteria. It was nearby, and we took a seat by the food vendor.

Trudie was checking her phone in-between talking. She was an IT major and a real tech-junkie. She practically lived off the dark energies of the internet.

"So," Trudie said, flaring her nostrils. "Late night?"

I frowned. So, she could smell it.

"How could you tell?"

"Because you always have a late night. And…"

Trudie whipped out a surgical glove and leant over to pick something from my hair. A flake of skin. I would have retched last year. Was the norm now. Seems Trudie had even become accustomed to it – if reluctantly.

"Aren't there any day-time jobs?" Trudie frowned, putting the flake in a plastic bag and tossing it in the bin. She was too prepared for this…

"Undead are most active at night."

"So, get some jobs hunting non-undead. Maybe hunt unicorns."

"Most people don't categorize unicorns as monsters," I replied, smiling faintly as I *stealthily* picked fries from Trudie's lunch.

"Those people are wrong. Damn one-horned bastards."

"Remind me, why do you hate unicorns so much?"

"'Cause nobody else does. Everybody loves them. It's not like they're prettier than everything else. They're just horses with a horn. Still fine to kill fairies for their parts, but the Rifts all collapse on us if you dare think of harming a precious unicorn."

Trudie bit into a handful of chips and muttered, mouth full, "Wannabe horse bastards."

I snickered and stood to go buy myself some lunch. My previous mirth subsided as I handed over some of the money. I hoped the cashier didn't notice the black-red stain on the note.

"You've been pretty out of it lately," Trudie said as I sat down again. I shrugged. Trudie took some bites of my noodles in exchange for my previous marauding.

"History has me running ragged."

"Not the late-nights?"

"Slaying is quick. It doesn't get dull. You track your target, which is easy due to the moaning, and then cut its head off. Finished. History is interesting, sure, but not all of it. After three hundred pages of badly-written prose on the Cataclysm, I'd rather be facing down an armoured and armed wight."

Trudie's frown deepened. "So, you do it because it's fun?"

I shrugged again. "I do it because it's a way to put food on the table. Not all of us have a family paying for tuition and lunch."

That seemed to sting Trudie a little. I looked down at my food.

"I'm just worried, Kat. It's dangerous."

"And I can handle it."

Trudie nodded, slowly. She stood up and checked her phone.

"I better be off to class."

She pushed the remainder of her lunch in front of me. I nodded in thanks.

"She is concerned about you," Treth said.

There were too many people around for me to reply without looking mad. I didn't need to reply. I understood why Trudie was worried. She didn't understand or like magic. Weylines meant nothing to her, just wi-fi. And her family was alive to pay her bills.

Maybe Trudie's concern was justified. But it didn't matter. I had a job to do. Not just to feed myself and Alex, but - as Treth would so often remind me - because it was the right thing to do.

***

I got to history on time, energised by my double pseudo-breakfast of noodles and fries. The air conditioner was on full throttle, and while unpleasant, would hopefully keep me awake. Fellow students filed in, and finally, the lecturer.

"I like this man," Treth commented.

"Because you don't know if he's wrong or not," I replied in a whisper.

"He reminds me of my mentor at the Order."

"Morning...I mean afternoon, class," Professor Crowley stuttered, and then calmed. "Today we're revising some post-cataclysm history of Hope City."

This was a topic I did enjoy. Despite all my complaints, this was my city and I liked to know as much as I could about it. The lecturer began, his stuttering abating as he got into his topic of expertise. I hastily took down notes. Treth was silent. He must've been interested.

But, despite my interest about the discovery of the ancient primordial titan asleep under Table Mountain, the escapades of last night were finally catching up with me. My writing became gibberish and my vision blurred. Darkness engulfed me as I embraced the hard wood and papers before me.

Chapter 3. Ghost in the Shell

My parents had been killed when I was still in school.

My aunt, Mandy Caleb, looked after me for as long as she could, but she had her own life and an important job. Despite me being a seventeen-year-old girl in a hell-hole of a city, Mandy had to go back to New Zealand. I couldn't follow. Border control was strict and New Zealand wasn't much better than Hope City. The elves and human denizens of the country periodically engaged in brutal civil wars that made the gang battles in Hope City look like pillow fights.

New Zealand was no place for me.

But, neither was Hope City.

My aunt still sent me a stipend, when she could, but being a mediator between two sides that didn't see eye to eye did not pay well and Hope City had a high cost of living. So, at the age of seventeen, entering my first year of university the following year, I had to become self-reliant. This took the form of odd-jobs, freelance work and anything that a high school education could give you.

One such job brought me to a leafy suburb of Hope City, where I was babysitting two children as their parents went hobnobbing at a magicorp function. The pay was reasonable, and jobs were scarce, so I was thankful.

But gratitude wasn't endless, and I soon learned that money couldn't buy patience. That night, I found myself in a battlefield of entitled shits, bargaining with halflings – if not demons.

"Your mom said to be in bed by 8pm," I stated calmly, restraining myself as much as possible, hands on my hips. The room was dark, with just the glimmer of the TV painting a translucent blue light show across the lounge.

"My mom isn't here," the imperious little imp, who was allegedly a human child, retorted, ramming a fistful of chips into his mouth. I do not know when or how he got hold of them.

"Our bedtime is way too early, miss," the imp's sister added. She was much more agreeable but still played the accomplice to her rebel brother.

"Take that up with your mother. I received instructions to have you in bed by 8 and I'm going to stick to them."

"I'd like to see you try."

I should have been thankful for the lights being off, as my glare may have been capable of burning a hole in whoever saw it. Finally, I sighed and left the room, making my way to the extravagant kitchen. It was almost the size of my entire apartment.

Two hours till their parents get back. Two hours to get them to bed.

I just needed to ensure that they didn't get into anything that would keep them awake till ten. I opened the fridge and began moving all the caffeinated drinks to the top shelf. I hoped that the parents wouldn't notice nor mind. I couldn't be sure with this family. I got instructions to be strict, but the kids acted like they'd never been given orders in their life.

I sighed. I'd been doing it a lot tonight.

The parents probably couldn't rein their own kids in themselves so were hoping I could.

I closed the fridge and turned. A countertop dominated the centre of the kitchen. Perched on top of it was a knife-block. I winced. I hoped the imp wouldn't get any ideas. I wouldn't put it past him to think that he was impervious to stabs.

I heard gunshots and an explosion.

The imp had turned up the volume on the TV. Worst of all, it wasn't even a good movie. Just some mass-produced garbage checking all the criteria to take money from tasteless movie-goers.

"That's it," I said to myself. "No more Miss-Nice-Girl!"

I marched into the living room. The kids' faces were glued to a scene of the muscle-bound protagonist using a dirt-bike to destroy an attack helicopter. I proceeded to the TV. The kids didn't seem to notice, or care. I bent down, and the TV switched off.

"What the hell did you do?!"

I stared at my finger, only a sliver of moonlight illuminating it as it was about to turn off the power to the TV.

"Come on, miss. Please put it back on. I promise I'll go to sleep when it's done."

I stood up. The light in the hallway had also gone off.

"Turn it back on!"

I raised my hand to silence them and whispered. "That wasn't me."

A boom. Not thunder. Not like the gunshots and explosions of the action movie. Something otherworldly. The closest comparison would be a thousand speakers exploding from feedback. If it was thunder, no rain followed. Only an ethereal blue-white flash. I had seen the likes of it before, on a documentary about rifts. The rifts that opened portals to other realms, allowing all manner of beasts into our world.

"Kids, I need you to listen to me very carefully."

The imp looked about to speak.

"I'm serious."

My tone gagged him.

"Do you have a panic room?"

The girl nodded, catching some moonlight so I could see the motion.

"We must get there now and shut ourselves in."

Hesitantly, the pair stood and exited the room. In the halls, the moonlight lessened. I followed the children's semi-human shadowy forms in the dark. My heart beat hard and fast. It took all my willpower to keep my breathing under control. Fortunately, it seemed the children were just shocked enough to become obedient, but not so much that they became hysterical.

A thump. We stopped. Footsteps. Oddly human, but staggered. I stopped breathing. My head went faint. I had heard those types of steps before. And I had heard what followed. A moaning. A mournful, animalistic cry reverberating from the throat of something that resembled humanity. I could have cried then, the strain of the trauma becoming too much to bear. But I didn't. I nudged the kids onwards. I hoped that the panic room wasn't too far. But in this inky black, I couldn't be sure that we would even get there.

The children led me down the hall, a few open rooms with windows letting moonlight pool into the house. The moaning didn't stop. I knew it never did. It hadn't stopped from last time. It continued, forever, and ever and ever. A mob became a horde and they kept on coming. Rotting, moaning, shambling, devouring. The Dead never stopped…

"Miss…"

I had stopped. I looked at the shapes of my hands in the blackness. I felt them shivering, but I wasn't cold. A hand in the dark snapped me out of my reverie. It was warm. Small.

"Miss?" it inquired.

"Keep going," I said. "I'll keep you safe."

This was a big house. Much bigger than the one-room apartment I was able to afford with Auntie Mandy's stipend. Hopefully big enough to put as much in the way of us and the Dead as possible.

The thumping and moaning stopped. I almost breathed a sigh of relief, but I had seen plenty of horror movies before. And like all calms before a storm, it was ended by a loud noise. A breaking of glass and the pooling of shards on the ground.

A scream.

Was it me?

My mouth was closed. I grabbed in front and held the girl close, covering her mouth. Even then, I still felt the scream could have been mine. It would have been, years before. I must have screamed like that back then, when the Dead surrounded me, and through their rotting bodies, I saw my father chained to a rock, as a young man held an obsidian dagger towards the sky, chanting gibberish that made my primordial mind want to tear itself apart.

"Keep going," I whispered.

With a panicked haste, we all sped towards a room in the darkness. I heard the thud of flesh, the creak of wood. And the tinkle of disrupted glass pieces. The moaning was now inside the house. I wanted to tell the kids to remain calm. That they should be calm. But I'm not a hypocrite.

At least, I tell myself that. And how can I tell them to be calm when my vision is blurring, my throat is tightening and the only thing veiling the pain in my chest is the numbness of oncoming hysteria?

I couldn't. But I kept them moving. And then, lightning did strike. Another verse in the poetic horror of nature. The flash and boom made us all halt. Liquid coated my face. I was not sure if it was sweat, tears or both.

Another boom. Another flash. And a silhouette. Approaching. Closer. Closer. And with it – the moaning.

"Run," I whispered. They did nothing.

Another flash. It was a man. His clothes were ripped and foreign. A torn, fading red doublet and frayed hosen. He looked like an unemployed Shakespearean actor. He had holes in his cheeks and rotting, pale flesh was falling from his exposed ribcage. His sickly yellow eyes, shining in the dark, were simultaneously mindless and predatory, his pupils fixed on us, cowering before him. He staggered forward another step, and I shouted:

"Run!"

The children listened when it mattered most and bolted down the unlit halls. The zombie snarled and lunged forward. I felt the air move behind me as I ran.

In my head, it was more than one zombie. It was a horde. And as I ran, skidding into furniture and sliding across smooth wooden floors, with the undead in tow, I saw a different time. I wasn't alone. There were four of us. Four of the living. Me, my parents and a man wearing a black robe.

I saw the children at the end of the hall, struggling with a knob. I went the other way. My vision changed. I saw a horde of the undead, holding me down, salivating over me. Only the strict control of their master kept them from devouring me to sustain their endless hunger. I felt the wetness on me now, and the touch was almost the same. An unnatural clamminess. If hell had moisture, it felt like this. Pure decay.

The zombie was on my tail, its shamble turning into an efficient run. I needed to get out. To get away from it. But, what if it stayed here? Stayed with the children as I ran through the night.

I was back in the hallway near the TV room. Grunting, moaning and thumping followed. The kids were still in the house. The bratty, entitled kids whose names I couldn't even recall. But they hadn't seen what I had seen. They didn't know fear like I did. And I wouldn't wish it upon them.

I turned around and saw it coming, obscured by the shadow.

These things. And the man who had controlled them…

They had taken everything from me.

I turned into the kitchen, knocking over a chair and falling to the ground with an oomph. I grabbed for something to pull myself up as lightning struck. The zombie was right above me. Salivating. Snarling. The light of the outside sky flickered, feverishly. Like a crackling light bulb. The light faded, and the zombie fell upon me, sending a waft of rotting flesh my way. I kicked back, hitting a rib with my sneakers. It caught my leg and brought its teeth to it. I forced its head away, desperately. The first blow dazed it, and then it attempted to bite again. I kicked again. And again. And again. It let go and I pulled both my legs away. Appliances and kitchen apparatus clattered to the floor. A glint of metal. I crawled towards it and felt cold wrap around my leg. I was pulled back.

I saw the rotting teeth, sharpened to points through the dark magic of necromancy. The zombie looked me in the eyes and bared its teeth; it lunged towards my neck. I grabbed onto its shoulders, pushing as one could only do instinctively to keep the vile thing away.

But the living always succumbed to the dead, and even my strained groans waned as my arms became afire with the pressure of the monster on top of me.

And I knew I was going to die. That all that time since then was just borrowed time. That the cause of my fear that had been with me all these years had returned to finish the job.

But it was then that I felt an anger. A rage roiling deep inside of me at the thing before me. And at the black robed man who had taken everything from me. A rage against the Dead, the undead and this bastard who would eat the children I was meant to protect.

And then a voice in my head spoke to me:

"Wrap your legs around it."

What?

I hesitated. The voice spoke again:

"Wrap your legs around it and shift your weight. Get on top of it."

I didn't understand the alien voice within my head. Sure, I knew what it was saying, but not how, or where.

But as my arms approached jellification from exertion, I obeyed.

I flanked the snarling corpse with my legs and locked it above me. I felt its fragile flesh give way to bone as I squeezed. I was close to the thing... I felt bile rise. But adrenaline took over.

My arms strengthened and in one push, I flipped the zombie onto its back.

"Great work! Now punch it."

I did so without hesitation. I held it down with my left hand and with my right, I delivered a hard blow to its temple. Flesh tore, and bone shattered. My hand stung.

"Quickly, stand and get a weapon."

The glint of metal, I remembered.

I scampered off the dazed undead, towards where I saw the sparkle of steel. The zombie groaned, and slowly began to stand.

"It won't be dazed for long. You must skewer its brain."

Skewer...

Skewer...

My hands searched frantically across the black pit of the kitchen floor. I heard the phlegmy gurgles behind me.

They would have nauseated me before, but I was different now. Something had changed.

My hand touched something colder than the tile flooring. It tinged as my nail hit it.

"Hurry!"

The gurgles were becoming growls. Growing louder. More vociferous.

I reached for the blade and felt its point. It stung. I reached for the other end and stroked its rough, plastic handle. I grabbed.

"Stand."

I did so and faced the zombie in the dark.

"What do I do?" I asked, my now bleeding hand clutching a knife before me as the shadows roiled and the groans increased.

"Courage, my lady. Stand your ground. That is all one can do against the Dead."

The shadow-veiled zombie became clearer in the moonlight.

Stand.

I was standing. My hand shivered. I reached over and held the blade with both my hands. Alone, they shook. Together, they froze. Steady.

"Stand your ground."

I stood my ground.

A snarl. A flash of pale, rotting flesh. And pressure, an immense pressure. I heard the crack and felt the squelch. My gut wrenched, but I did not vomit. My anger transformed into cold calculation. My fear shifted. It was still there but was no longer the debilitating trauma towards the thing that had taken everything from you. When faced with a cat, a rat either runs or it bites back. I was biting back.

I kept pushing the knife into the zombie's skull. Deeper and deeper. Every bit of sinew, bone, skin and flesh held the knife back. But I pushed. And it broke through. The creature went limp and collapsed. I let go.

As if by some poetic miracle, the lights came on. I gazed at my hands. They were covered in black blood. My own red blood was kept to a small cut on my finger and palm. The blood wasn't touching, thankfully. Necro-sick wasn't a pleasant experience. The kitchen was a quagmire of black blood, strewn flesh and clattered cutlery. The zombie lay on its stomach, crumpled like a dead animal. Truly dead.

And I had killed it.

I looked at my hands. Covered with blood, bruising from the punch.

I had killed it.

And while I still feared it, and whatever master had brought it into the world, I knew that fear was a tool. It had a purpose. And I knew what its purpose was.

"Do not relish the kill, my lady."

"Who are you?" I asked. It felt odd to speak to a voice in my head, but I did it all the same.

"I am Treth of Concord, Knight-Paladin of the Order of Albin."

"Okay."

"And, who are you?"

I had been biting my lip. I again noticed the beating of my heart. My breathing was easy, though. I felt no hint of nausea.

"Kat. Kat Drummond."

"Well, Kat Drummond. It is an honour to meet you. I look forward to an enriching partnership."

"Partnership?"

"I find myself without a body," Treth said, sounding a tad embarrassed. "Through some cosmic fate, my spirit has been sent to you in your time of peril. I can only guess that the gods wish me to continue my quest through you."

"What quest?"

Treth hesitated. His voice lowered, filling with a fiery determination. "Something I failed to do in life. Something I may never truly complete, but I must do all the same."

"What is it?"

"Slaying monsters."

"All of them?"

"The ones that deserve it."

I looked at my hands again, covered in undead blood. I remembered the zombies that had held me down, as my parents were sacrificed by a necromancer for a ritual I did not understand. I remembered being released as the Puretide Agency burst in, too late to save my mom and dad, and too late to catch the necromancer who disappeared in a cloud of black smoke.

Monsters...

"I'll do it..."

Treth didn't reply, but I somehow felt him nod.

The parents of the children arrived early. The relief in their eyes at seeing their children unharmed was only surpassed by the look of fear and revulsion that they had when they saw the corpse in their kitchen, and my bloodied hands.

Despite the safety of their offspring, despite the slain monster in their kitchen, this blood-stained teenage girl was too much for them.

I left the house at their behest. I didn't receive any pay. I'm sure I could have threatened them for it, but I was tired. Too tired.

"Do not lust after reward," Treth said. "A hero acts for valour alone."

My stomach rumbled as I rubbed it. "I hope valour tastes good."

Chapter 4. Struggles

I awoke to the hustle and bustle of students hastily packing their notes and laptops into bags. Many attempted to make a break for the door, just to be stopped by the inevitable mosh-pit of students all with the same idea. The professor had already made his escape through the staff entrance. I blinked, my head still resting on the desk. As I realised that the class had ended, I sat upright with a start. I reached for my pen and my notepad, to salvage what I could off the white-board. My paper wasn't in front of me. I looked around, and then felt the paper fall off my cheek and drift harmlessly onto the table top.

Too late. The notes were gibberish without their context. Professor Crowley was a traditionalist. He didn't like using digital notes or spoon-feeding information. This made for an active and attentive class, but also meant that I was lost.

"I got most of it," Treth said.

"Thanks," I whispered, and smiled faintly. Treth didn't need to sleep. From whatever incorporeal chamber he resided, he was able to watch around me, including these lectures. I just hoped he had been paying attention.

I stood up, collected my things, and left. I felt sticky. The congealed sweat of my exertions was getting too much for even me to bear. Thank the Rifts that the day was over! I needed to get some sleep, right after I finished my history assignment, and right after a shower.

Mercifully, the buses were running on time on the way back home. I lived relatively near to campus, in a residential area called Rondebosch. Well, it used to be residential. The discovery of an untapped weyline led to several magicorp – corporations specialising in magical products and services – building their obnoxious skyscrapers in the historic district.

On the way home, I told Treth to fill me in on the lecture. His interests were focused on monsters and Earth's development of lawmancy, but he did absorb enough info on other topics to help me. As much as his holier than thou, perpetually heroic and chivalrous attitudes got irritating, I appreciated him.

After the incident with the zombie and the babysitting, we got to know each other, as much we could and were willing to do so. Treth was from another world – one much more magical than Earth. While Earth had only been experiencing the onslaught of monsters and the mystery of magic for the past few decades, Treth's world had been suffering the plague of necromancy and dangers of fantastical beasts for millennia. In his world, he was a knight of an order dedicated to hunting monsters. Then he died. He never said how. I didn't press. Somehow, after his death, his spirit had travelled through a rift and onto Earth, where it became fettered to me.

We soon learned that while his voice sounded like it was coming from my head, he wasn't in my head. If anything, he seemed to be an incorporeal and invisible spirit, chained to me. This meant that I still had to speak out loud to him, but also meant he could see what I didn't – watching my back and keeping watch as I slept.

Together, we had been hunting the undead for over a year. It started small. I was young, after all. I was not sure my parents would have approved. But I wouldn't have been doing this if they were still around. First thing I did was post a hand-written notice (I didn't and don't own a printer) at the local grocery store, advertising my services as an undead slayer.

I had no bites for a long time. Treth was anxious to get hunting but, as I reminded him, I needed money and couldn't just go tracking down zombies and ghouls wantonly. I needed this to be sustainable – and profits sustained.

Finally, while I was doing some data-entry for Trudie's dad, just before my first semester of my first year in university started, I received a phone call. An old lady was convinced that her dog had been taken by ghouls. I doubted that, but the money was good. It would be enough to keep me fed for a few days. And I didn't really think it was ghouls. She was basically paying me to find her missing dog.

And I was right, it wasn't ghouls. It was a nightkin.

That had been a hard fight. Treth didn't know what it was. I had only ever heard about them in passing. It was an undead, but not exactly. It resembled a monkey, but if a monkey's flesh was made of charcoal, covered in black flame and had eyes of magma. The dog was still alive. Nightkin, I discovered later at the behest of Treth to research the beast, were an undead/spirit hybrid with connections to vampirism. They collected their prey alive in order to feed later. They needed fresh blood and preferred fresh meat, right off the writhing carcass.

Somehow, Treth and I managed to defeat the nightkin. The pay wasn't worth it, but Treth enjoyed himself. I also couldn't help but smile when the dog ran up to its owner.

Things sped up after that point. My studies began, and I was on a deadline. While my family had saved up money for my tuition, this was not a stable economy. The investment had since devalued, and I was sitting with enough money to finance a single year of studying.

"That's enough," I told Treth. I had already decided I wanted to become a monster hunter.

"It is never enough when it comes to learning. Study comes before the quest. Knowledge is power."

He was full of adages.

But it motivated me.

After the nightkin, I was allowed to start listing my services on the MonsterSlayer app. That was the real godsend. People started hiring me. First, because I was the cheapest, and because my age was a novelty, but then because I ended up doing a good job. I took almost every job I was hired to do, and I delivered. Typically, delivered heads. Sometimes hands. Mostly pictures, because clients didn't really like the smell. Neither did I, but as I said, I got used to it.

And Treth was with me every step of the way. The annoying conscience telling me to serve valour and glory, and not just the allure of mammon. But annoying or not, I couldn't have done it without him… Didn't mean I had to put up with everything, though. Especially the constant talking over everyone.

But that didn't mean there weren't challenges. I was just one girl, trying to take down monsters normally reserved for agencies. And the types of monsters I could handle were not the type that paid well. Sure, I was surviving – but as Trudie constantly pointed out, not in a way that any human should live.

We arrived at the bus-stop and I walked the rest of the way to my apartment. Treth was still regaling me about the lecture. He was putting disproportionate detail into his explanation about the establishment of the Spirit of the Law of Hope City.

Five years after the Cataclysm, when the Vortex Rift opened in Siberia and led to many people gaining the Spark and becoming magic-users, the nation was in turmoil. In everything but name, it had split up into separate states. In the east was the Zulu Empire, ruled by a powerful sorcerous emperor. In the north, was the

Goldfield Magocracy, run by a semi-democratic but ultimately oligarchical body of mages. At the southern-most tip, was Hope City. The last bastion of democracy in southern Africa, for all that was worth.

It was bloated. A toothless council with ineffective functions. The best thing it did was occasionally get out of the way.

But it had done one thing right. Five years after the Cataclysm, a group of lawmancers emerged. They were hastily trained – the first of their kind on the planet. Through a system of complex compulsion, purification and divination magic, they formed a literally living constitution to govern Hope City. A document that judged all laws, defended democracy and kept the already swollen city council from getting any fatter. This was the Spirit of the Law.

Treth was truly intrigued by the concept and neglected the main gist of the lecture to describe this topic to me. Beggars couldn't be choosers, and I listened attentively.

Once home, I greeted Alex and showered. Treth was always silent during these times. Despite all this time we had spent together, he still seemed embarrassed. Tentative.

In many ways, it was inefficient that he had been linked to a girl. He didn't seem used to them.

Blessedly clean, at last, I dried my now loose hair with a towel and made my way to the couch. I was still tired, but I had an assignment to write, and then monsters to slay. The constant cycle of my life. Hopefully, I would find time to put sleep in there.

My phone buzzed on the coffee table, where I had left it while I got dressed. Hair finally tied up, I checked it. I almost dropped the phone.

"What is it?" Treth asked.

"The..." I had to stop to calm down. The excitement was overwhelming. "The new Warpwars novel is out!"

"Excuse me?"

"It's a series that has been on hold since I was in high school."

The speed of my dressing increased tenfold.

"What's so great about it?"

"Well, amazing characters, amazing world-building, high-stakes action..." I said, as if it was obvious.

I put on my black leather jacket, the one I use for low-power undead hunts and checked Alex's food.

"You're going to go buy it now, aren't you?"

"I've been waiting for it for years, Treth."

"You'll spend money on some frivolous fiction, but not on a decent weapon?"

I didn't respond. I gave Alex a final pet and locked my apartment behind me.

Treth sighed as I walked to the mall.

Chapter 5. Shopping

Despite Treth's protestations, I found myself at the entrance of the Riverstone Mall in Old Rondebosch. It was home to my favourite non-magical book store and my one-stop shop for all my grocery and entertainment needs. My friend, Pranish, worked there part-time, which got me all the super-secret release details long before other readers. It was Pranish who had sent me the message, telling me that Warpwars was now selling at his bookstore, without any official announcement from the author or his marketing team. Hopefully, I would beat any ensuing queues due to my inside knowledge.

"You have hardly enough time to study," Treth said, still pleading for me to reconsider my purchase. "When do you think you will find time to read this?"

"I'll make time."

On entering Riverstone Mall, my hair stood on end and goose bumps covered my arms. The air was cold. And while I could hear the traffic on the street and the chatter of people throughout the building, there was a sense of unnatural silence. As if something was muffling the sounds of life, obscuring it and attempting to make it as dead as it was. It was a pseudo-silence and it unnerved even me, and I hunt monsters for a living!

"I feel something," Treth said. His voice didn't sound normal. It was no longer haughty and self-assured. It had become tremulous. I imagined a deer considering running away from the headlights of a car. "It feels familiar."

"Anything familiar to you isn't something I want to face unprepared. Should I go back and get my sword?"

"No…" Treth considered. "This is not something that falls to steel. Go on."

"I thought you didn't want me to buy the book," I tried to chide him.

Treth grunted in reply.

I proceeded through the mall. Other customers were not acting out of the ordinary. They chatted and they shopped. Old Rondebosch was located within the safer parts of Hope City. Its people felt protected from the big bad monsters of the slums and overrun districts. That is, until a rift opened in their backyard – and then they'd hopefully call me. But until then, they were content with their lives, benefitting from the boons of the rifts and the clean weylines that the agencies and people like me helped protect.

My uneasiness grew as I trod deeper into the mall. It felt dark, despite the bright lights flooding the white-tiled floors. The quiet that was not, continued to deepen.

And then, I heard screams.

Before I knew it, I was running. Joining the screams were shouts, bangs, crashing, smashing and the cacophony of wanton destruction.

A horrific thought crossed my mind:

Pranish!

As I feared, the sounds were coming from the *Riverstone Book Shoppe*. The place where my friend worked, and which contained Warpwars.

A crowd of onlookers had gathered around the entrance to the shop. Many covered their mouths with their hands in shock. I noticed wet marks on the pants of many. Must have been a hell of a fright. The deeper, bitterer side of me didn't think it would even have to be. So many of my fellow Hope City-dwellers were cowards. They just didn't know it. They'd never had to face anything to clarify it.

The lights in the shop were flickering, as if deranged. I heard bangs. The crash and snap of furniture.

I pushed my way to the front of the crowd. Many were too shocked to care. From the front, I saw a storm of books, paper, bookshelves and other debris being flung in a veritable cyclone. A wave hit me. Like a gust of wind, but a wind made out of torment.

"Pranish!" I shouted.

I heard muffled cries from within.

"He's still in there," one of the onlookers said, sweat pouring down his pale face.

"Shit," I whispered.

This wasn't my forte. I hunted undead. Sometimes, lesser vampires. This was a spirit and, seemingly, a powerful one. Neither Treth nor I had much experience with spirits – despite Treth, in all likelihood, being one. Spirits were different. You couldn't just stab them to death. Most of the time, steel just passed right through them. Had to use enchanted weapons, or silver. But even then, many incorporeal spirits didn't care.

I was no exorcist.

But...

My friend was in danger.

I advanced. Some people cried out, but nobody came closer to stop me.

"It's going to be dangerous, Kat."

"And?"

"Let's go."

I stopped involuntarily at the threshold of the shop – the line separating open mall and the book shop within. A force field of palpable unease barred me.

I wracked my brain for all the info I had on spirits. Flinging stuff around. Feelings of unease. I looked within the store and saw no obvious signs of a monster, besides the hurricane of literature.

"A poltergeist. It has to be," I offered.

"I think you're right, but there's something else…" Treth hesitated. "It feels familiar."

I gazed through the tumultuous floating and flying debris before me to see if I could find Pranish. I could not.

"You're a spirit. It's a spirit. Mingle."

I felt Treth shake his head. "My recognition is faded, but memories are coming back…"

"Kat?!" I heard a voice shout through the buffeting spirit-wrought tempest.

"Pranish?"

"Help!"

Barrier or no barrier, I stepped forward, breaking into a run. I needed to find Pranish and get out of here – maybe retrieve a copy of Warpwars while I was at it. The initial resistance of the threshold gave way, and I popped out onto the other side. If there was a fake silence outside, then this was where all the sound had been stolen. Screams, pops, bangs, the whistling of wind…sounds that belonged and sounds that did not, all cooped up in the bubble of this shop.

I ducked, narrowly missing a hardcover, and looked around hastily for my friend.

"Up here!"

I looked up. Pranish was glued to the roof. His fingers were an icy blue. He must have tried to cast a spell out of sheer desperation. Pranish was a sorcerer, with a natural affinity for cryomancy. By natural affinity, I mean that it was the only element he could conjure – and badly. His powers were typically restricted to making ice cubes.

I examined my friend closely. Nothing seemed to be holding him up. It was as if invisible shackles chained him to the ceiling.

This was going to be tougher than I thought.

And then I felt a sharp pain in the back of my head.

When my eyes opened, I was looking down at the floor, the mosh pit of debris now below me. I couldn't move my head to look around. My arms were splayed to my sides, with my legs together. It was not comfortable.

"Well, shit…"

Pranish didn't speak.

"Pranish?"

He must have passed out – I hoped. Poltergeists were not the most dangerous spirits, I had heard. But what did I know? If it wasn't rotting, then it wasn't in my area of expertise.

"I sense great anger in this spirit," Treth said.

Duh, I wanted to reply.

"I…I think I know it. Kat, repeat what I say."

Out of ideas, I did so:

"Gorgo," I began, shouting Treth's words over the cacophony. His voice sounded sad. I could not help but echo the sentiment, as if acting off a script. "It's me. Treth."

The tempest seemed to calm. The cyclone of books slowed to a hover.

"I don't know what happened to you back home, Gorgo, but you must be strong. You were the greatest cleric at the monastery. My best friend. Don't let yourself be consumed by the ruinous powers. You are better than being a spirit. Fight it. Reclaim the light."

The books slowed. Some debris fell soundlessly to the hard-carpeted floors. The discord ceased. I breathed a sigh, and then everything exploded again – a gush of torment surpassing the one before.

"I think you made it angry," I shouted.

"She is too far gone."

"Who is she?" I cried louder, to rise over the din below.

"A friend. She was a cleric at the monastery where I lived. She…was sacrificed….to feed a lich's ritual. It must have driven her spirit mad. Sullied by dark magic, her soul cannot move on. It writhes in torment."

Treth paused and whispered. "Oh gods, why Gorgo?"

I didn't respond. I could not. That was Treth's trauma. I couldn't begin to understand it.

Or could I?

I did not know what happened to Treth, but I now knew what happened to Gorgo. It was something I knew all too well. The hatred, the loathing, the fear and trauma. The cold stone table. The undead all around. A

76

necromancer, more monster than man, thinking they had the right to my life.

I understood.

"Gorgo. This is Kat. Not Treth."

It was faint, but the storm seemed to calm, as if the poltergeist was listening.

"I know what it's like to be scared. To be in a place where all you know is terror. I may not know exactly what you went through. I never could. But I know that we all have memories. And we both have memories of what the dark has done to us. And I know that every second of my life, I want to scream. I want to cry. I know that I'm angry. With all these feelings, I want to give up. To let despair take me. To embrace the horror. But I cannot, Gorgo. 'Cause then it wins."

The storm was visibly waning. I felt an invisible presence before me, as if the incorporeal Gorgo was staring into my eyes.

"You let the memories rule you, and you have truly lost. And for all they have done to us, we can't let them win."

I fell slowly to the ground, landing on a pile of soft-covers and torn papers. All the debris fell, calmly. None so fast that the fragile material could break. Pranish awoke as he was slowly lowered, looking around like a lost puppy.

The winds focused, and sucked into the centre of the room, and then glowed. A warm, light-blue glow. Tranquil. It floated wisp-like to me, where I still sat precariously on the books.

"Can Treth hear me?" it said, a woman's voice, reverberating as if being transmitted from another world.

I nodded.

"You were a moron, Treth," Gorgo said, "But I miss you."

She disappeared.

Despite the pain in my haunches, and the bruises on my arms where I had been pelted by books during my brief unconsciousness, I stood. I waved my arms as I almost slipped on some books but managed to get off the pile. Pranish had awoken, and was looking at me, a hint of awe.

I limped to the back of the store and picked up a book. Its spine was only slightly scuffed. I hobbled back to the front, Pranish's eyes following me the entire way.

I placed a crumpled ball of notes on the cashier counter, and then I left. The crowd stared, as I limped, book in my arms. They parted like the Red Sea and watched as my back shrunk farther and farther away.

Chapter 6. New Ventures

"I've got to hand it to you, Kat. You said you'd find the time and you did. But I got to say, this doesn't seem worth it."

I was reading Warpwars in the shade of a copse near the central plaza on campus, resting on the grass. It was a period between lectures for me, and the faint ambience of footsteps and chatter contrasted with the tweeting of birds and hum of casual casting as students with spark used it for everything from lighting cigarettes to attracting mates. I had managed to finish my history assignment in a mad rush, at the expense of sleep. Straight afterwards, I began reading.

"You haven't read the others. Can't really judge it without reading the rest of the series."

"It's all aliens and spaceships. No honour. No glorious melee. No valour. Just self-interested freelancers doing their own thing. Horrendous!"

"I'm a self-interested freelancer."

Treth let out one of his characteristic and incorporeal derisive snorts.

I smiled faintly and amusedly, but I couldn't focus on the book. Maybe it was that I had waited so long for it that the hype now outstripped the book itself. But that wasn't it. It was a great read. All the stuff I loved from the previous books. It was a welcome addition. But I just couldn't focus. Perhaps, it was the slight pain in my leg from the fall the day before? Or that the last years of being a monster hunter had made reading dull?

But those didn't seem right either.

My mind kept drifting to the poltergeist. Gorgo, Treth had called her. Someone he knew. She was sacrificed. Like how I almost was. I couldn't help but wonder if Treth had met a similar fate. I knew very little about Treth's life, despite all the time we had spent as one. To be fair, he didn't know much about my past either. Our relationship was professional, as much as it was forced. I didn't want to exorcise Treth, and all the spirit-seers I had visited so far couldn't detect him. I didn't think he was part of my imagination. I trusted in my own sanity enough for that. Gorgo's wisp speaking to me only further validated that Treth did exist. Nonetheless, we were stuck together, so we made the best of it. Didn't mean we were going to speak heart to heart. But, maybe we should?

"Treth?" I whispered, eyes glued to the third sentence on the page, but not reading it.

"Yes?"

"About Gorgo…"

"I'm sorry, Kat. I would rather not speak about it."

I nodded, slowly. I tried to continue reading.

"It isn't that I don't trust you," Treth continued, interrupting me as I almost finished the sentence. "There is nothing to trust one about. But it is my burden. I wouldn't be a knight if I placed my burdens on you…"

"Because I'm a lady?"

"Because you're someone else. Don't be caustic with me, Kat. You should know that I think you're capable, if a bit impetuous. But this is my problem."

I shrugged, hoping that was that, and looked back at the page. A shadow loomed over me and before I could look up, a sliver of paper blocked my view of the page.

"Your receipt," Pranish said, beaming ear to ear. There was no sign of any injuries or trauma from the day before. He wore a dark-grey waistcoat over a white-buttoned up shirt. Always over-dressed for the occasion. Around his neck was a glowing green stone on a golden chain. Pranish's mage-dominated family were trying everything to enhance his measly powers. And as the heads of the prosperous Nightsilver Industries, they had plenty of resources to waste on the effort – including the money to buy a gold necklace, a metal meant to strengthen casting, with an enchanted jade-stone. I hadn't seen any improvements yet.

Trudie was next to him. I was glad to see a faint smile on her lips. It had become the norm for her to look at me with a creased forehead of concern and a glare of disapproval.

"I'm glad to see you back to your high school self," Trudie said, taking a seat on the grass next to me and stealing a glance at the book, receipt now deposited in my pocket. Trudie lit up a cigarette, sending a cloud of acrid smoke across me and Pranish, who winced as he took a seat as well, flanking me.

"It good?" Pranish asked, trying to hide his disgust at the cigarette smoke washing over us. I did not smoke, nor liked the smell of smoke, but I hung around rotting corpses for a living. I could handle a little bit of tobacco.

I nodded and hummed in the affirmative. I kept the book open, as if I was going to get any reading done.

Trudie took another puff and looked like she was restraining herself from sniggering at Pranish's expense. Her black lipstick stained the white butt of the cigarette as she withdrew it and began playing with the ribbon in my hair. I swatted her hand away and she grinned before her face soured.

"I heard about what happened yesterday."

I shut the book with a sigh. I knew that they wouldn't care. This would have been their goal all along.

"What about yesterday?" I said, attempting to hide all hints of apprehension in my voice.

Rift-damn Pranish, running his mouth off...

"I also shop at Riverstone, Kat," Trudie frowned. "Even if Pranish wasn't raving about you all this morning during maths, I would have found out. When a ghost haunts a shop and a student exorcises it, that gets around."

"Was a poltergeist," I muttered.

Trudie took a drag and waved the comment aside.

"You were amazing, Kat!" Pranish said, excitability overwhelming his usual restraint.

I shrugged. I didn't think so. All I did was talk.

"You seemed out of it for most of the time I was there."

"I was awake when it counted. Saw you staring that glowing orb down until it went poof."

Pranish made a poofing motion with his hands for emphasis.

"You didn't look afraid at all. I was involuntarily casting from fright and you were staring this thing down as if it was a disgruntled kitten."

I snorted. "I'd show much more concern for a disgruntled kitten."

Pranish's beam grew, as if that was possible, and he practically shook with excitement. "So cool…"

I rolled my eyes but couldn't help but feel a tinge of pride. Despite not being able to read my mind, Treth said:

"Pride cometh before a fall. Humility, Kat."

"Cool or not," Trudie said, voice seething with thinly veiled irritation. "It is dangerous. You're an undead hunter, as much as that is already a stupid idea, not an exorcist! What were you thinking?"

"She doesn't need to be an exorcist if she can handle spirits like she handled that one," Pranish interjected.

"Exactly," I said. "I handled it."

"But you didn't know that beforehand."

I sighed. I knew Trudie was just concerned. She was my oldest and best friend, after all. Me becoming a monster hunter had hit her hard. But it was my life. And she couldn't understand what it meant to me. She hasn't seen what I've seen, and she doesn't have a medieval knight living in her head.

Pranish and Trudie didn't know about Treth. I considered telling them on many occasions, but after spirit-seers couldn't detect him, I decided to keep him under wraps. I didn't want them thinking me any more eccentric than they already did.

"Pranish was in trouble. Didn't have much of a choice."

"Thanks, Kat," Pranish said, puffing up his chest a bit. Proud, for some reason.

Trudie let out an almighty sigh.

"It's just that…it's impulsive. This worked out okay, but what about the next time? I'm almost used to you fighting zoms, but there's so many more dangerous things out there. Yeah, a spirit yesterday. But what if it is a werewolf today? A dragon tomorrow?"

I put up my hands, conceding. "I'll be more careful. I'll do my research. Sharpen my blades, so to speak."

That didn't seem to satisfy her.

"What if it is a case like with me yesterday, though?" Pranish asked.

"Then," I said, stifling a yawn as my repeated late-nights threatened to catch up with me. "I'll be impulsive."

Pranish grinned. Trudie rolled her eyes.

"Regardless," Pranish said, changing to his serious voice. "You are getting really good at this. I must say, I used to agree with Trudie. I was worried you were gonna get bit and die of necro-sick."

"Didn't really show me much support," Trudie grumbled.

"But you didn't... and now you've been doing this for almost two years."

"Much to my chagrin."

I put my arm around Trudie. "Sorry about that, hey."

She gave me a small grin. Satisfied, I let go and clutched my book, trying to send some subtle hints that I wanted to get back to reading.

I heard the muffled sound of *The Smith*'s playing and felt my phone vibrate in my pocket. I reached for it.

"Unknown number," I muttered.

"Don't answer it," Trudie added.

"May be a client. Let me take this."

I answered.

"Is this Kat Drummond?"

"Yes. Speaking?"

"I'm phoning on behalf of a client. I heard about how you exorcised a poltergeist from Riverstone Mall yesterday."

"News travels fast."

"Especially when a poltergeist is exorcised at all. I have a haunting I want you to look into."

"That was a fluke. I specialise in undead."

"Not necessarily a fluke, and this should be a good way to test that. The spirit seems, for the most part, harmless. Just irritating to my client. The local weylines have also shown some signs of corruption. I suspect it is a lesser poltergeist, or just a ghost."

"Hmmm." I rubbed my chin, thoughtfully. I saw Trudie's eyes. They were telling me to hang up.

"How much?"

"For a purification of the building? $500."

I almost choked on nothing. That was more money than I've ever been paid for a hunt! But spirits weren't my forte…

"I'll do it."

"Superb! I'll forward the case signature and details to your MonsterSlayer account."

"Thanks."

We both hung up.

"Another hunt?" Trudie asked.

"A haunting."

"Rifts, Kat! What was I just telling you?"

"It was one of those impulsive situations."

"How?"

"If I didn't accept a chance at that much money, I'd be in grave danger of hurting myself."

Trudie rolled her eyes, again. Pranish's grin remained.

Chapter 7. Research

It all started with a spark. The Spark. The Cataclysm didn't start with monsters and demons. It started with humans. Glowing orbs rising from the hands of office workers, fireballs being flung by homeless people, and an overwhelming arrogance by people who had gained immense power by sheer luck. Arbitrarily, or so I and many people believe, people gained magical abilities. This was called the Spark – a magical energy residing at the core of its owner.

When the big rift opened – the Vortex in Siberia – it released tendrils, like roots from a tree. These spread throughout the world. Where they passed, the new magic-users of the world felt immense power. These were dubbed weylines, inspired by the elves who subsequently colonised northern New Zealand and parts of Ireland. People flocked to weylines. Enchantments were stronger there. Magic-users flourished. And people in their vicinity just felt good. Weylines exuded a sense of purity. But not all weylines were good, and not all good weylines necessarily remained so.

While I may seem quite disparaging towards my friend Pranish, I do respect him. While I may mock his inept use of magic, this is mostly due to my own distaste for magic-users. When it comes to the theory behind magic, there is no one else I'd trust more than Pranish.

"What spirits corrupt weylines?" I asked of him, sitting in an isolated part of the library as he studied runemancy. He was in study-mode, and his usual silly grin was replaced by a forehead wrinkled in concentration.

Without looking away, he answered. "Technically, none necessarily. Well, that's what Caroline Gerdavoire argues."

"It is commonly thought that all monsters corrupt weylines…"

"And common thought is commonly wrong. Only a few monsters definitely corrupt weylies. Demons and greater vampires. Their presence is, as this fine establishment refuses to acknowledge, innately evil."

"I like this guy," Treth said. "But many undead types also corrupt weylines, according to the studies on my world."

I touched my bottom lip with my index finger, thoughtfully, as I sat down. I had phoned the client earlier and their main concern was weylines corruption. But they thought it was a spirit.

"What exactly is weyline corruption?" I asked. I understood the rudimentary stuff, and had observed its effects, but it wasn't my area of expertise. I knew how to stab things, not fix magical powerlines.

Pranish put a bookmark in his runemancy textbook and closed it. I could not help but feel a small sense of justice, as he had interrupted my reading earlier.

"Think of weylines like a river. You get water from a river. People close to a river get more water. Now, this doesn't mean that people far away from a river don't have any water. People can carry water with them. And: people have water inside them already."

"Sorcerers?"

"Exactly. While being near a weyline helps with all manner of casting, enchanting and rituals, sorcerers strictly don't need to be near one to use magic. People like me have their own innate magic. We don't need weylines to cast."

"But sure helps, I presume."

"That's the thing. It is sorcery if you use your own power. It is wizardry if you tap into a weyline."

"Even husks like me?" I smirked.

Pranish winced at the term. Husk – a non-sorcerer. Someone without a spark. He had his own spark, but it was weak.

"Yes. Wizards don't have their own spark. But with enough knowledge and practice, they can tap into weylines and then use magic."

"Back to the topic. You were explaining weylines corruption."

Pranish nodded. Despite his jovialness earlier today, his studies and the topic at hand had brought a serious expression to his face. Magic was a sore point for Pranish, but that didn't stop him from wanting to master its theory. As a result of his weak spark, Pranish sought to enhance his wizardry rather than his sorcery. I admired that. Wizardry was earned through intense study. It wasn't just some arbitrary privilege.

"If weylines are a river, corruption could be thought of as pollution. Not everything we do with water is nice and harmless. We need it for chemical treatment, sewage, cleaning of vile substances…etcetera. When people, or things, use weylines for bad ends, the magic they use will inevitably find its way back into a weyline. If the magic is what we call dark magic, then the weylines start becoming dirtier. Corrupted."

"What does that mean?"

"Well, observed corrupt weylines are darker in hue than the usual glowing blue."

I did not know weylines could be observed, just detected.

"I mean practically."

"This is all up for debate in the academic community, but the school of thought I find most convincing is that corrupted weylines improve the casting of dark magic, while lessening the effectiveness of other types of magic."

"It has to be more than that. A lot of non-magic users complain about corrupted weylines."

"While unscientific, many report that corrupted weylines bring a sense of unease. A discomfort. People living near them become grumpier. Crime allegedly rises. Domestic abuse, and such."

"Nothing about monsters?"

Pranish sighed. "Some believe that monsters are attracted to corrupt weylines. There has been no evidence to suggest this. I think they're getting their order wrong.

The monsters are already there, and the weyline is corrupted due to dark magic."

"What about the theory that evil acts can corrupt weylines?"

Pranish waved the question aside. "Weylines are not agents with moral frameworks. They don't and can't judge acts to be good or evil. Dark magic is something measurable. It's a language of nature. Morality is manmade. It has no bearing on weylines."

I shrugged. Treth seethed.

"Thanks, Pranish. Last question: are there any spirits that you know of that can cast dark magic?"

Pranish shook his head. "Monsters, even non-undead, are more your speciality, Kat. I'd read up on the spirit section in the library."

I nodded my thanks and departed.

"I disagree with him on quite a few things," Treth said.

"And you know better?"

"My world had weylines, even if we called them something else, long before Earth did."

"But we have the scientific method, Mr Medieval."

"Regardless, I believe corrupted weylines do cause more than unease. They are caused by acts of evil, manmade or not, and absorb that energy. Then, the evil energy is exuded, causing discomfort and angst in the population. Go to corrupt weylines and close your eyes. You will feel the impurity."

"And monsters?"

"Many monsters are magic users. Wights, for instance, as we both know. Dark magic is stronger within corrupted weylines."

"And spirits?"

Treth shook his incorporeal head. "Spirits were not that common where I came from. We had purity rites. When you've been fighting the undead for centuries, you learn how to properly stop the dead from being raised."

"From what I know, spirits are often not necessarily the departed dead. They seem like their own species. Wraiths and banshees are aspects of a departed dead. Their rage. Their lust for vengeance. Their torment. But then there are gremlins, gheists and haunts. They don't come from the dead."

"Seems like a flaw in their categorisation."

I snorted in amusement.

"Regardless, let's go check out the site. Can test your weylines testing eye-closing whatchadoodle there."

***

No rushing in, I had promised Trudie. And I'd stick to it, at least most of the time. While for most of my hunts, I just tracked the beast and put it down, this required a more delicate touch. Research. Investigation. A plan.

Treth was torn.

"You need a plan!" he would often say, right after I successfully decapitated a ghoul.

But when it came to this, his tune changed.

"Just go in. Let's get this sham case over and done with."

"A sham case worth a lot of money."

"So, get it done so you can get paid."

"I thought you'd condemn my lust for riches, Sir Knight." I grinned.

"The sooner you get this fool errand out of the way, the sooner we can get back to real slaying."

"Not into exorcisms?"

"As I said, spirits were a rarity on my world. I don't understand them."

"And neither do I," I sighed. "And that is why we need to be careful."

The afternoon sun was warm on my back as I walked along the concrete pavement. My destination was near the Old Town. One of the middling parts. While a main weyline had kept the central part of Hope City bustling, many parts without any magical energy had fallen into ruin. People still lived there, sure, but magic was the main industry. Without weylines, non-magic users – or husks, as they were so affectionally called – had to rely on the mundane industries of the pre-Cataclysmic variety.

This part of town was inbetween. It wasn't located on a main weyline, but it was near some tendrils. Like splintering streams from a river, to continue Pranish's example. While not as powerful or reliable as the main weylines, these tendrils provided adequate energy to the casual wizard, sorcerer looking for a pick-me-up, or a demon looking to sup on the fruits of the Vortex.

All this culminated in a neighbourhood that wasn't too great but wasn't too bad. It was in these neighbourhoods that I found most of my clients. Rich enough to hire me. Poor enough to have to.

The street was quiet. Most of the houses were walled off. Pre-Cataclysm politics had people scared. The undead that came after the Vortex made it even more important to erect a concrete barricade around one's residence.

I stopped outside a house without a wall. I checked my phone. The yet unnamed client had sent me the details.

"This is the place."

"I think they're mixing up a bad weyline with bad maintenance."

I couldn't help but agree.

Instead of a concrete wall, the client's property was behind a broken-down wire fence, currently lying flat on the ground. Dry grass had overgrown around it. This too long, dead grass, peppered with weeds, stretched up to a dilapidated triple storey house. Facebrick could be seen where paint and plaster had been chipped away by the weather. Peeling paint adorned the rest of the veritable shanty. I swore I heard creaks as the wind whooshed past. I heard a whistle as air passed through the house, indicating an open or broken window. In its day, it may have been a manor house. A happy home. Now, it was a ramshackle ruin, bringing down the property prices of its neighbours.

"The client hasn't been living in the building for years. They want to sell but can't do anything until the spirit is out."

"If there even is a spirit."

"Spirit or not, this place looks unnaturally decrepit."

"Nonse..." Treth stopped. He thought for a bit. "Now that you mention it..."

"Let's do your weyline test."

"Get closer to the house. Won't be able to feel any points of corruption this far away."

I frowned. "Do I have to? It looks like it'll fall on me."

I felt Treth stare at me disapprovingly. I sighed and made my way to the door of the house. It had a roofed porch up a short flight of stairs. I stopped by the steps. I did feel something. An uneasiness. But who wouldn't feel uneasy near a house that looked undead?

Could a house be undead?

"That unease may or may not be as a result of weyline corruption," Treth said.

"Some test."

"Shush. Close your eyes."

Reluctantly, I did so. A breeze passed by and sent chills through my body.

"Clear your head. Expel all natural discomfort at being in such a place."

"Easier said than done, Treth."

I breathed in and then exhaled. I thought about Warpwars, about Alex, and then with those being my last thoughts, cleared my mind. I focused on nothing in particular, and let my inner senses do the thinking.

Nothing, as expected. Then, I felt a tingle on the back of my neck. I thought nothing of it. This place gave me the creeps. Any dead building would do that to you. I calmed my breathing and focused on the blackness of my closed eyes.

But the tingle increased.

It felt like a gust of wind, focused on my neck. But then it hardened. And it stroked my nape, with its cold, icy hand.

I opened my eyes and the sensation left. But I still felt its after effects. A numbness where the incorporeal had touched me.

"What is it?" Treth asked, sincere concern in his voice.

I began walking rapidly towards the street. Back straight, tense. I was holding my breath. My heart beat like a machine-gun. My skin felt hyper-sensitive underneath my jeans and top. I felt every dry blade of grass brush across my ankles.

As I arrived on the pavement and parked myself in front of the neighbour's house, I breathed again.

"What happened?" Treth asked once more, worry rising in his voice.

"Didn't you feel that?" I gasped, still struggling to breathe.

"Feel what?"

"A…thing."

"A what?"

"Some sort of presence."

"A spirit?"

"Maybe. I don't know about the weyline, but I have little doubt this place is haunted."

Treth was silent, then spoke in a hesitant whisper.

"Are you sure we should continue?"

I hesitated as well. Should I? I was an undead slayer! I knew how to stab things. Not how to exorcise spirits. I took the job because I thought it'd be the usual. Most people didn't understand the magical. A rat in the floorboards might as well be a wraith to them. But this was the real deal. Could I handle the real deal?

"I must," I finally said. "I took the job."

Treth didn't say anything, but I felt him exude some sort of emotion. Perhaps – pride?

"Let's get back home. I have research to do, and then shopping."

"You have enough noodles and tinned cream corn stocked up to last a few more weeks."

"Not for food. The research is one thing – but I need the proper tools."

***

Treth condemned my use of the "shining box" to research spirits. To him, only leather-bound tomes enchanted by druids counted as reliable knowledge. Lucky for me, plenty of these leather-bound druid tomes had been transcribed onto the internet.

My research took a while. I didn't have the right search terms. I didn't know what to search for in the vast labyrinths of the web. How could I? How does one describe what I felt? How does one put pure sensation into words? Eventually, I found something half-way sufficient. I gave up on the easy research route and downloaded a document detailing different recorded spirit types. I recognised a few. Ghosts were common knowledge. I knew about wraiths. Had a run in with a poltergeist, of course. Others were less familiar. Wisps, banshees, revenants, terrors, haunts…

And among all of them, two stood out. They were perhaps the vaguest of the bunch. Disturbances and presences. Both could be confused with just a feeling of disquiet but were potentially much more sinister. They were incorporeal, non-visible spirits who had limited interaction with the physical world. This limited interaction could be felt, however, in the touching of mortals and the making of noise. As was the case with so many other-worldly topics, the information on these two spirits was limited – but one thing was certain. Both disturbances and presences were there, and that is what made my experience earlier today so uncomfortable.

"Which do you think it is?" I asked.

"Not much to go on," Treth replied. "The client reported noises, right?"

I nodded.

"Then probably a disturbance."

A pause.

"But what you described sounded much more sinister."

"My imagination, perhaps. My uneasiness at diversifying the business. It can't be too evil. It had a low weyline signature."

"Or something else…"

"Just in case, I will overcompensate with the kit."

"The kit?"

"I need to buy some exorcism equipment. Moonsilver dust, enchanted water, purity seals, a sigil of undoing…"

"You'll spend coin on all these knick-knacks, but you won't invest in a decent weapon?"

I closed my eyes. I liked Treth, but he could get on my nerves. Constant nagging could do that to anyone. Alex stroked himself up against my leg and I petted him on the head. He rewarded me with a deep rumbling purr, much larger than his size. Treth continued.

"You won't reach your destiny if you don't take your proper slaying seriously. A knight always makes sure they have the best armour and weapon they can get. These spirits are a sideshow. The real monsters are out there."

That shocked my eyes open. Treth often alluded to destiny. Fate. Mystic crap. But I never thought much of it. He was a medieval knight. I cut him a lot of slack due to that. But he had been acting odd lately. A small part of me wanted to be diplomatic, to humour the poor, disembodied fool. But an even larger part of me wanted to prove him wrong.

"I am not a knight. And what destiny?"

"Your destiny. The fate we rush towards. Or should be rushing towards if we weren't distracting ourselves with harmless ethereals."

I snorted. "My destiny to do what?"

"To slay monsters."

"I do that of my own accord. Destiny, fate…has nothing to do with it."

"Do you truly think that?"

"Yes."

"You think our paths crossed by accident alone, and not the cosmic will of the gods and amorphous fate?"

"Yes," I replied, tinging the word with an even greater note of finality. As much as I wanted to argue, I also did not. I hope that makes sense. I wanted Treth to know he was wrong, but at the same time, I wanted to end the conflict.

"Really?" he whispered, sounding disappointed.

I sighed. Resignation was starting to overwhelm my irritability. "I have become a monster hunter because of my actions and you tying yourself to me. Destiny had nothing to do with it. Some cosmic randomness, or equally arbitrary will of some magical science nonsense linked us together. Not fate, and, I sincerely doubt, the gods."

Treth didn't respond. Silence.

"I can't believe in fate," I finally continued, whispering. Alex jumped on my lap and rubbed his head on my chest. "If I believe in fate, I must believe my parents were meant to die."

"Maybe, they were."

"Shut up." I was surprised by the icy-cold venom in my voice as I spoke before even thinking. Treth must have been stunned to silence. Seconds changed to what seemed like minutes, of silence.

Finally:

"I'm sorry," I said.

"Don't be. What I said was inappropriate. I'm sorry."

I didn't reply immediately. I stroked Alex's head, and then stood.

"Let's go. I've got stuff to buy."

Chapter 8. Horror

I arrived at the client's ramshackle manor at nightfall. The sun had finished its slow descent and the city was bathed in the darkness of night.

I had spent the rest of the afternoon perusing the magical shops of Long Street, Old Town. While I was by no means an exorcist, as I have stated plenty of times before, I had found some reliable guides on exorcism. Well, reliable was an overstatement. I had found swathes of texts on the expulsion of spirits, some dating back to pre-Cataclysm. I ignored those. As far as I was concerned, there had been no genuine spirits on Earth before the Vortex arrived. Just hocus pocus and opportunists. Now was a different story. There were scientifically provable incorporeal beings that we could consider spirits, and we had some ways of getting rid of them.

Silver was anathema to many spirits. Silver swords could pierce the normally ethereal flesh of wraiths. Silver dust could make spirits semi-corporeal, allowing their swift execution through sheer force. Enchantments and magic could be used to force spirits to flee, as they became wrestled from their fetters. But not all spirits were so easily dealt with. Spirits were here for a reason. While many could be dealt with simply, many others could not.

Disturbances, as I believed this spirit was, were much more complicated. I couldn't just toss silver on it to make it corporeal. It didn't even have a visible incorporeal form. It was like the wind. How does one find the origin of the wind?

Solving complex hauntings required delicacy, and a plan. I was not used to that. The undead were much simpler. Cruder. You look for its head (or equivalent) and destroy it. Use fire, and it becomes even simpler. Spirits were a whole different ball game. But I had promised Trudie that I'd be careful. That I'd do this properly. That meant a plan. And while Treth may be irritated that I was taking this more seriously than more normal hunts, there was a reason for this. I had proven I could take care of the undead. I hadn't proven I could take care of spirits. So, I needed to work hard. Smarter.

Disturbances were relatively harmless. They did, however, damage weylines (according to some) and did steal from people's sleep. It is not nice knowing something is watching you as you sleep, and then has the audacity to break a vase and stroke your neck with icy hands. They were also one of the harder spirits to exorcise. They didn't respond to seances, couldn't be peppered with silver and couldn't be directly exorcised with plain purification magic. Rather, the most reliable method was to trap them to their fetter with purification seals, vellum enchanted with purification magic, and then close them in. It was like a genuine hunt of yore. Surround the prey. Close them off. Tighten the noose. Strangle them until they have nowhere left to go. And then, kill them.

But it was hard work. I had to place a seal at strategic points of the house, starting with the furthest points from the centre and then slowly placing more until the only place not covered by the holy rites was a small portion of the haunted abode. Then, I would trap the spirit using a rune of entrapment drawn with moonsilver powder mixed with salt.

The entire plan was complex. It required everything to go as perfectly as possible. My timing had to be on point and everything had to be done in the proper sequence. I'd much rather be tangling with a wight, even without demanzite.

It had also been expensive. I had to spend my entire last pay check on the supplies. If I succeeded, the pay-out would be worth it, though. And if I didn't – then plenty of zombie parts to sell in the slums. That was, of course, if I made it out.

But that was silly talk. It was creepy, but I'd faced much worse than creepy. It was just some mischievous and possibly depressed spirit. A gül or wight was much scarier in practicality.

Streetlights adequately lit up the suburban street, but no lights shone from the manor. Only the moon lit my path to the front door. I stopped at the porch.

"Second guessing?"

"Pah! Never." I said that, but I must admit that I did consider leaving.

I looked up at the shadowy house before me, silhouetted by moonlight, took a deep breath, and ascended the steps. The door was unlocked. No point keeping an abandoned and haunted house locked.

I turned on my bag-strap mounted torch. Dust shimmered in the light-beam. I stepped forward. The floorboards creaked.

"Can this get any more cliched?"

"If the disturbance is wearing a rubber mask, then yes."

I couldn't help but laugh. I didn't know where Treth picked up that reference. I also noted that he seemed back to his old self, at least for a bit. That was good.

I checked my kit one final time before continuing into the rest of the building. By my side, a satchel full of the vellum and wax purity seals, on the other, my surviving short sword (just in case). In my backpack: moonsilver powder, some salt and vinegar crisps, a spare handheld flashlight, a lighter and Warpwars – in case I got a chance.

"Let's take this nice and slow."

"Sharpen your sword for as long as it takes but strike swiftly when the time comes."

"Another quote?"

"Indeed," Treth affirmed.

"Who said it?" I asked, examining the doorway, my hands on my hips. I saw what seemed like a good point for the seal and placed it. The wax was sticky, and its enchantments helped the seal adhere to the wall with ease.

"My master."

"Tell me about him."

"You've never asked about him before." Treth sounded just a tad apprehensive.

"Let's say I want a distraction roundabout now."

"He was a great man," Treth replied, and then silence.

"And?" I finally asked, examining a smashed mirror.

Treth sighed. "What else am I supposed to say?"

"Perhaps, his name?"

Treth didn't reply. I shrugged and continued down the dank hallways of this crumbling excuse for a home. Even the brick walls seemed brittle. As if they had been rotting, like willows in a swamp. The swarm of dust, combined with the darkness all around the arc of my flashlight, made me claustrophobic. I was thankful that many of the windows were broken. They let in some fresh air, as well as a merciful glow of moonlight, which pooled onto the decaying carpets and wooden floors, and glinted on the broken glass shards still surviving in their long-abandoned frames. Without this fresh air, I may have seriously contemplated Treth's suggestion of reconsidering this entire thing. But then the weight at my sides reminded me that I was way too invested already. Had to press on.

The open windows were prime places to place seals. While incorporeal, most spirits couldn't pass through solid objects. They needed holes, cracks. Rather than phase through walls, they had to sieve through small openings – like smoke. I couldn't account for all the cracks, but I could create a relatively stable zone of purification to keep the spirit contained. At least, I hoped.

"You're normally chattier, Treth."

I reached up to stick a seal above an open window. I could see into the neighbour's house. They were having dinner. This late at night? They better not be going to bed soon. Very unhealthy. Says me…

"I have little to say tonight," Treth finally answered. "I am usually giving you advice, but this is not my regular hunt. I can do nothing but wait for it to be over, and then we can go back to the real monsters."

"Spirits aren't real monsters?"

"Some are. Wraiths, definitely. But this disturbance? It is basically a less dangerous rat."

"They corrupt weylines."

"Minimally. I can also detect corruption, remember, despite my lack of body. I have not detected any severe corruption here. It seems to be the same as any other rundown building."

"Rundown buildings corrupt weylines?" I snorted.

"Ever felt comfortable in a rundown building?"

I wanted to say yes, but that would have been a lie.

"Exactly." Treth took my silence as assent. "There is order, growth and life – good. And then there's chaos, decay and death – evil. Evil corrupts. This decay is evil."

"I struggle to put this on the same level as necromancy and murder, Treth."

I bent down by a hole in the wall and placed a seal over it.

"And it is not. But it is on the same spectrum. You wouldn't consider a pickpocket on the same level as a Lich, but both are no doubt bad."

"If you say so."

"I do."

I giggled, reaching into my bag for another seal, as I entered a furnitureless room.

"What's so funny?"

"Nothing…nothing. Just that…got you talking again."

The front of the house done, I proceeded down a hall. There was more furniture here. Old stuff. Antiques, neglected and caked in grime. I turned into a room and my flashlight glinted harshly. I squinted until my eyes adjusted. A mirror on a dressing table. And on the dressing table, some wax candles stuck to the surface.

"Let's make some ambience."

Treth grunted his agreement.

I took out my zippo lighter and held it to the wicks. Some people thought me a smoker when they saw the shining steel case, but I couldn't stand tobacco. I kept the lighter to immolate dead bodies. One by one, the flames bounced off the mirror and sent a warm glow across the room. The flames, while small, warmed my hands. I didn't know they had been cold until then. I was wearing my work gloves and it was early autumn. It shouldn't be that cold.

But I was cold. Cold enough that I felt that I should be able to see my breath. I exhaled and saw nothing. The air wasn't cold. It was just me. I shivered and turned, but as I did, I caught an image in the mirror.

My sword clinked as I pulled it clean out of its scabbard. I turned away from the mirror, towards the doorway – sword at the ready and my legs ready to bolt.

Nothing.

I turned back to the mirror. Nothing.

"You okay?" Treth asked.

I shook my head and clutched the bridge of my nose with my thumb and index finger.

"No…I mean yes. It's fine. Just, the house has me on edge."

"It is wise to fear…" Treth began.

"But right and glorious to stand your ground," I finished and sheathed my sword.

"I've said it before?"

"Many times."

"Sorry…" Treth sounded chided.

"I'm not annoyed. Consider it a sign that you're a good teacher."

Treth didn't respond, but I felt a warmth emanate from him. I was glad. I didn't like fighting with Treth. Couldn't really get away from him to cool off.

Eventually, I coated the bottom floor with purity seals, covering every major opening and ensuring that the effective radius of the seals coated every inch of the outer wall.

I was standing at the entrance again. A faint fiery glow shone from parts of the house, where I had found candles and lit them. I unsheathed my phone and checked the time. I had been circling the house for an hour!

"Oh Rifts, this is going to take all night."

"Then no more wasting time. To the next floor!"

"Starting to like this job?" I asked, a hint of false mockery in my voice, jogging up the stairway. Mercifully, it didn't creak and seemed quite stable. The light shook as my body vibrated up the stairway.

"We're committed to it, so might as well get into it."

"That's the *spirit*!"

"Har. Har."

The stairs opened into another hallway. Symmetrical doorways flanked a torn, patterned rug. Its imagery was obscured by the damage and the dark. Chairs and small wooden tables were scattered throughout the passage, strewn like they were being sold at an unenthusiastic yard sale.

"Chaos," Treth commented.

"Evil?"

"Getting there."

Treth may be a tad OCD.

I entered the door on my left. An unmade bed with torn sheets dominated the room. I felt a draft coming from the window. It felt good. Natural. It wasn't like the whistling gales that felt like a conscious foe. I made my way to the open window and took another seal out of my bag. I reached to the top of the window and heard a crash.

I dropped the seal and spun, drawing my sword – for all the good that would do me against a spirit. The crash had come from this floor.

"That was no ghostly sound," Treth said.

"It could be."

Silence. And then a thump.

"It doesn't sound calculated enough," Treth continued. "Strike now. If it is a physical foe, take them off their guard, strike before they can prepare themselves."

I charged, trained by over a year of Treth's tutelage, and skidded into the hallway, shifting the torn rug below me. A tearing sound. Fabric. Curtains. I darted down the hallway towards the noise. A human wouldn't be tearing a curtain, but neither would a spirit. But an undead or other beast…

I knew how to deal with those.

I stopped at a door beside the stairway to the final floor. The noises had become incessant. Scraping, tearing, crunching.

I took a breath and kicked the door open.

"Back, ye bloody bugger!" screeched a petite voice. I narrowed my eyes and couldn't believe what I was seeing.

Hovering off the ground, giving off a faint golden glow, was a tiny elfin figure with butterfly wings. In its minuscule hands was an equally minuscule spear, crafted from a shard of tiny glass, a wooden skewer and the torn threads of the curtain.

"En garde, vile ogre!"

"I didn't know pixies spoke French." I couldn't help but grin ear to ear at the unexpected sight.

"And I didn't know ogres could speak at all," the pixie squeaked.

I raised my eyebrow at that. Ogres were well known for their comprehensible, albeit crude and brutal, speech. They used their handle of human languages quite effectively to conquer swathes of territory and maraud across the plains.

I sighed. "So, you're the one making bumps in the night."

"I don't negotiate with ogres trespassing on my property."

"I wasn't negotiating, and this isn't your property."

"I live here, so it is mine."

"That's not how things work…"

I shook my head. So, this is what I was getting all worked up about.

"This thing must've been the source of all the trouble," Treth said.

"Pixies can send out creepy sensations?" I asked, aloud. The pixie stopped its spear waving and cocked its head. I noted that it looked distinctly male if a bit androgynous. I decided to consider it male.

"Pixies are magical," Treth answered. "May have been putting up wards to scare away intruders."

"Then we've probably found our disturbance."

"I was wrong," the pixie squeaked. "No ogre is as mad as you."

"Yeah, none," I answered, in agreement. "Now, pipsqueak, you gotta get out of here."

"Bugger off, maddy."

I would have laughed, but my vision was blurring. I had been wide awake from the adrenaline of the job but finding out that the threat was just some measly excuse for a faerie was causing my body to realise it was tired.

"It's been a late night…" I stopped, prompting him to give his name.

"Duer," the pixie said, puffing up his chest and stating the name with a rolling R.

Treth snorted. "Doesn't fit the name."

I didn't know what he was talking about, but I could warrant a guess. Pixies may have come from Treth's world, or one like it. They may share the same naming conventions.

"Well, Duer, I'm Kat."

"I don't like cats."

"Kat with a K."

Duer cocked his head again. I got the distinct impression he didn't know how to spell.

"Regardless," I said, my patience ebbing away as I felt the time rushing by when I could be reading or sleeping. "You need to leave. This home belongs to a client of mine. You can't stay here."

"Right bloody likely, maddy with a K."

That didn't make sense...

I sighed, trying to remain calm.

"If you don't leave, I'm going to have to make you leave," I hissed. "Don't make me make you leave."

"That a threat?" Duer asked. I caught a hint of what sounded like a Scottish accent.

"Guess."

I was glaring now. A tired Kat wasn't a happy Kat, and I was very tired.

"Then I have no choice..."

I calmed.

"But to charge!"

I dodged out of the way just in time as Duer whizzed past with his glass shard spear. His movements were silent. No wonder I hadn't heard him until he had started crafting his weapon.

I stumbled into the doorframe with an oomph. The butt of my blade hit the doorframe with a thud. Duer corrected his flight trajectory and flew back at me. I ducked just in time and Duer's spear snapped on the doorframe.

"You're disarmed now. Give up."

"Never!"

"He's got spirit," Treth added.

"Another pun?" I grunted.

I rolled out of the way. Duer was still coming at me with his tiny bare fists.

I backed away. "I don't want to kill you."

"You won't be able to!"

My legs hit the end of the bed and I stopped. Duer charged.

"Calm…"

I felt a sting on my chest. I looked down and saw a needle protruding from my chest, stabbing through my shirt. I pulled it out, causing an unpleasant tingle.

"Now you've done it," I hissed, through gritted teeth, and swiped a wide arc with my sword. I heard a whip as the blade cut through the air. Duer flew towards the roof, avoiding the cut by a wide margin.

"That really necessary?" Treth asked.

"Self-defence," I replied.

"You really are an aggressor, then? Just a mad marauder marauding madly," Duer said in a sing-song voice. He seemed to actually be enjoying this.

"You attacked first."

"And rightly so."

"You kicked out the real owners of this place. You have no rights to stay here."

"This abode, maddy, was abandoned when I found it."

I raised my eyebrow at that. Duer could see, as he said:

"Really. Swear on the fields and trees and all that nonsense."

"Then...why was it abandoned?"

At that moment, the house heaved. Not an earthquake. We didn't get those in Hope City. The walls shook, causing dust to cascade onto the floor. Rumbling. Like a deep growl, coming from the bowels of this undead house. The floor shook. But not like a building was supposed to shake. It felt alive.

"Probably…that," Duer finally answered my question.

I exited the room, Duer's glow followed soundlessly behind me.

I looked down the stairway. No light. Not even the faint glow of the candles. Not even the moonlight. I investigated the other room, where there had been an open window. No light – at all. No moonlight. No distant glow from the streetlights outside.

An all-encompassing darkness.

And then my flashlight died.

"Treth, I think the pixie wasn't the problem."

"My names not Treth," Duer said. "And duh!"

"The weyline is changing, Kat. I feel a veil lifting. It…it wasn't what we thought. Something was masking the corruption, or keeping it at bay, but no longer."

"How bad is it?" I whispered.

"Run."

Without hesitation, I bolted down the stairway.

"Wait up!" Duer shouted. It came out as a squeak.

I navigated by memory and touch, but the roiling of the house and the growing inferno in my chest made that increasingly more difficult. The house shook and shifted to the side. I tripped and caught a railing.

But it wasn't a railing. It was flesh. Cold, brittle flesh. The lights flickered on, and as they did, I screamed.

My hand was holding the arm of a corpse, and it was snarling at me, pointed teeth bared within a lipless mouth with black, bloody gums. White and black eyes with red veins popping out stared at me with a rage not found in human or beast. A gaze of evil incarnate. Snarls deafened me, as the floor below the stairway churned with the quakes of the house, and zombies rose from the floorboards. Not just several, but a horde. A mosh pit of seething, rotting flesh, rising towards me. They clambered on top of each other. Clawing, crawling, pushing to approach their prey closer and closer. They reached out, bloody saliva dripping from their bestial twisted maws. Their flesh seemed to meld together. An abomination of fluxing, rotting, pale and greying flesh.

And I felt a fear I hadn't felt in the years since I met Treth. My chest tightened to the point of paralysis, and I couldn't breathe. I let go of the corpse's arm and jumped back. Duer stopped mid-flight and doubled back, his glow disappearing.

I couldn't tear my gaze from the rotting horde. It was as if I was caught in the headlights of a train – rushing towards me. But this was much worse. The horde clambered up the stairs, snarling. No groans. Just the roars of a hive minded predator.

"Treth! What do I do?" I cried.

He didn't reply. I could only hear my heartbeat, and sobs. I turned to face the top of the stairs. To run. To hide. To do anything…

Another horde blocked my way. Arms outstretched. Blood dripping. Fresh flesh protruding from bestial teeth in an uncanny and defiled human form.

I keeled over and shook my head. Willing them away. It couldn't be…it couldn't…

The noises grew closer. Their cold grasps. And a frigid sensation on my nape.

I looked up. The zombies approached, slowly. Unlike the undead, they were savouring the moment. But necromancers controlled their hordes, and they often played with their victims. They played with people like me.

And I hated them for it.

I hated these things that I feared. I hated them because I feared them. For what they had done to me and done to others. And I hated them enough that I couldn't let them do it again.

I stood and picked up my sword where I'd dropped it on the step below me.

The zombie horde seethed on either side, moving like a pock-marked flesh tide.

Zombies – the undead – were my fear. The thing that kept me awake at night. The stuff that made my nightmares. They had been my reason to fear for the better part of my life.

But I fought my fears every day.

I charged. My blade forward, steady. It made contact, and the zombie stopped moving. I unsheathed the blade from the zombie's head. Silence. And then a roar. I ducked, slicing tendons, letting limbs fall, and letting the zombies dogpile on top of me as I cut through them.

Blood flew, and sprayed, showering zombies in the sick blood of their kindred. I mowed into the horde, slashing, stabbing, pirouetting and maximising my arcs. Blade met neck, limb and tendon. And the zombies fell. Swathes of them.

And with every zombie that fell, the house heaved, and groaned. Objects flew at me and the lights flickered. It was the stuff of a low-budget horror flick. It wasn't enough to unnerve me – not anymore.

The spirit had made a mistake.

I couldn't fight what I couldn't stab, but my greatest fear was very stabbable.

The zombie horde did not thin, but I didn't care. This was my lot. My *raison d'être*. To slay the unhallowed. To make the dead truly die.

And as I did what a gardener would do to weeds, I laughed. I asked for more. I shouted at the house. The horde. The necromancer who had put me here, all those years ago.

And with my laughing and derangement, the house screamed. It rose, and it fell. And then it started to shrink.

The zombies dispersed, in puffs of smoke, and the lights went off. I heard crunching. I looked above me. My flashlight was working again. The roof was cracking.

I ran, and then fell. I cried out as a piece of the roof dropped on my leg. I couldn't see clearly as dust and debris fell. I tried to crawl, and then the stairs collapsed under me, and I closed my eyes.

***

The street was alight with the blinking blue/red sirens of the City Police. Vans from a multitude of private agencies were parked haphazardly, facing the dilapidated building as it glowed purple, jumped into the air, seethed like a thing possessed and began to collapse. Brick by brick, it crumbled and imploded, as if being sucked into a black hole.

The cacophony of voices, sirens and shouts to, "Evacuate the area!" were clouded out by an inhuman scream of a spirit being torn from this mortal plane.

Exorcists, wearing their white robes and covered in vellum scripts of sacrosanct runes, were chatting in motley groups near the edge of the property. None agreed to approach the building. They said that the death throes of the spirit within were too hazardous. No pay check was worth them risking shrapnel in the face just to sprinkle some enchanted water on the reeling mass of brick and wood.

Brett of Drakenbane stood by his agency's van, smoking a cigarette. His ZomBlaster-13 shotgun was slung behind his back. Clients of the agency had called in responders just in case they became threatened by the supernatural occurrence. It was unnecessary, but Brett got paid a call-out fee regardless.

"Damn night shifts," he said, shaking his head and tossing the still lit but flagging cigarette onto the street.

"What?" his partner, Guy Mgebe, shouted over the cacophony.

"I said…" Brett shouted, just as the noise stopped and silence fell. His voice echoed over the silence, but nobody looked his way. Brett and Guy turned to look at where the seemingly demonic house once stood. It was just rubble now, and on top of the rubble, lay a prostrate and unconscious figure.

Brett walked forward, drawing another cigarette and lighting it.

"The terror has dissipated," he heard an exorcist say. The group nodded, but still looked disbelieving.

"It must have been overwhelmed by something. Would need a full circle of mages to exorcise a terror of that calibre."

"Terrors retreat, and even dissipate, when they can't scare particular individuals."

"That's impossible. Terrors reach the darkest fears of the mind. It would take a mythical-level hero to take one down."

The discussion faded to silence as Brett distanced himself from the gaggle of exorcists, walking across the dry grass towards a group of paramedics who were attending to the unconscious hero who had chased away the terror spirit.

Brett's cigarette fell from his mouth as the prone figure came into view. She was splayed, as if spat up by a monster that couldn't digest her. Her tied up hair had become undone and was messily covering her face. A torn backpack, spilling crunched crisps and shredded paper was still stuck to her back. Purity seals were scattered around her. A broken sword was still clutched in her hands.

"Katty?"

"You know this woman?" a blue and white clad medic asked.

"She's a monster hunter."

"Agency?"

"None."

The medic frowned. "How'd she survive?"

"Katty's pulled through worse," Brett said, retrieving his cigarette before the grass set fire. "She'll be fine."

Chapter 9. Recovery

I woke up to a setting sun casting a reddish-orange tint on the clinical white hospital room. I immediately tried to sit up. That was a mistake. A deep pain wracked my body and I instantly stopped moving.

"Well, great."

My voice came out hoarse. I needed a drink. I winced at the thought of sitting up again to get one. I hoped I would recover soon. I needed to get back to work.

Another thought hit me. How was I in the hospital? Sure, I knew why. Crushed up, eaten and then spat up by a house. But who paid for me?

Healthcare was not extortionately expensive in Hope City – thankfully. I had been in enough scrapes to know it was not the greatest of my financial concerns, but if I hadn't been awake to pay for it, who had?

I doubted it was Pranish. His parents could afford it but wouldn't waste money on a husk like me. Especially for a friend of their almost husk son. I hoped it wasn't Trudie or her family. I had promised I'd be careful... It would just add insult to injury if she had to pay for it.

But despite my hopes that it was not the case, I was pretty sure Trudie had covered the bill. I would insist on paying her back. She would refuse. I winced.

"You awake?" Treth asked.

"Yeah," I whispered. I didn't want to risk turning my head to see if I was alone in the room. Best keep my voice low. If there was someone, they may excuse it as fevered muttering. "How long has it been?"

"A few days…"

A pause.

"I'm sorry, Kat…"

"What for?"

"This past week…I haven't been in form. Haven't been the help I should be. When you have needed me most, I have let you down."

"It's fine, Tre…"

"No, it's not! I laid my quest on you and you have helped me achieve what I could not. Cannot. I should be spending every moment helping you. Every moment redeeming myself…"

Treth stopped, suddenly.

"Redeeming yourself for what?"

Treth whispered now, a hushed and intense tone. "I lived a life I am not proud of, Kat. I did bad things. And when I realised it was evil, and that I had to redeem myself, it became too late. But now, with you, I have a chance."

I felt him shake his head. "But after seeing Gorgo again… It reminded me of what I have done, and what I have lost…"

Before I could respond, I heard footsteps approach.

Soon enough, Trudie, wearing her usual getup of black mascara and lipstick, was peering over me with the twin looks of relief and dismay. Pranish joined her, smiling weakly.

"Hi, guys," I smiled. My voice sounded like sandpaper.

"Let's get some water down that throat," Pranish said, slowly helping me up. I wasn't as sore anymore. I felt a refreshing chill on my back. Pranish was casting his cryomancy to ease the pain in my back with cold. Like ice on a sprain. I became increasingly appreciative of his powers, and a tad guilty for internally mocking them. I was now sitting up, comfortably. He offered me a glass of water. His fingers were glowing an icy blue. The cold water tasted wonderful.

"Thanks," I said. He took the empty glass and put it on a side table.

"Your copy of Warpwars didn't survive as well as you did," he said, pulling a book out of his bag. "So, here's a replacement."

"Thanks, Pranish," I smiled, deeper, but not as energetic as I would have liked. I was still feeling weak. "You're the best."

Pranish shook his head and indicated Trudie, who was standing at a bit of a distance. "She's the real best. She attended all your lectures. Took notes for you."

My eyes widened.

"Really?"

Trudie shrugged. "I didn't understand a word of it, but I wrote it down all the same. Already emailed it to you."

I frowned. "You really didn't have to…"

"But I did."

I held her gaze for only a second. Her eyes, highlighted by her bubble-goth makeup, were the saddest I'd ever seen them. I looked down.

"I'm…."

"Don't," Trudie interrupted. "Just…please take it easy. Recover. If not for me, for yourself."

"Not like I have much of a choice." I tried to grin. It felt forced and I stopped.

"You soon will, Ms Drummond," a voice said. We all turned to the doorway. I realised I was in a private room. How did I afford that? I really hoped Trudie didn't pay for me now...

A man approached the bed. He had a square, cleanly shaven jaw. Greased back, black hair. Eyes like a predator, and snow-white teeth.

"We've spoken before, Ms Drummond," the man said.

I thought for a second and nodded. "On the phone. You didn't give me your name."

"Conrad Khoi." He offered his hand. I shook it, despite the ache permeating my body. Mercifully, if a bit iffy, his handshake was soft – even approaching limp. I chose to believe that it was him taking note of my condition.

"You did a splendid job with the terror, Ms Drummond."

He kept saying my name, as if using it to punctuate his remarks. He reminded me of a used car salesman.

"The house was destroyed," I replied, deadpan.

"And the contract was merely to get rid of the spirit. The survival of the house does not matter."

I snorted. "Are you sure your client is fine with that?"

"There was no other client."

I raised my eyebrow. Conrad grinned. It looked exaggerated. I could have sworn I saw a sparkle on his pearly white teeth. A well-practiced, marketing smile.

"All a test, Ms Drummond. A test that you admirably passed. I owned that property. It has been haunted for years. No exorcist has been able to crack it. I had pretty much given up on it. That was until I heard about a student who exorcised a poltergeist out of the blue. A student known for her affordable and efficient undead slaying."

Conrad was giving an even wider smile now. Despite the pretentious overtones, I felt some sincerity behind the expression.

"You don't seem so upset by the house…"

"Of course, I'm not upset! I'd given up on it. And now, I can sell the property. But that isn't why I'm happy. As I said, it was a test. I'm a fixer, you see. I act as an agent for non-agency aligned exorcists, monster hunters and purifiers. I find the jobs, handle the payments, sell the bits, and ensure my clients get a generous cut."

"So, you live off other people doing the work?" Trudie asked. Conrad seemed unfazed by her glare.

"I ensure my clients actually get work. Ms Drummond…can I call you Kat?"

I didn't reply.

"Kat – what is your average haul for a hunt? What is your average hunt?"

I remained silent.

"Under $200? Hunting vampire rats and rogue zoms?"

I bit my lip. He noticed.

"MonsterSlayer registries are public, Kat. I know all your jobs. Complete transparency in this industry. I also know that your talent is being wasted. You're a damn good slayer. Your track record slaying the undead is unparalleled by any other in your age group. Rifts! There's no one else hunting in your age group. That makes you a novelty, Kat. And novelties bring in bucks – but only if people trust you. I trust you, and that's why in addition to your payment for a job well done, I've paid for all your medical bills, post-operation purification and an executive level rushed magical healing, so you can get back to studying and work."

"What is your proposition?" I finally asked, wondering if I was about to make a deal with the devil.

Conrad grinned again, the fading light glinting on his unnaturally white teeth. Many may have found the smile inviting. I could not help but think of a wolf, which made my later decision all the more surprising.

"I'd like to become your fixer, Kat. You're going places, and I want to help you get there."

"Terms?"

"I take 15% of the job's cut as a finder's fee. I'll sell the parts and loot for a 60% cut."

"35."

"I'll be doing most of the work with selling the parts." His grin didn't fade.

"You going to be cutting up the corpses?" I gazed down at his suit without a tie. "Might stain your shirt."

"50."

"40."

"Deal." He presented his hand. I didn't shake it.

"What type of jobs can you get me that I can't get myself?"

"I've got a reputation, Kat. That lets me fish in ponds others can't. I won't be able to get you the jobs you'd get in Puretide or Drakenbane, but I can get close."

He leaned in, his smiled faded and his eyes became intense. His tone lost its announcer-like tone. It was hushed. Honest. "Real horrors, Kat Drummond," he said. "Real stakes. Real money. Ghoul hives, vampire cartels, marauding ogres, demonic invaders…"

I was still.

"You're strained as it is, Kat," Trudie said, genuine anxiety in her voice. "If what you've been doing isn't real jobs, I don't want to see you after this… You could die!"

I winced but didn't respond to my best friend. She couldn't understand. She hadn't seen what I had seen. And she didn't know what this meant to me.

"Okay, Mr Khoi. I'll do it. I'll like to see a contract, but you have my tentative acceptance."

Trudie covered her face and turned away. Pranish bit his lip.

Conrad Khoi smiled wider than he had before. "Call me Conrad."

We shook hands. His grip was tighter now.

142

Trudie left without a word. Pranish whispered that he thought I was doing the right thing. Soon, I was alone with the setting sun and a faint hospital light, humming and glowing a clinical white near my bed. A nurse, wearing the white and red rune-covered robes of a healer, came in and checked up on me for a minute, and then left.

I was alone. Well, as alone as I always was.

Treth was still with me and was still silent.

"Treth?" I asked.

He didn't reply.

"You okay?"

"Sir Arden of Drambyre," he finally replied, a tone of relieved if strained concession in his voice.

"Excuse me?"

"That was my master's name."

I had almost forgotten I had asked. It had just been an idle question. Something to distract me from the dark eeriness. With the action that ensued after that, I had almost forgotten the question.

"I watched him die, Kat. The man who saved me from the gutter of depravity."

Treth didn't sound sad. He never really sounded sad. I only ever recalled him being joyful, proud, angry and disappointed. And more recently: melancholic. This didn't sound sad, but neither did it sound like anything I had heard from him before. It was cold. As if he was reading from a history book about events distant from him. I knew he didn't truly feel that way. The earnest Treth, so honest and naïve, didn't recount such important things with a feeling of steely distantness. Treth only spoke like a morose scholar now because it was all he could do to hold back the weakness he probably promised himself to never show.

"I watched him charge on Gallant, towards an unassailable horde of the dead. Towards a Higher Lich. Alongside him was every surviving friend I ever had. My only pride was that I charged alongside him. I was scared, but there was no room for retreat here. It was the precipice. The last stand of a dying world. But despite my bravery, when it counted most, I failed…"

He stopped. I felt his lip quiver. I willed him to be strong. For all he had done for me, and simply because nobody wanted their friend to cry.

"I failed, Kat. And I saw my failure again. That spirit - the terror - showed me my darkest fear. My failure. For when my master and comrades charged into the jaws of death, I had the opportunity to slay the Lich at the head of the ruinous horde."

…

"But I didn't."

Silence.

"Why?" I prompted him. I felt guilty for doing so.

"Because I still saw my brother in the monster that he had become. And I saw what I could have become if I had continued down my old path. The terror spirit showed me. I saw myself as the evil I now swear to destroy, and I saw the brother that had defended me for so long as a child. That failure was my fear. My most hated memory. It burns me even more than the vivid memory of my own death."

I didn't reply. I couldn't.

"Now you know," Treth said, voice as cold as ice. "I failed as a knight. And when that failure came back to haunt me, I failed again."

"I have survived this long because you helped me, Treth."

I felt him about to respond, I didn't let him.

"I've never told you my story, have I?"

He shook his incorporeal head.

"I watched my parents die. Sacrificed by a necromancer. I couldn't do anything, yet I still hold myself responsible. And every time I close my eyes, I see that obsidian dagger hovering over the chests of my parents. And while they chafed against their chains and bled from the necromantic runes engraved into their chests and gut, they cried out for me. Their last breaths…about me. I survived that night. And while a failure or not, I knew I had to avenge them, somehow."

I gulped and took a breath. "You died, Treth. But I didn't. And now, you're here to help us both get what we want."

"What is that?"

"I don't know. Redemption? Revenge?"

"A quest. To finish what I…we have started."

I nodded. I was getting tired. I closed my eyes.

"We're in this together, Treth."

"I know, Kat. Thank you."

Chapter 10.   Home

Through the wonders of medicine and magic, I soon recovered from my injuries suffered through being eaten up and spat out by a house. Conrad had paid for a speedy recovery, and a full body purification. I didn't only feel recovered, I felt better than ever. The latent curses that cling to necromantic entities must have been dragging me down. While before, I had felt sluggish, a tad irritable, and dreadfully tired, I was now ready to take on the world – and probably pick up some new curses along the way. At least, if Conrad was able to get me these jobs, I'd be able to afford regular check-ups and purifications.

Blessedly, it was a Friday afternoon when I was discharged. No classes till Monday! I sniffed my new copy of Warpwars and shivered with pleasure. New book smell should be classified as a drug.

"Weekend of relaxation ahead of us," I said to Treth. The street was empty, but not ominous as empty streets often were. I could hear the hooting of traffic and the chants of Titan pilgrims, praising…I'm really not sure what. Definitely not the Titan Under the Mountain. Or were they? I really didn't understand the Titan Cult. The sun was shining down, magnificent and golden, yet the temperature was still pleasant. All in all, a decent day.

"What does relaxation entail?" Treth asked. His voice was back to his enthusiastic, if haughty, tone.

"Reading. Hanging with Alex. Hunting a monster or two."

Treth grinned. "Sounds like my type of relaxation."

Then I felt him glower. "You have that essay due."

I clicked my tongue, irritably.

"Which subject is it?" Treth didn't only help me as a mentor, but also as my personal diary. He had a memory like an elder dragon. The ones with good memory, that is. Not all of them had good memory. In fact, that was quite a poor example. Treth had a memory like…well, a memory card.

"Both. You have a three-thousand-word essay on the establishment of the Titan Cult due for Tuesday and a two-thousand-five-hundred-word essay about the proper classifications of wights due for Wednesday."

"As if the latter matters," Treth continued, under his breath. "That fool knave wouldn't know a wight from a revenant."

I sighed. It seemed that Warpwars would have to wait. I still smelled the scent of fresh ink and paper. I gritted my teeth.

Outside my apartment block, I was greeted by the sight of a portly lady with a poof of spongey white hair. She was hunched over, hammering a sign-post into the ground. When she stood and backed away from it, I could clearly see the cartoon image of a wraith, wreathed in black smoking miasma, with the text: "Warning: Wraith spotted. Enter at your own risk."

I restrained myself from chuckling.

The person in question, the owner of this building and my landlady, was named Mrs Ndlovu. The building was plastered with warning signs like this. Mrs Ndlovu had a pathological fear of lawmancers, lawyers and lawsuits. Which was odd, because (as far as I know) she had never committed a crime. Perhaps, her anxiety was because she was afraid she would. Regardless, in her desperation to avoid all risks of legal trouble, she ensured that no one entering her property could hold her liable for, well, anything.

I stopped by the newly planted sign and grinned.

"It's not nice to warn people about your husband, Mrs Ndlovu."

Mrs Ndlovu turned on her heels as she heard my voice, belying a grace hidden by her physique. She let out a throaty laugh, the product of a lifetime of pipe smoking.

"Reggie might as well be the wraith. Doesn't do anything about it, that's for sure," she said, hands on her hips. "But can't be too careful."

"I haven't seen a wraith for the entire time I've been here."

Mrs Ndlovu waved the comment aside. "The bastard isn't stupid, Kat. It stays away from you."

I nodded, pretending to agree with her. At least she hadn't tried to hire me to exterminate the non-existent wraith. I'd have to charge her, and I didn't like charging people I like for cases that I knew were made-up. I still did it, but didn't like it.

Mrs Ndlovu looked thoughtful for a second and then looked me in the eye, as if remembering something. "Been hearing noises from your room. Your friend that looks like a vampire doll, Trudie, didn't think anything was out of the ordinary but be careful besides."

I raised my eyebrow. I was sure it was nothing. Trudie would ensure nothing bad could ever happen to Alex. She may let her concern for me stop at nagging, but she'd become a monster hunter herself to help Alex. I'd have felt jealous, if I was the jealous type.

I waved Mrs Ndlovu goodbye and continued to my apartment. All was silent outside my door. Must have been Mrs Ndlovu's hyper-active imagination. I shifted Warpwars to my other arm and drew out my keys.

I heard a hiss.

Alex hardly hissed.

I half opened, half kicked the door, reaching at my belt for a sword that wasn't there.

My apartment was a mess. More than usual. Torn toilet paper adorned the now stained carpet. Curtains were streaked with claw marks.

I gritted my teeth. I felt naked without my sword. My belongings had been returned to the apartment. Inside, where a beast now lurked.

I walked forward, softly, my arms in front of me, ready to grapple with any assailant that charged my position. I needed to get to the kitchen. I had knives there.

A crash and meowling. Something primal took over, and I charged ahead.

My mounting rage dispersed almost immediately and changed to bemusement, as I saw a floating, glowing orb. Alex was arcing his back, hair on end and tail acting like an antenna.

"Finally!" Duer exclaimed in his sing-song lilt.

Alex pounced high, swiping at the pixie, who dodged out of the way.

"This beast is trying to eviscerate me, Ms Maddy Ogre Exorcist...whoever you are."

I proceeded to the kitchen, opened my tiny, second-hand bar-fridge and retrieved a bottle of Coke. Duer continued to dart around the room, Alex hot on his minute heels.

"I can't defend me self," Duer said, anxiety starting to break through his usual cocky accent. "Hurting felines is bad luck."

"And hurting pixies?" I asked, opening the Coke and taking a swig. That hit the spot.

Duer's lack of response was answer enough. I sat down, out of the way of the battle of pixie and feline and drank.

"Please, Maddy…"

"My name is Kat."

"Kat…please get your cat under control."

"Alex is his own man."

Alex's paw narrowly missed Duer's foot. The pixie retreated upward and found the lightbulb. He clung onto it, giving his golden wings a break. Alex let out a half growl, half meow. His tail swished irritably as he looked up with a predatory gaze.

I sighed. "What are you doing here, Duer?"

"I live here. This is my property."

"Lightbulbs get mighty hot when turned on, and Alex looks hungry."

Duer gulped. I could hear it even this far away.

"I hid in your bag after you destroyed my old home. When the witch…"

"Trudie."

"When the witch, Trudie, brought your bag here, I decided it was fitting that I make this my new dwelling. It has a clean weyline. It will be much easier to keep pure than that ramshackle manor."

"I don't think you can hold me responsible for what that spirit did…"

"I had him under control," Duer huffed. "That's my job, after all."

"Your job?" I couldn't help but snort. Duer's golden glow glowered, as if a glow could glower. Pixies, I had heard, were not only very vocal about their feelings, but could transmit them through their auras. Duer was not pleased.

"I'm a pixie! It's my job to keep the places of power clean. What you giants call weylines."

"Who gave you this job?" I finished the Coke and tossed the bottle behind me. A satisfying thud signalled that it had landed in the bin.

Duer shrugged, his glow twinkling as if uncertain. "It's just the way it is. Some creatures hurt magic, some creatures heal it. Pixies, like me, keep the rivers of life and incantation clean."

"How?"

Duer grinned. "With our presence. We're a balancing force of nature, Ms Ma…Kat."

"That explains things…"

Duer cocked his head.

"The weyline at the manor felt off, but not too off. Just like any ruined building. But that terror should have been darkening it to the point of blight."

Duer nodded swiftly. "That was me. Mr Terror kept trying to pollute the stream, but I picked up the darkness too fast for him."

Pride emanated from the petite figure. His glow doubled in intensity.

"So," I continued, putting my feet up on the counter. "You want to live here now?"

"Well, you destroyed my old home..."

"I don't react well to emotional blackmail, Duer."

He hesitated.

"You fight a lot of beasts, right?" his tone changed. More conciliatory.

I nodded.

"This weyline is much cleaner than my old home, but it is still dirty. I sensed the corruption clinging to you last time."

He sniffed. "You're clean now, but what about next time? What happens when you drip too much beastie blood into your home and then a demon decides to move in?"

"I'll kill it." I shrugged.

"Every time?"

"Every time."

"Even when you're sleeping?"

I felt Treth's presence. He was amused by the pixie.

"I've got an alarm."

"Come on!" Duer started to beg. "Let me stay."

I sauntered across the living room and opened a window. I gestured for him to leave.

"Please, Kat! I can help with other things. I can clean up the mess. I'll become friends with this beast." He indicated   Alex.
"I'll even lead you to my pot of gold!"

"You're not a leprechaun."

The glow was flashing, feverishly.

"Please don't put me on the street. People don't look kindly on pixies. They'll eat me, or cut off my wings, or use me for…unmentionable things."

"There's a reason people don't like pixies." I indicated where he had stabbed me nights before.

"I didn't know you then…please let me stay. If only for a bit. I'll prove that I can behave."

I raised my eyebrow. "No pixie pranks?"

He nodded his head, earnestly.

"No growing toad stools in my living room?"

He hesitated, and then nodded again.

"No ripping up my stuff to tinker?"

More hesitation, but he nodded again.

I sighed. "Fine. You can stay here. For a little bit. We can see what use you are."

Alex was still letting out that demonic feline growl that cats give when they remember their primal ancestors. I picked him up and while he shoved against me with his paws, he failed to struggle out. I placed him on the countertop and opened a can of his food. The allure of an easy meal was too great, and he turned away from his would-be prey and began nibbling on the long-dead remains of assorted less magical animals.

Duer let out a sigh of pent-up relief and flew closer. I could see him clearly now. He looked like a thin, young boy with golden butterfly wings. He wore a tunic made from leaves. Despite his boyish features, he bore a thin scar across his chest. He looked at Alex askance as I examined him, my one hand stroking my cat's head.

"What happened there?"

Duer cocked his head and then oh-ed. "This?"

He grinned. "A worthy tale. Worthy enough that it will need a proper occasion. Perhaps, when the moon shines bright, the dolmens are polished and some of my brethren will be here to finally hear of my valour."

Chapter 11. Upgrades

I tolerated Duer's sing-song folk music. He claimed it helped clean the weyline. I didn't know enough to dispute him. I only know that it didn't help my essay writing. But that was probably just my own lame excuse. Anything would have distracted me from an essay I didn't want to write. Fortunately, my discipline won out – even when Pranish invited me to go play mini-golf with a centaur – and I got the essays done by Monday. Class was uneventful. The protesters still kept up their half-arsed activism. The air conditioner was still too cold. The lecturer was still more effective than any sedative. A normal day on campus.

I received a message from Conrad after my last class. He wanted to meet in his office. It was located in the old Observatory district, just a short bus trip (if the bus ran on time) from campus.

"Time to meet our new employer," I muttered to Treth, as I descended the campus stairs.

While on campus, we couldn't see Table Mountain, nor the Titan Citadel built atop it; we were instead rewarded with another vista: a clear view of the simultaneous blight and paradise that was Hope City. Magicorp skyscrapers shone a brilliant glassy blue, surrounded by the occasional drake or radiant incantation circle. At their feet, a sea of houses and buildings, stopping at protected parks and the real sea itself. In the distance, the slums looked peaceful. It was a deception. Despite their colour and quaint façade from afar, they were rife with the dregs of this society. I had been called into the slums a few times. My rates were cheap, and slum-dwellers could afford me, even if they couldn't afford agencies. Zombies were a rarity in the suburbs and Old Town. Necromancers did live there, I'm sure of it, but they kept their ghastly heads low. The slums were where the necromancers came out to play, and the vampires fed. No agencies to keep the darkness at bay, and the Council didn't care. They had their hands full keeping the Titan asleep.

I hoped that Conrad would send me slum-way. It wasn't a pleasant place. Dirty weylines all round. But I felt a need to cleanse it. To help the people there scraping for a little bit of light. But I wasn't going to do it for free. I was a concerned citizen, not an activist!

The trip to Conrad's office was dull. I spent the time reading Warpwars until my stop.

I squinted as I exited the bus. Conrad said his office was right by this stop. But I didn't see any offices. No magicorps buildings, no glass facades. Just some bars and dingy housing. I checked his message again. Yep. Right here. Just in front of the bus stop. Between the old tome-store and the canvas shop. But that was a pub. The Gravekeeper Tavern. And quite a raucous one by the sound of clinking glasses and slurred chattering at…only 4pm!

My phone buzzed. Another message from Conrad.

"Look up."

I did so. He was waving from the second storey, pulling a curtain aside.

What have I gotten myself into!

A few drunken sots and a sticky stairway later, I arrived at a wooden door. Stuck to it was a plastic sign reading:

"Conrad Khoi. Monsters, Mysticism and Magnanimous Relations."

"Fan of alliteration, I see."

I stepped over a wet-floor sign and knocked. The dark, lacquered wood was hard. Good quality. An old building, maintained by enterprise. Even if a raucous enterprise…

Conrad opened the door and beamed his car dealer smile.

"Kat! Good to see you."

I gave a faint smile in return. It was all I could force. It wasn't as if I disliked him. It is just that his constant smile made up for my lack of one. If I was to smile, there'd be a glut, devaluing the value of smiles irreparably.

Conrad's office smelled of cologne. Old Spice. It wasn't unpleasant but made the space a bit inauthentic. The room itself was not what I expected, however. When I first pictured Conrad's office, I imagined a sleek lawyer's office. Shiny table tops, top-end computers, purification crystals to keep the local chi balanced. That's not what I found. Conrad's office was dark. But not a bad dark. The type of dark you find in a theatre, or a second-hand bookshop. That welcoming dimness that made you want to stay. Within the dim room, hiding the light with a maroon curtain, was a wooden desk covered with papers. Many looked to be the mundane – bills and invoices. Others were inscribed with Celtic and Nordic runes, another with the Elvish script of Sintar. Three chairs surrounded the desk. All were identical wood and pale leather. On the surrounding shelves were swathes of books, jars of ingredients and a troll skull.

I raised my eyebrow at the last one. It didn't matter how Conrad got it, it was an impressive artefact all the same. Trolls were renowned for their regenerative abilities. Agencies typically had to work together to take one down, let alone a marauder horde of them.

I pointed my thumb at the skull and inquired about its origin.

Conrad's grin deepened, if that was even possible. But it lost its pretentiousness. Became genuine. "A gift from my first client. A mountain of a man. Wrestled the troll naked, finally slaying it through sheer strength alone."

"Like Beowulf?"

"Just like Beowulf. That was his nickname."

"What happened to him?"

A hint of hesitation. A sign that Conrad was more than just a neon billboard. His grin didn't leave his meticulously stubbled face, but his tone did lose a bit of its enthusiasm.

"He moved on. Went to Scandinavia and joined the Thunder Corps."

"The Thunder Corps?!" I gasped. My surprise was genuine. The Thunder Corps were legends. A top-level

163

global agency run by Thor, the Norse God of Thunder himself. They handled the top missions and operations that this magical world could throw at them. When the legendary Fafnir decided to make Berlin into his own personal hoard, the Thunder Corps were the ones to send him spiralling into the abyss. With an assorted roster of demigods, top-level magic users, ancient and modern heroes, they were the best of the best. If Conrad's client was now one of them, then I had really big shoes to fill.

Conrad must have read my mind, as he laughed.

"Don't worry. I don't expect you to be at his level, just yet. I've got plenty of clients. You're already outperforming three of them."

"Great," I said, deadpan, but hiding my relief. I hunted undead. Trolls and dragons were on a whole other level.

Conrad indicated for me to take a seat. I did so and accepted his subsequent offer of coffee. I took it black – like my shirt, ribbon, and how Trudie described my soul.

"I like to know my clients well," Conrad said, pouring the coffee.

Well, of course he did. He'd be a crummy agent if he didn't.

I accepted the boiling mug and placed it on a coaster.

"I've been following your short career."

"Not too closely, I hope."

Conrad laughed.

"Close enough. You've been doing well. Got a lot of monsters under your belt. And more than that, you've put yourself through a year of university and almost two years of rent, not to mention other necessities, by yourself. That takes guts, kiddo."

I almost winced at the, "Kiddo."

Conrad leaned back in his chair and steepled his fingers, both index fingers pointed towards the roof. I could hear music and drunkards downstairs. But if Conrad had served clients that now worked for the Thunder Corps, then he had to be at least a little bit competent.

"Tell me, Kat. Why do you still study?"

I opened my mouth, about to give my usual ham-fisted reply. But I didn't feel "Knowledge is power", would cut it. I felt Treth listening in as well. It was more than that. Something deeper that kept me studying under pretentious academics while I spent my nights covered in black blood.

"Variety," I finally answered. Conrad almost spat out his coffee. He slapped his knee.

"That's great! It isn't a problem. It's just that, for someone who claims to be a part-time monster hunter, you work really hard at it."

"I want to be a monster hunter. I want to study. Best of both worlds."

"But which means more to you?" Conrad was looking carefully at me, examining my every pore. I felt a bit uncomfortable under his considering gaze but steeled myself and stared right back at him.

"I study to hunt monsters, and hunt monsters to study. Part-time student, part-time monster hunter."

Conrad stared a little longer, and then nodded, satisfied.

"I will be sending you jobs through the MonsterSlayer app. I'll sometimes phone you. You can take on other jobs, if you want, but I advise against it. I'm going to be filling up your already precious time, Kat. But don't let that goth friend of yours discourage you. We're going places. In a few weeks' time, zombies will be pocket change compared to the type of money we'll be raking in."

Conrad stood, and so did I. I hadn't finished my coffee. He put out his hand.

"Let's make some money!"

***

I yawned. A deep yawn. The type that makes you sleepier. The light was fading. I didn't have any jobs lined up. Conrad said things were pretty quiet at the moment but that he'd have some stuff later in the week.

I couldn't help but be excited. Finally, I was moving on from hustling jobs from old ladies and landlords too cheap to hire Puretide. I was going places. And those places would hopefully be filled with all manner of monstrosities to stab and slice.

I approached the bus stop. I needed to be getting home. Warpwars and sleep awaited – and a feast of polystyrene cup noodles. Yum! I also needed to check up on Alex and Duer. Alex was still trying to slay the pixie and I had left Duer home all day. As much as I trusted his word, pixies were notoriously mischievous. I didn't want him tearing up my notes to build sailor hats.

"What are you doing?" Treth asked.

I yawned again. "Heading home."

"Night market is still open."

"And I'm sure the night market customers are very happy about that."

"We're getting a decent opportunity here, Kat."

It was his nagging voice. The voice he took on when he wasn't quoting his mentors, and rather trying to mentor me by himself. I hadn't missed it during his funk. I resisted rolling my eyes. He could see it when I did that. He didn't like it.

"A great opportunity, and it isn't going anywhere. You heard Conrad. I've got the night off!"

"From hunting, not from preparing."

I pouted. "Come on, Treth. I'm tired."

"Hasn't stopped you before."

"Haven't had Warpwars waiting for me before."

"That book will be the death of us!"

"And a worthy death it will be, Sir Knight. But I concede. To the night market we go. We can finally buy a weapon befitting a warrior of my stature."

***

The night market of Long Street, Old Town, was awash with shoppers, partiers, hawkers, musicians and street mages. Floating red and gold lanterns lit up the sky. A cacophony formed from countless vying street performers. There was energy in the air. A palpable pulsing of good vibes and vigour. As much as I felt distaste for many forms of magic, I couldn't help but feel infused with a positive aura when I entered the night market. It was a welcome change from the dark magic I was usually surrounded by. It felt like I could breathe. The collective joy of the droves of people only added to the pure positive magic in the street. It rose up and lit the area, raising my spirits and giving me a heady feeling of excitement and peace.

The night market was renowned for its clean weyline, but I felt it was more than that. It was a demonstration of some of humanity's best characteristics. Its desire to get along. Its comradery regardless of backgrounds. Its determination and happy perseverance to prosper. The connection we all felt, consciously and unconsciously, through commerce. There was nothing like the market, with all its non-fantastical magic, to remind one of humanity's virtues.

I decided to treat myself to some of the usual food you find around open markets such as this – a nice bowl of noodles. Don't think me missing an opportunity for variety, though. This was different from the stuff I had at home. I bought *this* from a street vendor.

"So," I whispered to Treth, my voice masked to others by the chaos of the crowds. "What are we looking for?"

"A decent weapon. Armour. Replacement equipment for what you've lost. More demanzite."

"You want me to buy a shield?" I said, in between bites.

Treth shook his incorporeal head. "That's not your style. No point imposing my training on you. You specialise in dual blades. Best to perfect what you already know. A jack of all trades is a master of none, after all."

"You have that expression in your world?"

"No. Picked it up here."

"I should pick up some of your phrases. Just to be fair."

"Our phrases are dull. As dull as those swords over there. Stop, look. By the gods, those swords are terrible. I hope this market has something of worth."

Despite his complaints, Treth seemed to be enjoying himself. Being surrounded by so many diverse, happy people, and so many magical and martial wares put the knight spirit into a good mood. It was a welcome change from the melancholy he had been expressing for the last while. His new mood was infectious, and I soon found myself smiling contently. I browsed the stalls, carts and shop windows, occasionally entering for a closer look or to buy something I knew I needed. I refreshed my demanzite stocks, filling the front pouch of my backpack with the sachets of mercifully cheap minerals. Well, relatively cheap. Sure, the comet showers that led to them becoming abundant killed a lot of people but I couldn't help that. At least the minerals put me on a slightly more even footing against damn magic-users – the humans and monsters. I didn't buy any more purity seals. I had more than enough left from my last job. I also bought some poultices, some new arm polymer bracers and a hardier facemask, to avoid necro-blood splatter.

I checked my wallet and frowned. A few hundred bucks but dwindling fast. Monster hunting was expensive!

I was nearing the end of the market and Treth had rejected every sword we'd seen. I had since resigned myself to enjoying the other wares on display. Assorted tomes, rune-covered clothes and exquisitely decorated purification urns, to prevent loved ones from becoming hostile spirits. I couldn't help but appreciate their design, even though I knew their use was not that pleasant. Only people with unfinished business of a dark nature came back as hostile spirits. If a family was putting the remains of their loved one in a purification urn, their loved one probably didn't deserve the treatment. Or, they should be allowed to come back and avenge themselves. Spirit ethics were complicated…

Eventually, there was one weapon stall left, flanked by a charms shop and a place selling purple scarves. I approached the stall. All manner of bladed weapons were strewn across the plastic fold-out table. Curved swords, long swords, daggers, katanas, stilettos, falchions, axes, even a claymore. Some were engraved with Nordic runes and styled in the old Viking fashion. Others were more modern, with tactical grips and polymer blades. I surveyed the wares. Treth didn't speak up, which was a welcome sign. He hadn't found anything to complain about yet.

"How can I help you this fine evening, Miss?"

The shopkeeper, a bald goateed man wearing a leather biker-style vest, asked.

"I hunt undead," I responded. "Looking to upgrade my tools."

The shopkeeper gave me a warm and serviceable smile. It wasn't forced. He enjoyed his job.

"I'm no hunter, but I know a bit about weapons…"

One would hope…

"…You'll want something durable. An axe, perhaps?"

He indicated a long-handled double-blade axe. Its steel was engraved with runes, but I doubted it was genuinely enchanted for its price. Treth probably would have liked me to learn to use a weapon such as this. When we first met, he had tried to train me to use sword and shield tactics. A lack of shield and a lack of platemail made that hard. Treth's martial tradition was one of acting like a walking tank. He and his comrades were decked out in enchanted platemail, armed with two-handed heavy weapons, or one-handed and shields. They trained to work as a group against the undead hordes, supported by clerics and sorcerers. With teamwork and decent equipment, their style emphasised brutal efficiency and sheer strength. But I was one girl and the context of my hunts was very different. I wasn't fighting an endless horde of organised undead. I was hunting small groups and individuals. For me, speed and finesse was more important than strength. A two-handed monstrosity like this axe wouldn't fit my style.

"Need something shorter. Preferably a sword. Something fast."

"Rather a rogue, than a warrior?" The shopkeeper grinned. He indicated a katana, the iconic Samurai sword. I felt a pang of desire. Katanas were definitely something I've wanted to use in the past. They were one of the most distinctive blades out there, and Samurai were renowned warriors. They were even legendary before the Cataclysm and were the subject of many books and films. In the modern magical world, Samurai heroes were famous for their defence of Japan, as demons and spirits from Shinto folklore proved themselves very real and very dangerous. These modern Samurai wielded combinations of Shinto purification magic, Japanese-style wizardry and enchanted blades.

I really wanted to use a katana. But I knew it was a bad idea. The katanas of the Samurai in modern Japan worked because they were facing a specific type of enemy. Japanese yokai had informed the culture and mythos of pre-Cataclysm Japan. The katana was suited for slaying these beasts, because that was the reason it had been invented. But when it came to the beasts of other mythologies and worlds, katanas were not as effective. In my case, the blade was not that durable. It was designed for swift kills, against relatively unarmoured opponents. My fights with undead required weapons that could endure a lot of stress. Hacking, chopping, bone breaking. But I couldn't go with an axe, either. Axes got stuck, pinning me to a single enemy, and couldn't stab. One of the best ways to end a zombie was to skewer its brain. Couldn't do that with an axe.

Currently, I was specialising in dual weapons – using two short-blades to cover my angles. They were fast, allowing me to swiftly dispatch many weaker undead, and because I was using two, I could attack and defend in multiple directions. My current short sword (the surviving one) was not ideal, however. It was a pseudo-ninja blade. I bought it because it was cheap, and because I couldn't help but pander to my love of Japan. It had been a mistake. The blades were brittle. They couldn't handle repeated blows and chipped easily.

I shook my head and pointed towards a pair of black machetes.

"Those'll get stuck," Treth said. "If you hit a non-vital area, or are fighting a horde, that's a death sentence."

I withdrew my finger. The shopkeeper looked a bit irritated, but there were no other customers, so his service smile remained.

"So, dual-wielder?"

The shopkeeper began muttering and turned around, bending over to look through a metal chest. I heard the clanking of metal. He turned and presented me with two slightly curved blades. The steel of each blade formed the hilt and the handguard, creating a single piece of solid metal, with a single edge. It wasn't going to break that easily, if the metal was tempered properly. I examined the blade and found a product identification stamp. It was approved by Pure Joy, a reputable quality assurance corporation.

"Dusacks," the shopkeeper said, offering me one to hold. I tested its weight. It felt good. I looked around and the space around me was clear. I swung it a few times. A good heft. Not too heavy, but with enough weight behind it that it would hurt anything in its way.

My face must have looked impressed, as the shopkeeper's smile broadened, and he continued. "Czech cutlass. Reliability of a machete, but speed of a sabre or cutlass. These beauties will cut through almost any undead."

I passed the sword back, after a quick flourish. The air hissed as I sliced it.

"How much?"

"For the two? $400."

"Bah! I could bribe the Council for a gun license and get a gun for that price."

"Why don't you?"

"I like swords." I shrugged. "But I also like to pay for proper value. $200 for both. If that katana is only $180, then these short swords aren't worth $200 each."

"This is quality craftsmanship. You won't find a dusack anywhere else in the city."

"Always the internet."

"Fine, $300 for both. But not going any lower."

I turned around. I heard a heavy sigh.

"Fine. $250. But that really is final."

"Now that is how retail will survive!"

The shopkeeper grumbled as I passed him the notes. A glint of steel caught my eye.

"How much for that seax?"

I pointed at a solid hunting knife, with a wooden handle bearing pseudo-Nordic runes.

"$50. No negotiations this time. That's a fine piece for carving. Plenty of demand for them."

I usually cut up body parts with a handsaw. This looked much more effective, and it could make a decent last resort weapon.

"Deal." I handed him an extra fifty. His expression lightened. He passed me a paper bag with the three sheathed blades and threw in a sword-belt as well. I thanked him and departed.

"You know what, Treth?" I asked, entering the darkness as I left the night market towards the bus-stop.

"What?"

"I'm feeling good about this. I'm glad I finally agreed to this upgrade."

"I'm glad you're now taking this seriously. Putting your money where your mouth is."

"Another cliché?" I chuckled.

Treth snorted, but then asked. "Why did you refuse to upgrade for so long? It's not like you have more money now than in the past. You could have afforded this upgrade before."

"Things were much more uncertain back then. I didn't know when my next job would come, or if they'd even pay me…"

I hesitated. Treth noticed.

"But it's more than that."

I sighed. The night was getting colder. The street was dark, except for the distant lights of enterprise and Old Town apartments. I noted that someone else in my shoes may be frightened in such a place. I just felt a tad underdressed for the temperature.

"Perhaps, it was about the commitment," I finally answered.

"Hmmm?"

"I'm still studying. Quest or not, this was a side-gig. But then it's gotten out of hand now. Got to the point where I almost stopped studying. I'm glad I didn't."

"Why is that?"

"My parents wanted me to study."

Treth nodded, understandingly. I frowned. He didn't press. Part of me wished he had. It was more than just that – my parents' wishes.

"Buying proper equipment, going in with the agent, continuing down this path…it's something I do think I want. But it scares me. What if I change my mind? What if it gets too much? What if it isn't me who really wants this, but you?"

It was Treth's turn to hesitate. I pressed.

"What would you do if I wanted to stop?"

"I…I don't think I'll ever need to find out."

A retort was at the tip of my tongue, but I stopped. Treth was right. I sighed again, heavier. The bus was late.

"I'm going down this path, Treth. We are. Maybe I just fear what is around the corner. An upgrade for me may mean an upgrade for my enemies, and I am afraid to see what that means."

"Regardless, Kat, we'll face it together."

I snorted. "That's what you always say."

But I appreciated it all the same.

Chapter 12.   The   Nine-to-Five

I received my first call out from Conrad a few days later. A zombie. Total grunt-work, but I was happy to get it. The undead had wandered into an empty motel along the North-Coast road. A store owner working across the street from the peeling paint covered motel had phoned Conrad to put a bounty on the zom. People didn't trust the Council cops to get there in time, so they were often more than willing to pay a premium for the quick and efficient elimination of monsters. Conrad phoned me, just as I was getting out of the shower and about to write an assignment, telling me to get there and slay the zom. It was low-level wet work. The type of stuff I had been doing before. Conrad had plenty of clients and had to divide the work as best he could. I didn't mind. I should've been writing my assignment, but this was much more fun.

I had to call a taxi. I really needed to get a license and then a bike or car. But just…time and money, you know? Luckily, it was way past rush hour. A privilege of the profession. Didn't have to worry about traffic when most of my work was at night.

I arrived at the shop fifteen minutes after the call-out. No sign of undead. I asked the shopkeeper for details.

"Walking corpse, thin as a reed," the middle-aged and bespectacled shopkeeper explained. "Just across the street. Saw it on the balcony and then through the window."

"Sure it wasn't just an ugly neighbour?" I asked, resisting smirking.

The shopkeeper didn't appreciate the question.

"I know what a zombie looks like, miss. Get rid of it and you get paid."

Despite my usual scepticism of the common-man's reliability when it comes to identifying monsters, the wave of stench that hit me when I approached the abandoned motel was unmistakeable. A neglected undead. Something with a tenuous or non-existent link to a necromancer, which would keep it from rotting. A rogue zombie, without a horde. It would have felt loneliness if it had the capacity for such decent and human emotions.

The motel was dark, and I didn't know its layout or how broken down it was. I didn't want to go stalking a zombie in its feasting ground. Always better to make it come to me. For that, I would need bait.

My rustling in the trash brought out a neighbour. Luckily, the shopkeeper was there to confirm my identity. More onlookers arrived and turned their noses up at the disturbed trash. I didn't notice. It was a pleasant meadow by comparison to the rot of undead.

"Bingo," I said, finding a dead rat which had been crushed under the weight of tin cans and a car battery. I levered the trash out of the way with my sword and skewered the rat with it.

"Bait," I explained to the onlookers.

"Zombies want living meat," Treth said.

"Not one as skinny as a reed. They'll follow the strongest stench to get a meal." I indicated the rat on my sword. "This thing."

I hoped the onlookers didn't hear me talking to Treth, or thought I was talking to them. Thankfully, they wouldn't see my mouth moving. I was wearing my new face-mask. Flat goggles that wouldn't harm my peripheral vision and a hard-plastic surface that covered my face and mouth. Still needed to talk quietly, if at all. I was too used to the spirit and sometimes forgot that others couldn't hear him.

"Plan of attack?" Treth asked.

"Stake out the entry room. Set up the bait, ambush it."

"Simple."

"Effective."

I stifled a yawn. I had an early class today and not enough sleep the night before. But I needed these swords to start paying for themselves. Not to mention the bracers and other equipment. I let out a heavy sigh. I had really been overspending. Treth didn't seem to notice. But he wasn't the one who had to balance the budget. I'm sure he worked hard in his chantry and knightly order in life, but his lack of frugality belied someone who didn't usually have to handle the money.

The motel door creaked as I opened it. I stopped. Listened. No footsteps. Not even any groans. A noiseless corpse typically was just a corpse. I was starting to believe that it was just an ugly neighbour. An ugly and unwashed neighbour. I pushed the door all the way, but made sure to draw my blade, the rat still impaled on my other. The street light created a yellow pool within the motel reception, turning dust particles into fireflies.

"Let's get a nice stench up."

"You disgust me sometimes."

I grinned, mischievously. I had learnt a while back that my approach to hunting was a lot grittier than Treth's. He probably didn't like the thought of dirt on his platemail. I waved the impaled rat on my blade, swishing it like a flag. The stench trailed in its wake. With a flourish, I threw the rat across the room.

"If that doesn't attract it…"

I barely managed to bring my armoured wrist up as the zombie pounced on me, human-like teeth locked on my polymer brace. My heart skipped a beat, but I'd been jumped before. Plenty of times. None had killed me yet. Yet…

I delivered a sharp kick to its leg. Missed. It responded by trying to scratch my face with a decaying, puss-covered hand. I heard a thud as the grotesque, peeling and nail-less fingers jabbed at my mask.

"Use your off-hand," Treth ordered.

I did so and lashed out with my off-hand sword. I hit something hard. Its ribs. At least I now knew where its body was. It was hard to fight the thin ones. Not enough surface area to damage.

I pulled back my sword, still wrestling with the thing as it tried to gnaw through my bracer.

"This wasn't cheap!" I yelled at it and delivered another kick to its torso. I made contact, and it reeled back. I slashed with my one sword, but its stagger saved it. It growled at me and I slashed with my other blade. And found my mark. My blade drifted seamlessly through the fragile flesh of the zombie's throat. Caked black blood clung to the steel, trailing skin and fleshy tendrils in its wake. The zombie looked like it was gasping. As if it could gasp. Its humanlike teeth were covered in old flesh and guts. It hadn't had a meal in days. Its smell pinned it as a ripe old corpse. So did the lack of resistance of its flesh. Its master was long gone. Evidently, whoever animated the body didn't care too much about it. Necromancers liked to play with their toys. Give them modifications. Mutations. But this guy didn't have any. It looked like a moving human corpse. Not some monster from an old horror flick. Just a maggot-farm. The zombie staggered, its head lolling at an angle as the remaining flesh of its neck held on like wet tissue paper. I kicked it, sending it reeling towards the floor.

"You kill faster when there's more of them," Treth commented.

"Got to pass the time somehow."

I skewered its brain and it stopped writhing.

It was a now lifeless maggot-farm. Again, that is.

Threat averted, I let myself breathe. That was almost a close one. The zombie must have been in the room. Treth wasn't scolding me for my lack of awareness, so he must not have noticed it either. I surveyed the room. Streetlights let in just enough light. Dead rats scattered the concrete floor. They all had single, large bites marks. If the zombie had been an animal, I would have pitied it. It took a lot of starvation for a zombie to resort to eating non-human meat. They needed more than just flesh to be satisfied. They needed to fulfil that anti-human drive. That need to kill and spread their necromantic curse. But this poor zom was subsisting on rat corpses.

I felt a weird pang. A sense of anger not at the zombie, but at its creator. Sure, I hated necromancers. Their very nature was evil. But to raise a zombie – a being that exists to consume – and then restrain it from eating by leaving it in such a place and not upgrading its teeth… There evil, and then there was neglectful and evil.

I shook my head.

"What is it?" Treth asked.

"How many non-mutated zombies have we faced?"

"Never fought one, but I knew it was possible…wait, I have seen one."

Treth wracked his brain.

"We were storming a cabal of necromancers. They had holed themselves up stronger than dwarves in a hold…"

"So, you didn't get in?"

Treth snorted. "Okay, not as secure as dwarves. But they were secure. We managed to get in with some creative fire-casting. Plenty of normal combat undead in there. Some heavily mutated zombies, abhorrents, we called them. But further in, after we purged the first few waves of necromancers, we got into their living quarters."

Treth paused. I waited for him to continue while cleaning my blade.

"Dressed in finery that I imagine only the top royal servants wore, were zombies. They looked like humans. Like, fresh, living humans. But dressed up like nobles. Gorgo said that they looked like butlers. They didn't attack us, initially, but when some of the novice necromancers saw us, they ordered the zombies to attack. We struck them down easily but felt bad to waste the suits."

"So… civilian zombies?"

"That's kinda stretching it."

I nudged the corpse with my foot. I considered chopping it up for parts. But I was tired…

I made a quick value judgement, calculating the time to reward ratio and then decided against it. But I'd need to show evidence.

I drew my seax hunting knife and cut cleanly through the zombie's neck, pulling on its thin strands of hair. Its head didn't even pop-off. No resistance.

"What a pathetic specimen."

Treth nodded. "No self-respecting necromancer would put this on show."

"Probs why it was abandoned."

"As if you can abandon a zombie."

"You can abandon your problems – and I'd say zombies are a big problem."

"Yeah, yeah."

I skewered the head on my seax – really needed to get some hunting hooks – and exited the building. The crowd looked surprised to see me. They couldn't see my smug smirk. I loved dashing people's presumptions.

The shopkeeper was standing at the front of the crowd. I lowered my seax and the head slid right off, splattering on the ground.

"One ugly neighbour."

The shopkeeper stared at the rapidly rotting disembodied head, mouth agape. This was a sheltered man, I realised. Well, not necessarily sheltered in general, but from the undead. He, like his cohorts, hadn't faced the armies of the damned. Hopefully, this would be a wakeup call to them.

"My pay?" I said, breaking the man out of his stupor as I cleaned down my knife and sheathed it.

The man looked at me, and then shook. Consciousness returned to his eyes.

"Yes...yeah. Here."

I took off my glove and accepted the pay. Conrad would have already got his call-out fee. For larger paid jobs, we'd cut the money after the job was done.

The crowd of onlookers started to disperse. Probably spurred by the stench of the zombie head. I'd need to dispose of it. Sanitation? Nah. Maybe Conrad would know.

I took out my phone and stowed my mask, swinging it behind my neck. I was just logging in when...

"Kat..."

"What?"

"By the corner, in the shadows."

I looked up and felt a shiver.

The area was clear. The shopkeeper and crowd had dispersed. I was the only person in the open. Me and a hooded figure, watching me from the corner of a jutting brick wall. I couldn't see the figure's eyes. Only a black shadow within a black hoodie. But I somehow felt we were staring into each other's eyes. Considering. Were they staring at me as one would at prey, or considering me otherwise?

My instincts told me prey. But I was not some apathetic deer caught in headlights. I was a hunter.

When faced with terror, a person either runs or charges. When I was faced with uncertainty and the darkest of fears, I had made it a habit to charge head-first. To turn fear into opportunity. To stab it before it could stab me.

I took a step forward, slowly stowing my phone. The hooded figure didn't move.

"Hello?" I called.

No response. I edged closer. And then the figure bolted.

"After it!" Treth shouted. He didn't need to yell. I was already around the corner.

I didn't draw my blades. That'd just slow me down. And this bastard was fast. Too fast. Another turn. A darker road. I followed, my eyes adjusting to the dark. I could see well in the dark. Lot of practice. But the figure was all black. Camouflaged in the night. I focused on the sounds. I heard heavy breathing. Shit, that was just me. Heavy footfalls. I wasn't that heavy. Was I? And then...lighter steps. Further up. I turned. Blessedly, a streetlight lit my way, and I saw the cloaked figure. Standing. Inhumanity in human shape. It pointed at me.

My heart jumped into my throat. I felt something sinister. Something darker than undead.

Think about coal. That dusty blackness. Something which very essence is black. Not only does it make smoke, it seems smoky by itself. Now take that black rock. All that smokiness and smog. That black and dirty rock and inject it into your bloodstream. Have all that healthy red turn to ash. That's how I felt.

I gasped for air. None passed through my throat. An insidious, ashy blockage caught it all in my mouth. I felt the oxygen. That cold, ethereal lifegiving gas, caught in my mouth but not getting where it was needed. I only faintly felt the impact of my knees on the tarmac as I clawed at my throat and waterfalls fell from my eyes. My vision went blacker. Blacker. Blacker. As black as the coal I felt in my veins.

I heard muffled shouts. And then clearer. My breathing calmed. I could breathe! The shouts became more coherent.

"Kat! Kat! Kat!" It was Treth.

I stood. Staggered, finding my bearings. The cloaked figure was no longer there. I looked at my hands. Shaking.

"What was that?"

"I didn't feel it."

"I... I thought I was going to die."

Treth nodded. "Low-power dark magic. But must have caught you off-guard. First time it's used on you, you'll cry yourself to sleep."

"Let's hope I don't. Can't let Duer see that." I tried to smile. Failed.

"Are you okay?" Treth's voice was lowered. He sounded genuinely concerned. Was he now going to start seeing me as a case to pity? I hoped not! Trudie was more than enough.

"Yeah." I breathed. "Just tired. What was that?"

"It looked human."

"So do most undead."

"Doesn't look like any undead I've ever seen. Or act like it. Sounds like it used magic on you…." Treth shook his head. "I don't think it's an undead. Not a spirit, either. I'm pretty sure it's human."

"A necromancer?"

Treth hesitated, and then nodded. I felt some more sensation in that nod. Fear? I had seldom ever known Treth to be fearful. Prudent, maybe. Never fearful.

"May be the master of that zombie," I mused.

"That zombie was on its last legs. It had no master nearby."

"Perhaps – but perhaps it was a test?"

I felt incredulity come from Treth.

"Maybe it's the tiredness talking, but just maybe the cloaked figure is a newbie necromancer. That zombie was a test-case."

"To test what?" Treth asked, a hint of disgust in his tone. What ultimately drew us together, besides our unassailable circumstances, was our revulsion for the undead and the twisted powers that fashioned them.

"I may be twisted, Treth, but I'm not so twisted to understand the minds of necromancers." I replied, then yawned. "Rifts, I'm tired."

I looked around. Saw a street sign. Thank the Rifts for signage. At least the Council was doing something right. I dialled the taxi service.

"All cars are currently unavailable. Apologies for the inconvenience."

Shit.

It was late. Too late for buses – if I could even find a bus-stop. I frowned. I hated to do this, but I was too tired. Inhibitions collapse when all you want is a bed.

"Pranish?" I asked, after dialling his cell.

"Kat? It's 1am!"

"I know. I'm sorry. I really need a lift…"

Pause.

"Where are you?"

I gave the address.

"See you in ten."

"Thanks…"

He hung up before I could finish.

Pranish arrived soon after and I only knew how uncomfortable I had been after I entered the safe confines of his shiny magicorp-bought Corolla. Being on a quiet road at night was not the most pleasant of experiences. I had done it plenty of times, but this night was different. That no-feature hooded figure had me on edge. I felt the coal in my veins.

"Thanks, Pranish." I said, closing the door behind me and giving him a weak smile. He had bags under his eyes.

"You look like shit."

"Thanks."

We drove off, tires scraping on under-serviced tarmac. My eyes remained glued to the rear-view mirror. To the streetlight where I had last seen the figure. I half expected it to re-appear. And really hoped it did not.

***

"She weighs a tonne," Pranish grunted.

"Not polite to comment on a girl's weight," Trudie grunted. She wasn't handling Kat's weight much better herself. Even between the two of them, they were struggling to lift the comatose girl. "Besides, it's her equipment. Should've done it in relays."

"I've got an early class. Wanted to get this all done in one go."

"Counter-intuitive." Pranish grunted back. Much more a response of derision than one of strain.

Finally, they reached Kat's floor. It was a miracle she wasn't awake yet. Trudie was sure they'd banged her head at least once. She must be really out of it. All that strain. All that exertion. Hunt after hunt after hunt. Doing what no nineteen-year-old girl should reasonably do.

They arrived at Kat's apartment door and put her down. Trudie had a set of keys, to feed Alex and for emergencies. She opened the door with just a tad bit of strain. The door needed maintenance. Alex's meows and purring were audible from the other side of the shoddy door. Door open, they lifted their friend up again. Alex wound himself around their legs, claiming them in that cutesy way that cats do.

As they entered, Trudie swore she saw a flash of golden light. She shook her head. Must be tiredness. Rifts! No one should be awake at this time. Well, no one who wasn't at an all-night concert or party, that is. Trudie frowned at the thought. She had spent many nights awake at this hour. Parties. Concerts. And the inevitable all-nighters that came with academics and coding. The hypocrisy wasn't lost on Trudie, but she chose to ignore it. People of their age were meant to ignore prudent time management for fun and for the necessities of their job or study. And reasonable jobs! Not this senseless, violent and ultimately inappropriate stuff that Kat was doing.

Pranish left the room as Trudie stripped Kat out of her blood and grime strained clothes, and then haphazardly dropped her into bed. Trudie grimaced at the clothes. Shred marks. Old shred marks. And not the intentional shredding so popular among the youth. Tears from nightmares. From things Trudie had never seen and prayed she would never see. Trudie hoped none of the older stains of blood belonged to Kat. She couldn't be too sure. Healing magic and modern medicine did wonders, but it still took strain on the patient. You couldn't escape death indefinitely.

Pranish, signalled by the twang of bed springs as Trudie laid her friend to a hopefully restful sleep, entered.

"So peaceful…" he commented.

Trudie snorted, sitting on the side of the bed. Alex jumped up and demanded petting. Trudie obliged, but her attention was not on the cat. She stared at her friend. Pranish was right. So peaceful in sleep. A peace that Trudie hadn't seen for years in Kat while she was awake. They had been friends a long time, and Trudie remembered a time when this was the norm. And while Kat acted fine, Trudie could not help but worry that her friend was deeply sad.

"I miss her, Pranish."

"We see her almost every day."

Trudie shook her head.

"Do we? I see a girl burnt out with exhaustion, risking her life, covered in death."

"That's our friend, Trudie."

Pranish had his arms crossed. He was thinly veiling his irritability. He liked his sleep.

"And I miss her." Trudie stared Pranish in the eyes. She felt tears rise, but none fell. Pranish sighed.

"This is what she needs to do. It is her reason for living."

"She needs to go hunting nightmares in the early hours of the morning? Needs to snub us at every opportunity for this so-called part-time work of hers? Needs to keep me awake at night worrying if I'll ever see her again?"

Pranish nodded. Always matter of fact.

Trudie shook her head. Her raven black bangs swished in and out of her vision. She gave Alex one final scratch under the chin, and then stood.

They exited the apartment.

"Thanks for helping. Didn't want to wake her," Pranish said, breaking the silence. Despite his annoyance from before, this sounded sincere.

Trudie, fading fast, just nodded, and said:

"Let's go."

Chapter 13.   Burn-out

That night with the zombie and the mysterious figure was the start of a frenetic series of jobs. Conrad hadn't been lying. He promised to get me work, and he got me work. Possibly, too much work. Some weeks, I had a job every day. Sometimes two or three! It got so bad that I ended up recounting undead killing techniques in a test on their biology.

"Sever the front of the neck to stagger them," I wrote. "Then finish the decapitation or skewer the brain, being careful to avoid glancing off the skull."

That wouldn't have gone down well in the monster sympathising orthodoxy of my campus. Luckily, Treth had the sense to warn me that I wasn't answering the question – and I quickly scrapped the paper and started fresh.

After class, I got into the habit of sleeping in the afternoons. Alex appreciated it and would curl up with me on my bed or the couch. Wherever Duer wasn't glowing and keeping me awake. I ended up following Alex's borderline nocturnal sleeping schedule. It still wasn't enough sleep, though. More often than not, I still nodded off during class. So much so that I wasn't looking forward to checking my grades.

But despite the constant bags under my eyes, the exhaustion on campus, the inhuman sleeping patterns and my bloodstained laundry, I had never felt more alive.

The zombie at the motel had been just the beginning. Before entering employment under Conrad, my jobs were sparse. Common enough that they took their toll. Trudie could write a thesis on that. But still sporadic. A wight in a cave, a zombie in the street, a ghoul eating pigeons. But since getting this gig, the jobs were every day. This week alone, I had slayed a feral imp at a fast-food joint, a pack of undead seals (why in the Rifts would anyone re-animate seals?!) and a gheist keeping the old train station from re-opening. But that was just the odd-ball jobs. Every other assignment was filled with swathes of lesser undead. Zombies, flesh puppets and mundane abhorrent.

First, I thought that the influx of new work was because I had an agent. But even Conrad thought this was odd.

"There's never been this many cases of lesser undead in Hope City," he said. "Very few fatalities, but the number of appearances is astounding!"

"New necromancer?" I asked.

"Always new necromancers. But they usually stick to the slums. Fresh corpses and less law there."

"Can we do anything about it?"

Conrad had shaken his head. He had humanised as the weeks passed. I realised that his wolfish smile and car dealer mannerisms were just who he was. They didn't indicate any genuinely sinister intent. As far as I knew. I chose to trust this man.

"Just exterminate them as they pop up. Plenty of money for us, at least. And you like slaying undead, right?"

I couldn't argue with him. I really did. Slaying undead was not just a part-time job, paying the bills. It was a hobby. Profit was just an incentive to do what I already loved.

I was having the time of my life. And that's what made the time spent on campus so dreadfully dull. And while I tried my best to be upbeat around Trudie, I inevitably failed. I loved my friend, but she couldn't understand what this meant to me.

Things didn't remain so joyful in my part-time work, however. The rise of lesser undead didn't just remain a source of extra income, they became a pandemic. So much so that even the premium service anti-forces of darkness agency, Puretide, finally received a prerogative from the City Council to contain the undead hordes in the slums. Couldn't have them rushing into the suburbs, weyline districts and Old Town. Conrad had me working all evening. Even with his roster of monster hunters, he couldn't keep up with the demand. He even had me running joint jobs with Drakenbane and Puretide, much to my chagrin and Brett's amusement.

Treth and I undertook the jobs with the utmost efficiency, and I was making decent money. I had even been able to afford to upgrade to the premium cup of noodles and have enough to replace and upgrade my equipment. Oh, and I was able to pay the bills too. No more relying on the good nature of Mrs Ndlovu to delay the rent.

But despite all of this, and despite the feeling of satisfaction in my work, I was tired. Burnt out. Like a forgotten toaster filled with old bread.

And as I sat in the campus cafeteria, sipping on spicy ginger ale (a real luxury, indeed!), my head felt like it was in a vice grip. I was very much looking forward to bed after I got home – and then to slaying whatever horde had popped up overnight.

"Hey Kats," I heard Pranish say, grabbing my shoulder lightly in a futile attempt to give me a fright. He failed. Couldn't jump scare someone who hunted horror for a living.

"Howzit?" I asked. I infused myself with a temporary bout of energy. I owed it to Pranish. Calling him for that lift all those nights ago was very unreasonable.

Pranish seated himself and took a bite of fries liberally covered in barbeque sauce and mayonnaise. "Meh," he replied. "Have you finished Warpwars?"

I frowned. I knew how he felt. "Glorious and melancholic."

Pranish nodded. "Always this way with series. The longer the series and novels, the harder the fall. Seems that the wait also adds into it. Hard to think we won't be getting any more."

"Always room for spin-offs."

"A vain hope," Pranish waved the suggestion aside.

As much as I didn't want to, I had to agree with him. Warpwars had never received spin-offs in the past. No hope of getting one now, even with that grand finale. The only thing left was the melancholy that inevitably comes at the end of an era, and the small hope that the books will get a film or series deal. The latter was unlikely. Sci-fi wasn't that popular. When the fantastical was reality, science fiction became drab for many. They didn't see the value in speculation. Ingrates!

"Where's Trudie?" I asked, in between bites of magically grown fried chicken. Farmers enchanted the eggs to hatch quicker and their inhabitants to grow faster. "Thought you both had class today."

Pranish winced. Hiding something. I raised my eyebrow and leaned forward, examining him. He must have noticed my predatory gaze, as he seemed a tad unnerved.

"He's your friend, Kat," Treth said. "Not gül tracks."

I repressed a wince myself, and leaned back, embarrassed. Who could think Treth, the off-world knight, would be lecturing me on people skills?

"She should be coming now," Pranish said, not looking me in the eyes. Well, shit. Got my friend all scared of me now. Good going, Kat! I frowned. I really should be putting more effort in with them. Known them for long enough. Means I should work harder for their affection, not take them for granted.

I turned at the unmistakeable sound of combat boots impacting the tiles. Trudie was wearing a black leather jacket over a frilled shirt and black jeans. She had two bows in her hair. Like the one I wore. Trudie definitely had a noticeable sense of style. I was barely able to feign a smile as Trudie approached me, an equally simulated smile upon her lips. She thought I didn't notice her concern. I did. I very much did. But I couldn't stop now, regardless of what she, my best friend, felt about my activities. This was the usual interaction. Either, repeated nagging, or an insidious and unmistakable concern boiling underneath the surface. But this time was different. Trudie was not alone. By her side was a tall man. Early twenties. Olive, tanned skin contrasted with Trudie's almost vampiric pallor. He had short, brown hair. His shirt clung to his chest tightly. Either a sign of an impressive exercise regime or ineptness in buying clothes.

"Kat," Trudie said, giving me a hug. I hoped I didn't smell like the night before. Had been knee-deep in zombie corpses. Morons had charged right into my spear trap and splattered me with a tidal wave of blood. Hopefully, three showers would suffice to remove the stench. Trudie withdrew and presented the stranger with the too-tight shirt.

"Pranish, you already know Andy. Kat, please meet my friend, Andy Garce. He's a computer science major."

"Nice to meet you, Kat," Andy said, presenting his hand and a pearl-white smile. I imagined a cinematic glint shining off his teeth. He seemed the type.

I accepted the handshake. Strong. Unyielding. I raised my eyebrow. It wasn't the handshake of a limp-wristed weakling, or the weak handshake men usually use for members of the fairer sex. It was a proper handshake, reserved for equals. I returned it in kind and as one feels after a satisfying handshake, Andy and I came to an unspoken understanding.

Trudie and Andy sat down. I didn't say anything. Something was afoot. Trudie had never told me about Andy. And we told each other everything. Well, she told me everything. I didn't tell her about the grittier parts of my profession. Or about Treth. Or about my all-consuming desire to destroy all that comes from the dark. I didn't really tell her much, actually. Am I a bad friend?

Trudie spoke before I could ponder that thought. "Haven't seen you for a long time, Kat."

"We ate lunch together yesterday."

"You fell asleep in your fries."

"Long night."

"Aren't they always?"

The tone was casual. Banter. But I felt an intense energy in the air. I had known Trudie had a problem with my work, but it was always reserved to the occasional nagging and concerned expressions. Was she attempting her intervention now? I looked to Pranish. He looked irritable. Hopefully, he'd take my side. I hid my thoughts. Shouldn't be thinking about stuff like this. It wasn't about sides. Not some fight. Bad, Kat, bad!

Trudie sighed. This was it. The truth sallies forth. No holds barred. I feared this may be my hardest fight yet (and then reminded myself to stop thinking about it that way).

"You look burnt out, Kat."

Her tone was much more resigned that I expected. A feint?

I shrugged. "Conrad's got me running ragged."

"That sleazy guy from the hospital?"

"He's not that bad once you get to know him."

"I'd rather not have to get to know him."

"Who?" Andy asked, interjecting.

"Kat's boss," Trudie replied.

"Agent," I corrected.

"Like a movie agent?" Andy asked, grinning. A hint of joking flattery.

"Something much more virtuous," I replied.

"Trudie told me you're a monster hunter."

I nodded, hesitantly. Was Andy meant to be Trudie's backup for this intervention?

"Very cool! You with an agency?"

I shook my head.

"Even cooler! Independent. Like a noire private-eye, or a gunslinger from the Old West."

"The post-cataclysm bounty hunter," Pranish mumbled through his food.

I looked at Trudie while Andy and Pranish began lauding my profession. She did not look pleased.

"Andy," Trudie said, repressing a hiss. I got the feeling she hadn't expected him to act this way. "You're single, right?"

The question took us all by surprise. Pranish spat out his food. My head swivelled to my friend. Trudie was playing a dangerous game here. I didn't like it.

"Um, yeah…"

"So is Kat."

"That's not true," Pranish said, grinning mischievously. "Kat's married to her job."

I repressed a chuckle. I couldn't disagree.

"And that's a problem." Trudie turned to me and looked me in the eyes. "This isn't healthy, Kat."

I opened my mouth to respond with a quip, but she raised her hand to stop me. "Please. Hear me out."

I closed my mouth and nodded. All serious now.

"This isn't a healthy life you're living, Kat. It's worse now than it ever was in the past. Your grades are suffering, you have bags under your eyes and you're sleeping during the day! I don't want to begin to fully understand what you're doing at night, but I think I know enough as a friend to know that it isn't good for you. You're nineteen years old! You're not supposed to be working yourself to the bones. You're meant to be having fun. Meeting new people. Going on dates. When last did you go on a date?"

I grimaced. Trudie knew the answer. Second year of high school. Rodney Cavitts.

"These are your golden years of innocence, Kat. You should use them."

A pause. I pondered what she was saying. I reminded myself that she was saying all this because she cared about me, but I couldn't help but become exasperated. She didn't understand. Golden years of innocence? How could I be innocent? After all I've seen and done. I breathed and calmed. Before I could reply, Pranish did for me.

"Kat's a hero, Trudie. Might pain you to admit that. But she's doing something. She's cleaning up this Rift-damned city while we live in our high rises."

"You're the one living in a high rise, Pranish!" Trudie snapped.

"But we both benefit from her keeping us safe," Pranish answered, voice much calmer than Trudie's. He had always been the better debater.

"I never asked for you to keep me safe!" Trudie turned to me. I raised my hands. Wasn't my fight. I didn't think I was a hero, but I wasn't going to stop Pranish from calling me one.

Trudie's eyes were glistening. The hint of future and past tears. "I just want my friend back. To hang out. To catch a movie. To do something that doesn't make me fear you're not gonna show up to class."

Sadness for my friend, and concern for her, overwhelmed my irritation and embarrassment that she would do this in such a place. I placed my hand on hers and squeezed.

"Trudie, I'm sorry. I'll try to be a better friend."

A hint of hope. Trudie looked me in the eyes.

"But I can't stop hunting."

The statement hit Trudie like a tonne of bricks. She slumped into her chair. Pranish stood up and stretched.

"Come on, Trudie. Class."

He half dragged Trudie out of her chair and disappeared out of the cafeteria. Andy remained.

"I thought you were in their class," I half asked, half accused, crossing my arms.

"I am, but don't need to go immediately. I'd like to talk to you for a bit?"

"Me?" I tried to let out a quip. Failed.

"Yeah. I fear we may have gotten off on the wrong foot. A tense little exchange."

"Trudie is worried about me. Always has been. Thinks she can be my mom."

"I think you can figure out why she brought me here."

"First thought she had a new boyfriend. But she prefers shorter guys."

"How about you? How do you prefer your guys?"

I eyed him up and down.

"Rotting and decapitated."

Andy laughed. A genuine laugh that infected me and I smiled. When the humour subsided, he continued.

"Trudie wanted to hook us up. Thought that my allure would pull you from your dangerous deeds. But I see that I may be a little too alive for your liking."

"Don't worry. You'll get there eventually."

"I hope later, rather than sooner, despite your preferences. Ignoring Trudie's agenda, however, would you be open to…hanging out?"

Well, that was straightforward. Andy was something else. I must admit, I had little interest in him initially, besides the novelty of a fourth member at the table, but that was changing. Confidence was interesting – especially the confidence to so blatantly ask out someone you know owns weapons.

"I've got a busy schedule."

"I've heard. But even Thor takes a break from being the god of thunder every once in awhile."

I hummed my consideration, and finally answered. "I'll think about it."

Andy's grin shone like a movie star's.

***

I didn't feel tired when I turned down the street of my apartment block. My run in with Trudie had me on edge, but my subsequent discussion with Andy had me intrigued. It was a recipe for a lack of sleep and I hoped that it wouldn't cost me my work tonight.

Mrs Ndlovu greeted me at the front door. She was watering the flowers. An oddly normal activity to contrast with her usual advertising that this was a terrible place to live due to angry spirits.

"Kat! How are you?"

"Fine," I lied. "You?"

Mrs Ndlovu frowned. "Kat, can wraiths be small?"

I raised my eyebrow. "How small?"

Mrs Ndlovu held her thumb and index finger apart, indicating something around 5 inches tall. I shook my head.

"Wraiths are essences of human hatred and malice. Ergo, they are roughly human sized."

"Oh," she said, looking a tad disappointed. "Must have been something else."

It was like she wanted to have a wraith haunting the place!

I left my landlady to her gardening and climbed the staircase to my apartment. Duer and Alex both greeted me at different heights.

"You look like a beaten cloth sack," Duer said, twinkling and whizzing about. Alex claimed my leg, shoving up against me and purring like a machine gun.

"Hello to you too, Duer, Alex."

I closed the door behind me and entered my apartment. It was a lot cleaner than usual. I had mostly been eating out, just before jobs. For the rest of my usual mess, Duer had proven to be a very useful janitor.

"A clean weyline requires a clean middle-realm," he said, whatever that meant.

"You gonna get some sleep?" Duer asked. "Your usual time."

"Not tired and got a report to write."

"Work tonight?"

"Always."

"Can't you take a break?" Duer frowned.

"You want me to? It'd mean I'll be here to stop you from your pixie debauchery. Besides, need to keep earning so you can keep living here and I can keep paying you in honey and vodka to keep this place clean."

Duer considered the comment and didn't respond. He liked his honey and vodka. Wouldn't want to risk ending the constant stream of it.

"He's right, you know," Treth said. He had been pretty silent today. Awkwardness from the cafeteria talk, probably.

"About what?"

Duer cocked his head. I had tried to tell him about Treth (what was the worst that could happen?) but he didn't really understand. He thought I was mad. But I was the hand that granted him housing and treats, so he didn't point out my eccentricities.

"Conrad said you can take a break whenever you want. No skin off his nose. And you've got plenty of savings now. Your swords are holding up and you've got a decent set of armour. Well, decent enough. You can afford to take a break."

I took off my bag and put it down next to the coffee table, and then went to the fridge to get myself something to drink. Treth was right. With my frugal spending habits and the influx of new jobs, I was rolling in excess cash.

"It isn't that," I finally said. "I'd like to get some more cash so I can comfortably pay next year's tuition, but that's not the main reason."

"The quest?" Treth asked.

"Mmm," I affirmed. "This rise of undead has got me worried."

"Things like this go in cycles, Kat. The darkness never disappears but does ebb and flow."

"I think it is more than that. Ever since that cloaked figure, I can't help but feel that there's something more afoot. I find it hard to believe that all these undead are just coincidence. Rift-born undead are a thing, yeah, but not this many. And if rifts were becoming more common, we'd be getting more than just undead. I think this is manmade. A new necromancer."

"Or necromancers."

"Probably. But different from the usual casters working for the gangs. This is too organised. Too united. Not enough attacks. Very few civilian casualties. It's like someone is mustering an army."

"And you want to put a stop to it?"

I nodded.

Treth sighed. "I know what you're capable of, Kat, and you're capable of a lot. But facing a true undead horde? That is way beyond your abilities. Take a break. Avoid the burn-out. In the long run, it will be better for the quest. If you go down in flames now, then we won't even make a dent in our mutual foe."

I took a long swig of cola and then wiped my mouth.

"Okay, Treth. You and Trudie win. I'll take it easy for a bit. And I'll focus on what is supposed to be my priority."

Satisfied, Treth didn't respond and retreated to do whatever it was he did in his long periods of silence. I wondered if he had some sort of spiritual room. Some place where he could be his own person, and not just watch me live my life. I hope he did. At least, I hope he wasn't watching me all the time.

I contemplated Andy. If things were to go further with him...

My cheeks reddened. Treth would be there every step of the way.

I chased the thought away and set up my work laptop on the coffee table then, taking a seat on the couch, I opened up a fresh document and started outlining. Duer hovered down to see what I was doing, and I barely managed to stop Alex from taking an opportunistic swipe at my pixie roommate.

Chapter 14. APB

The buzz in my pocket woke me from my class-made boredom and reverie. The professor had been discussing pre-Cataclysm history. The time of impending civil war. The breakdown of society. A possibility of a united and democratic society if a bit corrupt. The type of stuff I felt would have mattered if the Vortex hadn't appeared but was close to irrelevant now. After the Vortex opened, allowing other realms to bleed into our mortal plane, a lot of the titbits of human history became a lot duller. Sure, it remained interesting to the historian, but as a way of seeing how we got here? Nah. End of the Cold War could have meant something if the nukes weren't replaced with dragons. Nobody could have predicted that, and you can't blame Harry Truman for the unification of Scandinavia under Odin. The Cataclysm was more than a watershed part of history. It twisted our reality. It was unpredictable, out of this world and changed absolutely everything. Well, that last part is a lie. Most things remained the same. Human nature, at its core, doesn't change – even if you give the human a magic staff and a set of robes that talk pseudo-Latin. There were still wars, as they were in the past, but they had taken on a different nature. As a result of the rise of extremely powerful individuals and groups, the required size for a nation had shrunk. While a few states remained whole, many others had broken up into city-states and territories more reminiscent of feudal Europe. Major wars were reserved for the surviving conventional states, but that didn't mean the city-states couldn't engage in some of the old state-sanctioned violence. The Zulu Empire, for instance, was well-known locally for expanding its borders into the micro-states of southern Africa. Against the sorcerous ruling clans of the Zulu state, only Hope City and the Goldfield Magocracy had a functioning enough defence force to discourage invasion. And in the case of Hope City, only barely. Most of the city's budget went into keeping the Titan Under the Mountain asleep.

I had been taking it easy the past few days, as per Treth's request. Conrad seemed a bit miffed. I was one of his rising stars, after all. He wanted to keep grafting me, so we could both make a lot of money. But he understood. I was still just a kid, he irritatingly implied. Needed time to be "hip".

I used the time to hang out with Trudie, Pranish and even Andy – who had become a more common member of our group. I did as was expected of a girl of my age. We went to the movies, we hung out on campus. We shared pleasant silences together, while doing our own thing. Trudie seemed to like it and as much as her nagging had been irritating me, I was pleased that she was no longer worrying as much about me.

My short hiatus didn't stop me from keeping up with the monster hunting news, however. I still perused MonsterSlayer and even chatted with Brett and Guy, my acquaintances from Drakenbane. Brett was an obnoxious fool, but was growing on me, and Guy was pleasant. He was a man of few words and extreme professionalism. I liked him.

By the entries on MonsterSlayer and between the rubbish messages from Brett (many sent while evidently drunk), I found out that the undead were getting more and more prevalent. Entire blocks had been evacuated as zombies poured out into the streets. Every time I heard this, I almost phoned Conrad to put me back on the job. Treth reminded me, however, that there was little I could do. Relax, and wait for the real quest to begin. So, I did.

Bizt-bizt. My phone rang again. Thank the Rifts it was on silent! Wouldn't do to start blaring 80's Manchester rock during a lecture. I stealthily pulled my cell out of my pocket and checked the caller ID.

Conrad.

He usually never phoned me. Always messages. MonsterSlayer notifications. Suited me fine. Phone calls were too intrusive. Too immediate. Messages worked much better and kept a more effective record of our communications. But if he was phoning me now, then this must be something big. Something worth ignoring my vacation for, and something worth risking my exasperation.

I looked up at the class clock. Twenty more minutes of class. The phone stopped ringing as Conrad's call timed out. He immediately rang again. Something was up and I couldn't shake the feeling that the time was at hand to get back to Treth's oh-so important quest.

I packed my notes into my bag and snuck out of the class. History could wait. It wasn't going anywhere.

"Conrad," I answered, just outside the class, walking to the exit of the building.

"Kat, this is big. Very big!" His voice resonated with an excitable energy. More than usual. No hint of that sleazy, hard-sell attitude. Genuine, child-like enthusiasm.

"What is it?"

"Vampire got downed in a downtown warehouse. Had a huge ghoul posse enslaved. The monsters have gone rogue but are trapped inside the warehouse."

"So? Let them starve. Ghouls without a master are just feral. They won't be able to get out if the cops get a barricade up."

"The warehouse is owned by Uhurutech. Top-level magicorp."

I knew the name. They were the manufacturers of my laptop and cell phone. They combined magic with technology, creating highly reliable hardware.

"They need their stock ASAP and need the building cleared."

"Sounds like they'd rather have Puretide."

"Puretide has no one available," Conrad answered, excitement rising further. "Neither does Drakenbane. And no other undead or vamp hunters are available. Just you."

I didn't reply immediately. Ghoul posse…

"How many ghouls?"

"At least eight."

Shit. Eight! I'd struggled to eliminate zombie groups of half that amount before. The terror illusions didn't count.

They didn't really exist. Couldn't really hurt me. In my normal hunts, I had to separate my foes, play on their idiocy and slowness. But these weren't zombies. These were ghouls. Effectively, lesser vampires. They were faster than most undead. Smarter, too. Being rogue would only dull them a bit. They probably wouldn't know how to use guns anymore. But with razor sharp fangs and claws, that wasn't a huge consolation.

"How much they offering?"

"Uhurutech is offering $2000 to you. My fee is separate. We also get to sell all the bits ourselves, as per the usual arrangement."

My eyes widened. A single ghoul would net me $50 to $60 usually. This was over triple the usual pay! Uhurutech must really want their warehouse cleared. I did a quick mental calculation. I could usually sell ghoul bits myself for $100 each. Conrad was much more discerning and had got me better deals lately. So roughly $200 a ghoul. After his cut, $120 a ghoul for me. I bit my lip. $1440 for the bits.

$3440…

"What's the address?"

"I'm coming around to your place to lift you. Can't risk the buses or taxis running late for this."

"I'll be there ASAP."

Conrad hung up.

"So, Treth. Seems the quest begins."

"Haven't fought a ghoul in ages. This will be fun."

I snorted. "If Trudie knew how bad of an influence you were on me…"

***

Conrad's car sped around the corner and stopped with a screech outside my apartment block. It was an old white Golf. Pre-cataclysm. There were blankets and pillows in the back, and a half-eaten tray of TV dinner. He opened the door and I got in, swords on my lap and a bag at my feet full of gear. I was wearing my new equipment. Black and white hard-plastic mask and goggles around the back of my neck. Black Kevlar and plastic vest. Polymer and fibre bracers. A hard and scratchy scarf with the texture of a doormat. Zombies struggled to chew through stuff like it. Not so sure about ghouls. Their vampiric fangs were a bit more effective at rending.

Conrad sped off again just as I closed the door.

"You ready for this, Kat?"

"Ready as I can be."

"This is the big leagues, Kat." He said my name again, as if grounding himself. He was sweating. His knuckles were white on the steering wheel. I saw the faint sign of a shiver. In a way, his anxiety calmed me. I was not sure why he was the one shaking and probably doing jumping jacks in his tummy. I was the person who was expected to solo a warehouse full of ghouls! But seeing him act this way, I couldn't help but consider him a proxy for my own fear. I was calm. As calm as I could be.

"Check the glove compartment," Conrad said, pointing to it in front of me.

I did. It got stuck but I wriggled it open. Within: a paper-wrapped package.

"Open it. But carefully."

I unwrapped it, careful as possible. Inside was a canister the size of my fist. A ring-shaped pin was stuck in it.

"A flashbang," Conrad explained. "Ghouls are hyper-sensitive to light, right?"

They were. "This looks military grade…"

"It is. Surplus from the Goldfield Extermination Corps. So, use it wisely. I'm late on the rent at the Gravekeeper. But this is worth going more into the red."

We sped into Old Town. The old skyscrapers of the pre-cataclysm, many of them converted into housing or magicorp buildings, dotted the skyline. I saw Council cop cars heading in the same direction we were. They would just be containing the warehouse. No Council stooge got paid enough to justify risking their lives the way I did. Besides, they got paid regardless if they did the job or not.

"What about your other hunters?" I asked. I was one of his new hunters, after all. By the look of his trophies and photos in his office, he had quite the roster of partners. Were they all busy as well?

Conrad frowned. "Dead or retired."

"Shit, sorry."

"They knew what they were getting into. Cowards who survived don't have your grit, though. So, time you surpass them."

I felt the pressure mounting. It wasn't just about me. Conrad needed this. For the work he had gotten me in this short amount of time, I owed him this much.

"They're just some ghouls. Not even vampires. You can buy me a round at the Gravekeeper to celebrate."

"You drink?" Conrad raised his eyebrow. He probably had the impression that I was all work. I got that a lot.

Serious, older than her years, Kat. Had that reputation in high school. It was earned.

"Only when I can afford it, or someone else is paying."

Conrad grinned. "I look forward to it."

I considered inviting Pranish, Trudie and Andy. Trudie would appreciate it. Could maybe make her see that I wasn't all just work. There was still some *fun* Kat to be had.

"Be careful, Kat," Treth said. I didn't respond. Couldn't with Conrad so near.

"Ghouls are much more dangerous than our usual fare. They're faster. They know how to use weapons. They have retained more of their darker side of humanity. Feral or not, it will be dangerous. We need a plan."

I cleared my throat, casually to avoid alarm from Conrad, but to signal to Treth that I agree.

"Ghouls are hyper-sensitive to more than just light. They also have enhanced hearing. The flashbang, if it makes a bang as well as a flash, will throw them off for a few moments, but it's not enough. We need more. Something incessant to throw them off."

I noticed Conrad's car speakers. They weren't built into the car. They were wireless, synced to a phone through a wireless connection.

"Can I borrow these?"

"The speakers?"

I nodded.

"I kinda like them."

"I'll bring them back."

"You need them for the hunt?"

I nodded again.

Bemused, Conrad indicated for me to take them. I did so and stowed them in my bag. The bag had some baggies of enchanted herbal remedy, in case of necrosick, and a whetstone to sharpen my swords. I did that for the rest of the drive.

We soon arrived at the warehouse. Council cop cars with blinking red and blue lights surrounded the warehouse. A deployable barrier had been erected on the metal door. I saw dents coming from the inside. I resisted gulping. I didn't know ghouls were that strong.

Conrad and I exited the vehicle. A man wearing the navy blue of a Council cop came to us.

"This is a restricted…"

Conrad flashed an official looking document.

"We're here to do your job, tick. Corps' on deadline and can't wait for a vote to get you to do something about these vamps."

The cop's face reddened, but he let us pass. Everyone's heads turned to us. A man in a cheap ash suit and a girl hastily strapping on her sword belt. I almost envied them. It must be a sight to behold.

I checked the straps on my armour. All secure. Swords sharp and ready. Seax, ready as a last resort. Prepped, I looked up at the warehouse. Grey-brick. Windows covered with…cardboard? Could get them uncovered. Ghouls didn't like the light.

"Have a layout of the building?" I asked Conrad, and any relevant person within earshot.

Conrad shook his head. I bit my lip. Typical of employers to skimp on what matters.

"I need a look inside."

I paused.

"And a way inside. Not going through the front door. Other entrances?"

"Garage door."

I shook my head. "Defeats the point. The ghouls will come rushing out."

"Won't they want to stay away from the sun?" This must have been Conrad's first detailed foray into ghoul extermination.

"Ghouls are lesser vampires and are over-sensitive to light," I replied, scanning the building before me to prompt some ideas. "But they aren't actually hurt by sunlight. They'll just get some minor sensory overload. But their desire for blood will overtake their prudence. Especially if they're rogue."

Conrad frowned. His hands were still shaking. His forehead creased.

"We still doing this?" Conrad's concern really surprised me. I had him wrong when I thought of him as sleazy, wolfish and like a used car salesman. That was just who he was. Nothing sinister about it. He was a man with a waning career, held on by a girl less than half his age. That couldn't be good for his self-esteem. I didn't show it outwardly, but I felt pity for this man, and a sense of new determination. This wasn't just about slaying monsters, or getting myself rich, this was about keeping this man alive – so he could continue to help me do the first two things.

"I'm still doing this…but I'll need your help."

Sweat glistened on Conrad's brow. I continued.

"That window looks promising." I pointed at a second storey window, covered from the inside. "I presume Uhurutech doesn't want any of their stock broken, but how about windows?"

"Go right ahead. Smash 'em. But gonna need a ladder."

Conrad looked towards the growing morass of emergency workers and onlookers. A large empty space of gravel and concrete separated us from the police tape. I felt everyone staring at me. I looked away from their gazes and scanned the warehouse for the bazillionth time. I wasn't one for the limelight. Conrad trod off. His footfalls were heavy and sure. An act? His façade of confidence to fast-talk a solution? He really was like a used car salesman, but if he was using those powers for good…

"We need that ladder," Conrad said, voice steady. No hint of the vocal shakes from before. His tone brooked no argument. It was a command.

No response from the victim of his abrasiveness. Conrad repeated himself. I heard clattering and turned. The owner of the ladder, a technician, and Conrad were carrying a ladder my way.

"Thanks," I said. "Put it up by that window, please."

They did so, and I climbed. Conrad stood at the foot of the ladder. The technician stood to the side, dumbstruck.

"I need a diversion. Start banging on the front door."

I hoped no ghouls inside heard me or understood me. They shouldn't. I knew quite a bit about ghouls. Had hunted them before. But there were always exceptions to the rule. I hoped that these weren't the exceptional exceptions.

"What's your plan, Kat?" Treth asked. I was far up enough the ladder that I could whisper.

"First, need to scout out the place. See what I have to play with. After that…I need to overload their senses. If I can set up these portable speakers and blare music through them, then that may confuse them."

"And if that doesn't work?"

I gulped. "Then we fight them the old-fashioned way."

"You could die, Kat."

On the surface, his voice was steady. His usual, almost pompous knightly speech. It was a statement of fact. He didn't want it to hold any loaded sentiments. But there was a quaver. The way he pronounced some of the syllables.

"And?" I responded. I hope I was better at hiding my own trepidation.

Treth didn't respond. He wasn't one to decry foolhardy sacrifice. Foolhardy sacrifice was his entire MO.

I'm not going to lie. I was afraid. Too scared to shake. But I also knew that this was what I had been training for. The real deal. Where my desire for vengeance and aimless hatred was upgraded to becoming a big-league monster hunter.

Come on, Kat. I told myself. I clenched my fists on the rung of the ladder. I took one deep breath, and then I nodded at Conrad to begin.

He started banging on the metal door to the warehouse, much to the chagrin of a cop, who was promptly chased off by his glare. The cops of Hope City may be spineless, but at least they seldom got in the way. A timbre of snarls and growls emanated from the other side of the door. The ghouls inside responded to Conrad's banging with their own. It all formed a rather unpleasant cacophony. I didn't know if ghouls had some sort of super sound discernment. I hoped they didn't. I needed them focused on their free, if unpleasant, concert by the door. As the noise reached the loudest I felt it could ever get, I smashed the top window with the pommel of my sword. Cardboard and glass tore away at the blow. I used the pommel to shift cardboard and glass shards out of the way. By this time, Conrad had strong-armed the technician and cop to help make noise by the garage entrance as well. If they kept at it, I may be able to eliminate the ghouls easy-peasy.

My pommel hit something hard. It shifted. I reached my hand through the window and grabbed the latch, undid it, and pulled the window open. Snarls and the product of Conrad's impromptu band filled the interior of the warehouse. Dim lights emitted a hazy yellow glow across the room. Before me was a metal viewing deck. Excellent! I pushed the remainder of the cardboard out of the way and climbed in.

I winced as I clanged onto the floor of the viewing deck. The cacophony from below didn't stop, fortunately. The room was poorly lit, but I could see clearly. I can see well in bad light, as I have said. The shelves were sealed with silver coated metal plating, emblazoned with Uhurutech's logo resembling Mt Kilimanjaro. Uhurutech must really value this stock. The silver also explained why the ghouls weren't attacking the stock. They'd already gone to town with some chairs and loose boxes. Feral ghouls were not a fan of…anything really. When the connection to their master ceased, they went into a blood frenzy. Everything, other than their fellow ghouls, needed to die. Charming creatures.

The metal floor of the viewing deck was a grid. I could see the quite irate ghouls underneath. A ladder was to my left. A welded metal one, attached to the viewing platform. The platform itself, kinda like an interior balcony, jutted out of the wall. Two thin support columns held it up. I didn't like the look of them. The ghouls had shown some immense strength already. Together, they could tear down the balcony. I had briefly thought I could lure them up here and use the ladder as a kill-zone, but they'd probably pull us all down. They'd need much less time to recover than I. In the smoking wreckage of metal bits, if I wasn't already dead, I'd soon be chewed up by ghouls. Not a fate I desired.

I was crouching on the grated floor balcony. Below me, I could see that not all the ghouls were entranced by the noises at the door. Only four, scraping and growling. Blackened, ash-like skin. Red, bloodshot eyes. They looked less human than some zombies. They also didn't smell. They definitely weren't undead. Vampires were a different beast altogether. Too simplistic to treat them like the undead, like so many ignorant people liked to do. Contrary to some mythology, vampires were very much alive. But even that was too simple. Despite being alive, they did have a strong connection to necromantic energy and dark magic. More than a natural affinity. It is as if dark magic flowed through their veins. Which was ridiculous. Because they didn't have a bloodflow.

The ghouls wore an assortment of clothing. Workman overalls, jeans and t-shirts bearing Magicorp logos and even a security guard uniform. Their master, in life, must have been very diverse in his or her feeding grounds. Away from the group at the door, I heard guttural slurping that sent my stomach churning. A lone ghoul was stalking between the shelves, like a large cat. It looked grumpier than Alex when I scolded him for trying to eat Duer.

"Conrad said eight?" Treth asked. "Five in sight. More behind these shelves."

I nodded. I know. It was going to be dangerous. Enclosed space. Vicious monsters. Well, time to start...

I took Conrad's portable speakers out of my bag and placed them on the balcony. I synced it to my phone. Was a good brand. A Uhurutech, in fact. No fuss. Just simple intuitive interface. The music app on my phone was less agreeable and froze up when I was getting it ready. Old piece of cheap garbage – even if a Uhurutech. Needed to get a new one. After this, I'll be sure to buy a new phone. If there is an after this…

Finally, I finished setting up the speaker and the phone. It had a good range. I'd be able to play music from my phone to the speaker from anywhere in the building. Hopefully, it would be loud enough to confuse the ghouls.

I watched the ghouls again. Another came into view at the far end of the room, and then disappeared behind the silver shelves. I'd need to watch my back.

Conrad's banging was waning. He and those he had pressed into service were getting tired.

I needed to get to work fast.

I scaled down the ladder, thankful for my gloves. The metal didn't look the cleanest. I stopped just before reaching the concrete floor, making sure to step off quietly. I froze. The ghouls were ahead of me, still obsessed with the door.

"Keep scouting," Treth advised. I nodded. No point going after the main group. Best to pick off loners – and to ensure I knew where everything was. Knowledge was the first step down the path to victory, as Treth would say.

I kept low, in that way people do when trying to be quiet. Swords already drawn. The flashbang bulged out of the front pocket of my jacket. I'd never used one. Only seen them in films. I hoped I wouldn't screw up. As much as it would stun a ghoul, it could just as easily stun me.

The one ghoul headed down that way...

I followed it, slow and methodical footsteps, sticking behind the cover of the shelves. I heard footsteps, even over the banging and ghoulish howls. I stopped by the corner of a row of shelves, took a quiet breath, and peeked. A ghoul, hunched over and examining the floor. It looked eerily human from this angle, like someone bent over tying their shoe, or picking up a coin. I felt a pang. Killing a human... It wasn't something I wanted to consider. Despite all that I killed looking so human, they weren't human. And this wasn't human. I needed to remember that. I steeled myself and proceeded forward, footfalls silent under the cacophony from the door.

Closer, closer. It felt quiet, despite the noise from a few shelves away. It was just me, overthinking every footstep. Overthinking every detail, and the target I was slowly approaching.

It twitched and lifted its head from whatever it was looking at on the ground. Its profile revealed a dark grey visage, with bloodshot red eyes. Eyes like the blood they craved. A small primal voice in my head told me to freeze. To stop my approach. To flee. But Treth spoke louder.

"Charge!"

I leapt forward, slashing my blades in unison. The ghoul didn't cry out. It remained crouching, and then its head fell off, hitting the ground with a quiet thud. Blood – red blood – covered my blades, dripping onto the floor. I wiped the blades off on my shirt. Ghouls were not attracted to other vampiric blood. If anything, it would mask my much more delectable scent.

One down, seven more to go. Hopefully, only seven more.

I proceeded down the shelf-lined aisles. Nothing out of the ordinary. Just a severed hand, drained pale of blood. I had seen a broken chair near the ghouls. There must have been a security guard in here. I frowned and scowled. Simultaneously angry and sad at the loss.

Around a corner, I did my routine peek and saw two ghouls feasting on an already finished corpse. Every bit of flesh that could be accessed had already been consumed.

They now chewed on the bones. That wasn't enough for these ghouls. It was never enough. My grip on my swords tightened. I felt my chest constrict. I smelt smoke. That angry smoke. That sting you get in your nostrils when you're angry. And I mean really angry.

These monsters. These darkness-wrought good for nothing shits! Nothing was ever enough for them. No pain was ever sufficient. They had to just keep consuming. They may not have been the hated undead, but I hated them all the same.

"Calm down, Kat."

How could I? They'd eaten this guy. This guy just trying to do his job. Just trying to feed himself – probably a family. And these bastards ate him. They made it so not even his corpse was identifiable to the family. They'd probably eaten the teeth! No dental records. And here's the kicker: they didn't even need to eat. Ghouls just needed a wee bit of blood. Just a glass of blood and they could last for a week. Not even human blood. Could be a fucking pigeon. But they chose to eat humans. They chose to eat my kind!

I stepped out from my hiding spot. The ghouls didn't notice. They were too busy gorging themselves – just for the sake of gorging. I cracked my neck, stretching it. I was walking upright now, swords by my side.

"Careful, Kat!" His voice was commanding. Loud. Good thing only I could hear him. Well, only barely. I wasn't paying attention. I could only hear their slurps and crunching. I could only see red. Behind the monsters, and they still hadn't noticed. I paused above them. Considering them.

Abominations.

I lifted my swords. Some blood still clung to them. They needed a polish. The faint light still glinted off them. Glinted, but then darkened…

I dodged out of the way as a being of snarls and growls barrelled past me, colliding into the feasting ghouls. But I cried out. Its claws had sliced into me, cutting my jeans into ribbons and leaving a hand-span sized cut. It stung. I hoped it wasn't infected. I knew I had no risk of getting vampirism – ghouls transferred ghoulification through bites and could only do so if their master was alive – but I could still get some sort of other necromantic-related disease. Ghouls and vampires may not be undead, but their origin was the same. Dark, necromantic energy. Bastards…

My would-be attacker had tumbled over the feasting ghouls, drawing their attention to me. The entire scene had also resulted in the group at the door turning around and staring right at me. First, they looked bemused. Like a cat wondering why this mouse would be stupid enough to enter its domain. Then, they charged.

I jumped back as a closer ghoul grabbed towards me, slashing outwards and delivering a shallow cut across its wrist. It roared in response. Well, shit. Just made it angrier.

I needed to get out the flashbang. I sheathed my one blade and drew out the flashbang, continuing to back up towards an aisle. Needed that cover.

"Do you like light, fuckers?" I yelled. They roared in response, coming at me faster than any zombie horde could manage.

I pulled the pin. "Then here's some light!"

I threw the flashbang and dove behind the aisle, covering my ears. Even with my ears covered, it felt like my head had exploded. Like C4 had gone off in my ears, and afterwards, they rang like a billion bees had made my ears their next holiday destination.

Groggy, putting it mildly, I took out my phone and pressed a single button. I couldn't hear the music yet – but when the ghouls recovered, they'd hear it. And hopefully, it'd confuse them utterly. And more importantly, it'd enthuse me.

"Let's kill some ghouls!" I shouted. I didn't hear myself, but I'm sure Treth did.

My hearing started to clear as I shot around the corner. Ghouls were still stunned, rubbing their eyes and flailing in every direction. I drew my off-hand sword as I slid between two, slicing the tendons of both. They collapsed, and I heard the thud, just under the sound of *Drowning Pool's* glorious symphony. And the bodies did, indeed, hit the floor.

And I felt powerful.

I dove forward as two ghouls charged at my position. Turned back, skewered them both in the sides of the knee. Twisted the blade and pulled. They fell. I beheaded them both. Clean swipes. Their heads lolled to the sides, held to their necks by thin strands of ash-black flesh.

Rifts, I loved these swords!

The vocals were coming in. Incomprehensible over the banging, the snarling and the thumping of my heart. Still blinded by the flashbang, the ghouls were attacking wherever they heard something. But the sound was everywhere.

I grinned, as one only could while revelling in slaughter.

"You're enjoying this way too much," Treth said. Despite his comment, I heard excitement in his voice. We both enjoyed this. The hunt. The slaughter.

This was what I was born to do.

Slaying monsters.

***

Conrad opened the door at my behest. They'd stopped banging a while ago. Through the dance of death, with the hard rock melody and the fountains of blood – the banging had become redundant. I first noticed that Conrad's hands were red. Swollen. I then noticed his eyes. Disbelief. Horror. Satisfaction. No semblance of that cocky, if anxiety-ridden man who had recruited me from my hospital bed.

The others looked even more shocked.

I walked out of the warehouse door, leaving red shoe-prints and drops of blood. The air felt cool on my skin. Chilly on the sweat staining my skin where blood did not. I smelt salt on the air. A fresh sea breeze.

The crowd had grown since we had arrived. Past the police line, only Conrad, the technician and two cops. On the other side, a motley crew of civilians, firemen, police officers and some recently arrived Puretide agents. Six of them, strapped with armour and submachine guns. I almost grinned. Beaten them to this job.

Every bystander had one thing in common. They were all silent. Eyes stared. Shock. Perhaps, fear? What expression would you show if you saw a blood-covered nineteen-year-old girl exit a warehouse? Did you expect me to die in there? I'm sure you did.

I held a severed ghoul head by its hair. I dropped it on the floor. It squelched and rolled a bit. Its expression was locked into a monstrous grimace. It stared at the onlookers and they stared back.

And then someone clapped. And then others joined. Cheesy as it may be, they all began to clap. And then others cheered. Even the Puretide agents joined in. And their shock turned to awe. And I couldn't help but smile broadly.

Despite the stickiness of my skin, the ache in my joints and the stinging on my leg, I felt good. I felt better than good.

I felt alive.

Chapter 15.   Priorities

I couldn't keep the news from Trudie. Everybody knew.

"They're talking about a monster hunter," Pranish said, his fan-boyish grin as broad as his new enchanted gold collar (another trinket meant to enhance his power). "A monster hunter that goes to our campus."

I grunted in response. We were at the gym. I was lifting weights. Pranish was treating his membership as a get-fit-quick card, without any real exercise.

"Trudie knows," Pranish said, further validating my suspicions.

"I know," I replied, lifting the dumbbell to its perch. Pranish helped guide it in and I sat up to take a swig of water.

I had been training harder than I'd ever had before. Not just the usual agility training and cardio. I wanted to get my strength up. Those beheadings had been fine on my sword, but the after-effects shocked my arms. My entire body had been stiff for days after that veritable dance of death. So, I'd make it even stiffer – at least for a little bit – so I could become stronger.

"What did she say about it?" I asked.

"Nothing."

I frowned. Trudie wasn't one for silence, usually. She was quite vocal about her views. Especially her view that I was going to get myself killed. I was honestly tired of her over-concern for me, and the mothering. She'd accuse me of not acting my age, but she was the one attempting to act like my mom!

"Not like her to say nothing," I said, standing up and walking across the gym floor, with Pranish in tow.

"Maybe she's learnt that being a busybody isn't going to help anyone – much less her."

I didn't respond. I agreed with Pranish, but the agreement did make me feel a tad guilty. Trudie cared about me. I knew that. And as angry and as irritable as I got at her for her nagging, I needed to remember that. And remember that she was still my friend.

"Oh yeah," Pranish said, considering something. "She did say something. Gave me a message to give you."

We stopped outside the changing room. Pranish continued.

"Asked me to remind you that you have an Undead Studies test tomorrow morning."

Pranish's grin didn't help my immediately tanked disposition. He said farewell and left.

"Well, shit."

"Why so concerned?" Treth asked. "You've got more practical experience of undead than your lecturers."

"That's the problem. There's a huge difference between reality and academics. Shit, I need to get home and study."

I took a quick but blessed shower. Upon exiting the shower and drying my hair, promptly tying it back into a bun, I opened my locker. My phone's screen was glowing. A message.

"Phone me."

It was from Conrad. Most probably a job. I frowned. A job meant temptation. A temptation I really couldn't afford right now. Undead Studies, at least how it was taught at UCT, was not a fun subject. Slaying the undead, vampires and other ilk of the dark was preferable to learning vacuous untruths about them. But despite my distaste for the subject, or more accurately the way it is taught, I needed to pass this test. No job tonight. But I'd need to phone Conrad anyway – even just to tell him that I have a test.

I got dressed and dialled Conrad as I exited the gym. The street outside the gym was bustling with cars and people. I smelled fast food – simultaneously tempting and revolting. I resisted the urge to buy some fried chicken. I had noodles at home. Sure, I had money to spend, but hey, I'm frugal.

"Hey, Conrad," I greeted.

"Kat!" His voice was back to his usual enthusiastic self. "You up for something big?"

I rubbed my leg. The cut was healed. Purified and magically healed for good measure. But its scar was a reminder. Needed to be careful. Especially when Conrad prefaced the job with "something big". Above that, I needed to write this test.

"We're both richer, Conrad. Lot less desperate. What type of big?"

"How do you feel about some detective work?"

I raised my eyebrow. I wasn't a stranger to investigation. Plenty of monsters needed tracking down before the kill. But they were also time-consuming.

"You been hearing about the rise of undead?" Conrad asked, before I could reply, his voice becoming sombre.

"Yep." Even more zombie sightings since my ghoul hunt.

"We think this may have something to do with it. New necromancer in town. Making a big name for himself among the gangs. Calls himself *The Purity*. He's been raising record numbers of zombies and having them take over slum blocks. Puretide and Drakenbane have been culling the undead by the suburbs, but none of them got a lead on the guy. If you take him down, you'll get a hefty bounty from the City, including a pool from the communities affected."

Tracking down a person wasn't my strong suit. But… it was tempting. Very tempting. A memory flashed before me. A black-robed necromancer. Someone I desperately wanted to track down. And I could take this job. Didn't have a strict deadline. Wasn't like I needed to get to someone's house before the wight broke in. Could accept the mission now and investigate it later.

"Sounds good."

"Super! I'll message you some more details. Let's get that bastard down and some more dollars in our pockets."

***

I froze in front of my study notes, as one often does when they don't feel like studying. I had already caught myself re-reading the same passage over and over again.

"Dr Young argues, convincingly, that the phenomenon of zombie mutation is isolated."

Bullshit. Isolated to 99% of zombies I'd faced. Dr Young'd probably never seen a zombie outside of his labs – supplied by junior necromancers selling zoms for a quick buck. But as bullshit as it was, I'd need to regurgitate it during the test. Undead Studies was not one for allowing dissent.

I read over the sentence again, for the 50 millionth time, and then sighed. Heavily.

"I studied the undead for half my life," Treth said. "I can help you during the test."

"Thanks, but you know as well as I do that while we are right, we aren't their *right*."

I leant forward and skipped a few paragraphs. Zombie anatomy. My eyes on the sketch scanned for places to dismember or stab. I could go for the head. The traditional spot. Stab it in the brain. Could also behead it. I glanced at my swords on the coffee table next to my notes. They were clean and sharpened. Never had to care for blades before. Never got the chance. All the previous ones broke. But these guys deserved some care. They'd earned it.

I shook my head.

"Can't do this."

"Can't study?"

"Shouldn't have phoned Conrad. That job has got me all distracted."

"It can wait. *The Purity*…" Treth emphasised the necromancer's name with a snicker. "…isn't going anywhere."

"How about a break from studying anyway? Can clear my head."

"Making excuses." I felt Treth shake his head.

"Don't go all Trudie on me now."

"Me? Never!" I detected a childlike grin. I wondered what it looked like on Treth. I never saw his expressions, only felt them. But he had been alive once. I wonder what he looked like. I didn't feel it appropriate to ask. Treth definitely wouldn't respond to questioning. He didn't like talking about his life that much.

I opened my phone to the leads Conrad sent me. Locations of attacks and sightings. Foggy photos. Eye witness reports. Was like notes for a test – but fun. I scanned through them.

Attacks were mostly happening in the slums. That was to be expected. But it was a problem. The slums were a quagmire of old and new dilapidated buildings. A veritable labyrinth of dark weylines and gang warfare. I was comfortable roaming the streets to fight the undead, but gangsters were a bit above my pay grade. I didn't kill humans. Especially, humans with guns. But some eye witness reports differed from the usual narrative. The attacks were slum side, but from the outskirts. The parts bordering the suburbs and wealthier districts. And at least three eye witness reports swore they saw dark figures loping and shambling in the dark near the border suburbs. Undead were rare in the suburbs. Only a few Rift-wrought buggers every once in a while. They had been my bread and butter before Conrad hired me. Too risky to go into the slums, so I only went in rarely. But because the undead were so uncommon outside of the suburbs, people didn't really know what they looked like. A shambling figure could just as easily be a drunkard.

But my intuition said otherwise.

"You should be studying," Duer said in a melodic lilt. He was carrying a bottle cap for Vortex-knows what reason.

I grunted in response.

The North-Road zombie, where I saw that hooded necromancer, had been unusual. It hadn't been Rift-wrought. It had been animated Earth-side. My gut told me by the same hooded necromancer who stunned me. North-Road wasn't part of the slums. It was considered a border suburb. But to have a zombie there – and what I expected to be a necromancer...

I needed more leads. And as much as it pained me, I knew someone who would break company policy to tell me.

"Hi Brett," I said, infusing my voice with as much pleasantness as possible.

"Oi, Katty! How goes it? To what do I owe the pleasure?"

I cut right to the chase. "The rise of lesser undead. Drakenbane is working on it, right?"

"Always about the job, eh Katty?" Brett laughed. "Yeah, Drakenbane has been commissioned to guard some communities at the edge of the slums."

"Any firsthand accounts?"

"No attacks in the suburbs that I've seen or heard about. Guy saw a zom near the edge of the slums, but outside our jurisdiction."

"No attacks at all? Despite all the sightings?"

"You know civvies." Brett called non-hunters civvies, including cops and even soldiers. "Don't know a hobo from a ghoul."

That's rich coming from him. He didn't know the difference between a zombie and a wight.

"Do you know the name of the place where Guy saw the zom?"

Hesitation. "Company policy, Katty. Can't go rattling off sensitive info."

"Come on. What harm could it do? Could say you were just advising me to stay clear of the area. Can't have a girlie being eaten cause she went for a jog in the wrong neighbourhood."

Brett guffawed. "Nobody would believe that you could be eaten, Katty, no matter the neighbourhood. But fine. The sighting was over the fens at Milnerton. You know? Old district near North-Road."

North-Road. Things were falling into place.

"Thanks, Brett. I owe you one."

"I'll hold you to that."

I hung up.

My notes were still arrayed before me. A dreaded chapter on zombie anatomy and mutation. I stood up.

"It won't hurt to go check out one lead. To clear my head."

"If you say so." Treth didn't sound like he believed me.

Chapter 16.   Stakeout

The North-Road was redolent with the salty scent of fresh ocean air. I breathed it in. Let its cold and saline essence crawl up my nostrils. And then exhaled. Refreshed. This was much nicer than being cooped up in my apartment, pawing over fallacious texts for hours and hours. Nothing like the scent of the wind and sea for a change of pace and to cover corruption and degradation.

I exited a fish and chips shop located in Milnerton, overlooking the fens that Brett had mentioned. On the other side of the brownish wetlands, I saw rising smoke from woodfires and a façade of scrap metal and concrete. I had no binoculars but could faintly make out people lounging on the shore of the fen. Moving blobs of artificial colour.

The shopkeeper of the fish and chips place hadn't seen any zombies himself, but the neighbourhood association had given many reports. Many had spotted zombies across the fen – like Guy. But that was to be expected. The slums were known for their prevalence of dark magic. What was unexpected were sightings of zombies on this side of the fen. Shambling figures in the dark, entering and exiting the wetlands. In the darkness, it could just be excused as overactive imagination on the part of naive witnesses. But it wasn't just that. There were streetlights in Milnerton, and in their illumination, residents saw the unmistakable rotting dead crossing streets, peering through their windows and heading towards the fens. Despite all the consistent witness reports, however, I still found it hard to believe.

"It's getting late, Kat," Treth said. The sun was taking on a reddish hue. Clouds were also rolling in. May rain tonight. Treth was right. I needed to get back home and study.

"This is odd, Treth," I said, ignoring his comment.

"What part of it?"

"The entire thing. Zombies disappearing in the fens. Zombies en masse outside of the slums. And most of all, zombie sightings without zombie attacks."

"I don't find any of it peculiar."

I took a seat on a concrete and wooden bench on the pavement and leaned back, peering up at the reddening sky.

"Then please provide clarity on this situation, oh Sir Knight."

"Zombies have the primal instincts to consume, right?"

"Ah-ha." Zombies ate and ate. Was their nature. Could always count on that. Well, most of the time it seems.

"But zombies linked to necromancers have their primacy overwritten. They are puppets of their master and will do whatever they are told to do – even if it means not consuming to sate their insatiable hunger."

"Necromancers need huge reserves of power to keep a zombie horde afloat, though. Unless they allow the zombies to consume on their own."

"Then this necromancer is relying on their own power reserves, a very powerful weyline or maybe even a cabal of necromancers. On my world, necromancers banded into groups to maintain undead hordes. Zombies are cheap, because they can consume the living to stay animated, but they aren't as powerful as wights, flesh-puppets or other types of undead, which require a constant stream of dark energy."

I frowned. Some cold air hit my cheek. "If that's the case, it means we're up against a strong opponent."

"Maybe, but maybe not. If the necromancer, or necromancers, is maintaining as many undead as it sounds, they will be exhausting their own reserves."

My frown started to wilt and was promptly replaced with a grin. "So, leaving them defenceless?"

"Yep. The necromancers back on my world were often too weak to even raise their arms against our swords and hammers."

My quick grin also soon wilted, as I considered Treth's words. Necromancers were creators of monsters. Terrible people. Criminals and scumbags. But they were still human…

Would I have to kill a human?

I remembered a black-cloaked necromancer. A young man, holding an obsidian dagger over the chest of my parents. Even then, I had resigned myself to hating the undead and their creators. After Treth, I had rushed towards my goal of slaying the undead. But was that truly effective? I could chop, stab and slice all I wanted, but they'd just keep getting back up. Always getting back up. There could be no real stop to them so long as they kept being risen.

Did that mean I had to eliminate their masters? Could I do it? Even if they were human…

I sighed, deeply, and sat upright.

"No point heading back home. Will study from my digital notes."

"What are you planning, Kat?"

"The zombies come out at night. They're doing something, Treth. Undead, to me, are meant to be predictable. This isn't predictable, and I don't like it. I want to find out what they are up to."

"You've got a test, Kat. This can wait."

I shook my head. "I've got the scent now. Won't be able to do anything else till I'm done."

"You expect to track down the necromancer tonight?"

I was about to nod, but then hesitated. "Maybe not tonight, but I need answers. I need to know why these zombies are roaming these streets. I need to know where they're heading and where they're coming from."

"If you find that out, you may well have found the necromancer."

I nodded. "Then so be it. We finish the investigation tonight."

***

The last shop and home turned off its lights and I only had the streetlamps to illuminate my patrol. I was underdressed. Only a thin jacket as the cold sea air gave me chills, forming gooseflesh along my skin. I had tried to study as best I could on my phone, only shutting it off at the last minute to conserve battery life. I was not sure if it would be enough studying to pass the test. It would have to be.

The streets were as quiet and as empty as one would expect at this time of night. I could even hear the distant waves crashing on the shore. After what seemed like hours of patrolling the streets, more worried that neighbourhood watch would think me a prospective thief, I started to doubt the testimony of the witnesses I had interviewed hours before.

"Typical." I rolled my eyes.

"Common folk don't know any better," Treth replied.

I rolled my eyes at that as well. Treth was right, of course.

"Well, best be heading…"

A faint sound. A thud. Something on wood. I held my breath, standing in the middle of the barely lit street. The sky was a cloudy red, giving me some light. I said nothing and neither did Treth. Then I heard it again. More thuds. Footfalls. Many footfalls. And then…groaning.

I told you corpses never shut up. It's what made my job easier. But it is also what made it so unpleasant. The groaning of zombies was involuntary. Didn't serve any evolutionary purpose, so far as I could tell. It didn't signal allied undead to its side or even act as a deterrent to predators. Zombies didn't really have enough self-preservation to want to deter predators. But even if they did, the groans weren't exactly terrifying. I had heard them countless times before. They sent shivers down my spine and while they did bring back memories that I would much rather keep away, they were not exactly scary. Rather, the groans of the zombies were sad. Mournful. The vocalisation of pain. Of loss. Of missing the life they had and regretting that they had never truly passed on. The sound of zombies was of lamentation. If anything, perhaps the victims of necromancy were crying out and warning their prey.

"Do not become like us!"

I moved carefully towards the sound of the groans. They grew louder as I approached. Not just in volume, but in quantity. More and more groans entered the chorus. A joyless and guttural choir of undeath. I heard the scraping of their feet on the concrete. The thud as they walked into bins, benches and fences. The dragging of fleshy feet. I heard many of them. Too many.

"Just because they aren't seeking out prey doesn't mean they won't attack you," Treth said.

I nodded. I wasn't prepared for a full fight. Only had my seax and some demanzite on me. Couldn't go starting a fight with a zombie horde. I had been training well for the past year, but I doubt that I was ready to fight the undead in unarmed combat. Only the foolish and powerful warrior-monks could expect themselves to best the rotting dead in such a fight.

A short alley channelled the noise from the street-over like a megaphone. A small wall at the end blocked my vision. Suppressing a huff, I pulled myself up, peeking so only my eyes and the top of my head could see. I gaped. I couldn't believe what I was seeing, much less that there had been so few witnesses.

The street before me was dotted with ranks and ranks of zombies. Shambling. Groaning. Gesticulating feverishly as if still in the throes of whatever had killed them the first time. They were all heading towards the fens. They were fresh. Skin a sickly pallor and some with nasty, but staunched wounds, but not rotting. They had died recently.

I scanned for bite-marks and found none. None of them had been given the zombie infection the traditional way. Every one of them had been animated after dying of some other cause.

"Even if you were armed, you'd struggle to take them all down," Treth said, unnecessarily. I was impulsive, not stupid.

I backed down and whispered. "I can't believe Puretide and Drakenbane haven't noticed this."

"Head home. Leave this to them."

I looked over the wall again. More ranks filed through. The houses nearby were gutted. An abandoned street. Must be the reason they were not being noticed. Drakenbane and Puretide were paid to guard residential communities, not abandoned streets.

I snuck away from the wall. Treth seemed to sigh. It was unlike him to warn me off danger. He must be really spooked. Or just much more prudent than I. I was almost sorry to disappoint him.

"Where are you going?" he asked, as I turned down the street, towards the fens.

"I need to see if they're really going into the fens."

"Just don't be seen." Real concern in his voice. Was Treth getting soft? Or was he always soft? Perhaps, he really thought I was in danger. "And then go home. There's nothing we can do now."

I jogged down the street towards the fens, trailed by the zombie groans in the street over. The fens were just by the end. They looked like an unlit void in this darkness. An inky sea. Upon reaching the end of the street, I ducked behind a fence. A lone streetlight lit the intersection. One by one, zombies were crossing under the golden light. Their clothes were also new. Not the medieval getup so popular among Rift-wrought undead. These were Earth-born humans animated after death. I felt sick to my stomach. I hated all undead but turning MY people into monsters. I'd make the necromancer responsible pay.

The zombies disappeared into the darkness across the island of gold formed from the streetlamp. I had to squint to see further than the light. The brightness had damaged my night vision and I was struggling to adjust back. I held my hand over the streetlamp and squinted harder. My knees were getting wet on the moist grass. I felt trickles on my nape. Rain.

My vision adjusted. Hazy figures in the inky dark of night disappeared into the even darker depths of the fens. Between the groans, I heard splashes.

Zombies didn't need to breathe. They could easily traverse the fens. Didn't matter how deep. They could crawl the depths, and then pull themselves up on the other side. So, they were crossing the fens. Or were they hiding within them?

I shuddered. That last possibility was not one I wanted to investigate. If zombies were hiding in the water, there was very little I could do to stop them, and their necro-blood seeping into the water would deal untold ecological damage.

"They're going into the wetlands. Probably crossing to hide in the slums, or to feed. Would be practically unnoticed in that godsforsaken scrap jungle," Treth said. "Let's go."

I didn't answer. I watched as more and more zombies passed under the golden light and sank into the darkness. What were they truly doing? And why?

I turned around, doubling back into the street. I kept low and my footsteps quiet. The zombies were not in their primal state, but that could change if they noticed me. I made my way back to the alleyway and then passed it. I reached an intersection, darkness ahead.

"Best find another place to call a taxi," Treth said.

"Not calling a taxi."

"Kat…" Treth's voice was filled with apprehension and accusation.

"I said we'd finish the investigation tonight."

"You impulsive…" Treth almost spat, but then calmed himself. "You could die."

"Doesn't seem to have made much of a difference for you. Dying, that is."

Treth shook his head. "If you die, I'm pretty sure I will die too. And I don't want that. We haven't even truly begun our quest."

"This is the quest, Treth. Finding the one behind those abominations, and then putting him down."

A pause. I almost winced at my own words. Putting him down – a human being. I had resigned myself to doing it, but the thought still didn't sit well with me.

"What's the plan?" Treth asked, resignation colouring his words, but a veiled hint of pride underneath.

"I follow the trail of undeath back to the source."

Treth neither decried nor appreciated my plan. Without any comment, I turned towards the street filled with zombies.

From a distance, the horde was thinning. Just a trickle of the dead still shambling towards the fens. I stuck to the shadows, partly to keep my eye sight attuned to the dark. The undead were entering the street from an alley between two gutted houses. I couldn't risk going through the alley myself, but it had to connect to the next street-over. I skulked through the darkness, wincing as my sneakers crunched on twigs, gravel and under-repaired tarmac. The zombies were visible in the next street, in an avenue of dead trees and even more ruined buildings. The urban degradation was really bad here. No Magicorps to keep it bustling. Without the lifeblood of commerce, the street was just a burnt-out shell. Windowless panes. Thoroughly peeled paint. Roof beams jutting out of ramshackle busted ceilings like ribcages from an eviscerated corpse.

It was typical that the dead were rising from a seemingly dead part of the city. It was not just a rule of weylines that darkness attracted and begot darkness. Decay as a rule manufactured more decay. Chaos exacerbated chaos. Such was the way of the world that when we fall, we can only fall faster. Until someone caught us...or we hit the ground.

I approached the zombie horde to get a closer look. Plenty of debris to hide behind. The wind was at my back. I was thankful it was keeping the undead stench away from me, but hopefully the salty scent would overwhelm my own.

The zombies were exiting through a small hovel. But that couldn't be their origin. There were too many coming out. I navigated around the ruined abode and my suspicions were confirmed. They were only passing through, entering a backdoor just to exit from the front.

Such a convoluted route. Their master didn't want them to be seen. But then why so many in such a short span of time? It was a risk. A huge one. But one only risked something if one was desperate. The necromancer must be planning something. Something big and something pressing.

"A few hours until your test."

I ignored him and watched for the trail of advancing zombies to return. But none came.

I gritted my teeth. The procession had all passed. No more trail to their origin.

Shit.

My prudence overwhelmed my frustration and I didn't look for something to beat. But at that moment, both my frustration and my finely trained hunter's judgement disappeared.

I felt an unnatural chill on the back of my head. A piercing gaze. It held no emotion. Just cold. I knew what it was before I turned to look at it. It looked back at me. No eyes. Just a dark void under a black hood. It stood around ten metres away. We stared at each other, and it started to rain in earnest. The light drizzle transformed into torrents. I couldn't feel the cold of the wetness coating me. Just the chill of the creature before me.

"Kill it!" Treth managed to choke out, real fear in his voice.

A pause. I couldn't move. And then it ran.

It couldn't be coincidence. The dark mage from before, here. The master of these undead. My target.

I gave chase. My feet made splats and crunches on the wet gravel. I unconsciously drew my seax and a sachet of demanzite. I wasn't going to let them get the better of me this time. Human or not, they were my enemy. I'd put them down.

The cloaked figure rounded a corner and I followed. Again, and again. When I lost sight, I regained it seconds later. The cloaked figure sped up and slowed down periodically. And I was gaining. Faster, faster…

And it disappeared.

Stunned, I stopped in an overgrown field, a large warehouselike building before me.

"It must have gone in there," Treth said. His voice was more confident. Thrill of the chase.

I squinted at the scratched sign on the building.

"Ice Cone Creamery – Manufactory," I read aloud.

An abandoned ice cream factory in an abandoned part of town. Perfect.

"Think this is the lair? The necromancer must have led us here for a reason. Careful, Kat. It may be a trap."

I scanned the foot of the building for entrances, pondering it and my encounter.

Ice cream…ice. The zombies had been very fresh. Recently dead, and none of them had been bitten by zombies. And what could keep bodies fresher than freezers?

"This is the source of the zombies," I said.

"Good…"

I walked towards a nearby doorway.

"What are you doing?"

"Investigating."

"I love slaying the undead as much as you do, but we aren't ready."

"No slaying. Just investigating. And if the necromancer is in a weakened state, as you suggested, we may get the drop on him."

Treth didn't argue. I felt some inner conflict within him. Discretion versus his true desire. The wise and mature Treth wanted to escape. To allow me to pass my test. The thrill-seeking Treth, the one like me, wanted to press on, and slay monsters.

The doorway opened to a room only lit by fogged skylights above. The rain beat down above. Tap-tap-tap. The noise covered the crunch of my shoes on some long-abandoned debris or trash. The hazy figures of machinery and furniture dotted the factory floor. There was no sign of life. Or unlife. No trail that I could see in this dark. But perhaps there was a trail. A thought occurred to me and I closed my eyes.

Clear my thoughts. Focus on the underlying essence of the world around me. Its ebbs and flows. Its feelings. Its darkness and light…

I opened my eyes suddenly. The real life dark felt so much lighter than the darkness I had felt. The weyline of this place was dark. Intensely evil. I no longer had any doubt that this was my destination. I had not only felt the gloom of this place, however, but also its concentration. I walked forward, following a memorised path to the other end of the factory floor, where I heard the faint voice of a human incanting phrases of pure malice.

I opened the door as quietly as a I could. Its lock was broken, and it swung open without much effort. Mercifully, it also made no noise. The voice became louder. Below. I also saw the glimmer of light. Faint and coming from below a stairway.

Treth didn't speak. His lack of warning made me much more apprehensive than his nagging before. I almost wished he'd tell me not to go down there. But he didn't, so I did.

The stairs were metal. Very well maintained for an abandoned building. My feet made no sound as they touched down on the first step, and then the other. The chanting grew louder and more loathsome. I reached the bottom of the staircase and went towards the light. I peeked.

Memory came rushing back to me. I had been in a similar room before. That was to be expected. Necromancy required rituals. Rituals required uniformity. This room was large. It may have been a square or rectangle in the past, but curved installation walls adorned with dark runes of unearthly design formed a circle, surrounding a concrete slab covered in books, scrolls and blood.

It was just like the room my parents had died in. The room I had almost died in. I clenched my fist. Rage overwhelmed my fear. I was going to kill this monster. For all it had done. For all it was planning to do.

On the far wall, green gems flanked corpses hanging on meat hooks. Around ten of them in total. They were barely human any more. Hooks, scythes and crude blades protruded from where their hands should be. Their teeth were jutting out like an angler fish. Their eyes were wide open, as large as a man's fist and white as milk.

Abhorrent.

The necromancer wasn't content to just have an army of zombies. He was crafting undead soldiers. Undead mutants. This was serious.

But where was the cloaked figure?

I promptly left the necromancer's lair. Treth's advice finally became convincing. I was not equipped to do this now. And it really was late. Far away from the ice cream factory, I hailed a late-night taxi and made my way home. The sun had risen by the time I reached home, and I had to take the bus to my test.

On the entire journey, inbetween dozing, I couldn't help but wonder if the cloaked figure was not my target, but something else entirely.

Chapter 17.   Test

You ever smelled your own burn-out? That scent of fire in your nostrils, as if you can smell your brain cooking like a breaking-down engine? Ever felt your brain sputtering, causing your vision to falter? Like someone is trying to forcefully blindfold you? Ever slept through half a test because you were up all-night tracking shadows?

I have and let me tell you, it isn't great.

I arrived at the Undead Studies test with three minutes to spare. These three minutes were spent in a feverish haze between trying to stay awake, remembering my notes and contemplating the dire immensity of what I had witnessed only a few hours previously.

When the invigilator gave the call to start writing, I managed to spew out some garbage. Not even accidental and inappropriate answers based on my job, just gibberish. Actually, I can't even be sure of that. I can't remember anything I wrote. I remember Treth trying to help. I remember skipping some questions. Correction: skipping a lot of questions.

But what I did remember was what I saw this morning. My target. The necromancer. Somehow, I had made it out despite the cloaked figure spotting me and practically leading me to the lair. Why did it do that? Why lead me to its place of power, and then let me leave?

I pondered this in between bouts of mental blankness as my fist dug into my cheek and my elbow into the desk. My pen scribbled mindlessly across the page. I swear some of my answers were doodles.

The call to drop pens was a relief. I was too exhausted to care about my results for this test. They didn't matter. All that mattered was the necromancer lair, the cloaked figure who led me there and the army of the undead forming on the North-Road along the fens. Not just zombies hiding in the fens and slums, but abhorrent. If let loose upon the city, they could kill tens, if not hundreds of people. And every death would be another member of their horde. So many people would die before the bigger agencies could do anything about it. And that's assuming they could do something about it.

I exited the lecture theatre with a temporary vigour and determination. There were real questions that needed answering. Questions with real consequences. If I got them wrong, if I slipped up or didn't solve them within the deadline, many people would die. I could die!

The biggest question, of course, was the nature of the cloaked figure. I knew he was evil. Nobody could use dark magic and remain good. The very nature of dark magic corrupted the user. And that wasn't mentioning that the figure had used its dark magic on me! I wouldn't forgive it for that.

I was convinced that the cloaked figure was my enemy. No question about that. But was *The Purity*, the necromancer I was hired to hunt, the same as the cloaked figure? And if so, then why would they lead me to their own lair and let me go?

It didn't make sense. Did I accidentally avoid a trap? Was the necromancer distracted by something, allowing me through temporarily?

Both seemed unlikely. If the necromancer wanted to, he could have made me bleed from every orifice with a single vile incantation.

I winced at that thought. I had been really dumb last night. If the necromancer had been in the lair, I probably would have died. But if I hadn't discovered the lair, then the necromancer's plans would still be unknown. I decided to accept that the information gained had been worth the risk.

But there was still the issue of the cloaked figure who disappeared after leading me to the ice cream factory.

Was the figure not my target? A third party? Did the cloaked figure lead me to the ice cream factory on purpose? To help me…?

Perhaps, but that thought made me even more uncomfortable. Hunting necromancers was one thing, but being helped by one…

I felt sick, and not just from exhaustion.

I yawned. I needed to sleep. I would move on the necromancer tonight. Would contact Conrad. Would hopefully get Puretide or Drakenbane reinforcements. Needed to make sure I was involved, though. Needed that pay-day. And more importantly, I needed to be there to know the job was done. That the threat had been averted.

"Kat."

I didn't turn towards the voice. Instead, I realised that I was hunched over, a bit like a zombie. My eyes felt heavy. Arms weak.

Trudie put her hand on my shoulder. I turned then and faced her. She wasn't wearing any make up. No black lipstick or mascara. Just her natural pale skin. She often thought she looked plain without her goth get-up. I

284

thought she looked normal. And for me, that was a compliment. Normalcy was something to desire. Nostalgia. Seeing Trudie without make up, as she often went during test season, reminded me of better and younger days.

Trudie didn't speak as she examined me. At least, I thought she was examining me. She usually looked me up and down to guess what type of monster I had spent all night trying to slay. But I found now that she was not surveying my body. Rather, she stared into my eyes and I stared back. Eyelids heavy. She kept staring, and I knew now that it was still an examination. She was studying my soul.

"Did you get any sleep?" she asked softly. No hint of that nagging tone she usually used. It sounded like a normal question one might ask a friend.

My expression didn't change, to my mind, but I felt that I couldn't lie in my exhausted state. Trudie was my friend, and for all my irritation with her, she deserved to know.

"No."

Trudie nodded, slowly. It didn't seem resigned. It was an acknowledgement of something she already knew.

"I heard from Pranish that there is a rise in undead activity."

Odd. She had never been interested in that sort of topic before. I didn't respond. I stared dully at her, waiting.

Trudie finally sighed.

"I can't stop you from doing this, Kat. I should've understood that this is your burden. Your reason for being. But...but..."

I heard the hint of a sob in the final words, but Trudie bit it down and continued, stoically.

"I'm your friend, Kat, and I hope you realise that. I don't want you to get hurt."

I opened my mouth to speak but didn't have the words in my present state. Trudie noticed my attempt and nodded again, as if something had been confirmed in her mind.

"I don't want you to get hurt," she repeated. "So...I want to help you."

"Help me?" I finally replied.

Trudie bit her lower lip and then nodded. "I want to watch your back. Make sure you come out alive. You don't have what the agencies have. You need a team. You need a friend behind you."

I smelled corpses then. Not real, of course. I was delirious from exhaustion. But in my feverish state, I smelled corpses, and I saw zombies. Zombies ripping Trudie to pieces. Not even eating her. Just tearing her limbs one by one as she cried out in pain. I was immobile. I could do nothing to save her.

I couldn't help but picture my friend being torn apart by the undead I hunted. Her artificial pallor would become genuine. Blood would ooze out of every orifice. She would be torn apart. And there would be nothing I could do about it. I couldn't accept her help. Not if that's what her help meant. For her sake, and my sake, I needed to do this alone.

I shook my head, as slow as Trudie had nodded hers. Her lower lip quivered at the display and then she tensed up.

"Is there anything I can do, Kat? Anything?"

I tried to smile. I managed a small upturn of my lips. I shuffled forward and put my arms around her. She didn't hug back as I supported my weight upon her.

"Just be my friend, please. That's all I need."

And that was the truth, but I doubted Trudie believed it. But that was what she was like. Intrusive, overbearing, a busy-body – but caring, concerned and genuine. I realised that I couldn't be angry at my friend for caring about me. This was who she was. I needed to accept that, as much as she needed to accept me for who I was. And if my profession led to my death, so be it.

Chapter 18.   Showdown

I fell asleep on my couch immediately as I arrived home. It was dark when I awoke. I had managed to sleep for well over ten hours. The day was gone, and most of my prep time. But I needed this. I no longer felt the stab of exhaustion or even grogginess. I was ready to hunt. I needed to put down the necromancer tonight. I couldn't let its plan come any closer to fruition.

I didn't even take time to shower. I only wet my face and got dressed into my monster hunting gear. Sword belt was attached to my thick denim jeans, with extra pouches attached filled with demanzite sachets and shoe polish tins filled with poultices for treating necro-bites and scratches. I put my leather jacket over my t-shirt and a black plastic breastplate usually used for contact sports over it. My bracers were put over my wrists, with longer versions over my upper arms to protect them from bites. I tightened the straps on the small segments of armour and felt a pressure. It was a comforting pressure. While the armour was not comfortable, I liked to know I was wearing it. It could save my life. Probably already had a few times.

Lastly, I sheathed my twin swords and seax, and draped my scratchy, carpet-like scarf around my neck. In a way, its scratchiness was also comforting. I'd also be a lot warmer than the previous night.

I moved towards the door of my apartment to leave, and then stopped.

I needed to attack tonight. Couldn't let the necromancer get away, or worse, complete his plans. But I couldn't just storm the lair alone. I needed help.

I drew my cell, moving towards the door and locking it behind me.

"Conrad?" I asked. A pause, a beep.

"I am currently away on business. If you are hearing this, I am in transit and cannot answer right now. Please leave a message."

"Shit!"

Wasn't like Conrad to up and leave without telling me. Must be something serious. But that didn't dissuade me from my irritation. Without Conrad, I lost my most certain partner and the guy who could get me some real reinforcements. He could get some freelancers behind me – even Puretide or Drakenbane. He may have a scummy reputation, but he could get things done.

I winced and chose a new contact. Put my cell to my ear. I was outside now, standing on the pavement. If Mrs

Ndlovu looked outside her window, she might think me a wraith.

"Brett?"

"Kat?" he answered. I heard gunshots in the background. A roar. His voice was anxious, surprised. Not that cockiness I was used to. Didn't even call me "Katty".

"I'm heading to knock over the North-Road necromancer. I need backup."

"No can do." Pause. More gunshots. A screech and the explosive, searing roar of flames. Drakenbane must be doing what it does best – slaying firebreathers. "I can't talk. On the job."

I was about to hang up.

"Kat, don't do anything stupid."

I hung up.

Shit. Drakenbane unavailable. That left only Puretide. I breathed heavily. Puretide didn't like working with freelancers, but I had to try.

"Puretide is currently purging the filth of the world. Please call back when more operators are available. Thank you," recited a clear, corporate automated message after I phoned.

Well, shit.

"What are you going to do?" Treth asked.

"The necromancer is planning something big. With that number of zombies being churned out last night, and with abhorrent that close to being done, I'm pretty sure they are close to finishing up."

"And that means?"

"I proceed. Alone."

Treth hesitated. He was still spooked. But Treth valued bravery, even if said bravery bordered on foolhardiness.

"Be careful, Kat," he finally said.

"No need to tell me that."

I dialled a taxi with a shaking finger.

***

I entered the ice cream factory in complete darkness. It wasn't raining tonight. No red cloud cover to guide my way. Just dark clouds, covering the moon and stars. Only the slight glimmer of lights in the distance silhouetted the dark monolith before me. In the silence, I was able to hear the faint rush of cars on the distant North-Road proper. It was a comfort, the sounds of motor vehicles. Despite the lateness, despite the monsters, the slums and the dire politics of the region, traffic stayed alive. Couldn't kill commerce.

I navigated the exterior of the factory by memory, only tripping occasionally over litter and rubble. Every crunch made me wince. I hoped that the thick lair walls and incanting by the necromancer would overshadow whatever sound I'd accidentally make. I also hoped that any patrolling undead would also make a noise. They had the benefit of dark-vision. I had to rely on their stench and their unstealthy footfalls.

Throughout the taxi journey and my traversal into the abandoned block, I felt an array of emotions from Treth. Worry, fear, anticipation and, for some reason, shame. I didn't question him on any of it. We didn't speak. We both needed to be on high alert. But I had my suspicions about his true feelings. He didn't want me to go on this mission. He only remained silent as he knew I wouldn't listen to him. But also, because he understood why I did it.

I needed to kill that necromancer. For all they were planning to do and simply for what they were. An abomination. Evil must not be allowed to live. I hated this necromancer who so pretentiously dubbed itself *The Purity*. I hated it with an all-consuming passion that prevented me from even humanising it at this moment with the benefit of a gender pronoun. In a way, this necromancer came to embody my hatred for the necromancer who had slain my parents and had almost slain me. My hatred for the darkness. For the walking corpses that had become my lifeblood, my reason for being and my passion. I told myself that I came to this dark place late at night, by myself, because I was worried about what would happen if I did not stop this human-monster. But the real reason was much more selfish. I hated this being. And that hate needed to be quenched. So, more by impulse than calculated reason, I entered the lion's den.

I had a faint memory of the floorplan of the factory from the night before, when a lighter sky illuminated it. Fortunately, the factory floor was relatively empty. Conveyer belts, machinery and everything I guessed belonged in a factory was long gone – either sold off or stolen. Only rubble and scrap were left to block my way. I'd need to be careful not to turn them into a form of alarm system.

Swords drawn, I managed to reach the end of the room, slowly trudging across the hard floors, without making much noise. I explored along the wall until I felt a crevice. A cold, metal door. I pushed it lightly and it opened. No noise. Greased. As if new.

I saw a faint greenish glow below and felt the temperature drop ever so slightly. I moved towards the faint glow, down some stairs identical to the ones from the night before. This wasn't the room from last night, but I needed to check out as much of the facility as possible any way. The glow was coming from a light on a large door. In the past, it must have been sealed tight, but entropy had proven greater than human engineering yet again and the door was letting through cold and some light from the other side.

I took out my phone and turned on its flashlight, sweeping it across the doorway. In faded lettering: freezer.

I put my phone away and pulled at the vertical bar on the door. It opened cleanly. At least its hinges were as maintained as the door upstairs. The escaping cold would not be good for whatever it was storing, but if the goods were only there for a short timeframe, it would not be too much of an issue.

I went through the door and was greeted by the hum of freezers. A wave of frost hit me and I saw mist coming out of my mouth. Luckily, I was warmly dressed. I preferred fighting in the cold. Got sweaty too fast otherwise. Even my scratchy scarf couldn't hold back the chill. The room was dimly lit, but much lighter than outside. Lining the room were large fridge doors, frosted up so to obscure their contents. Unfortunately, I'm pretty sure of what they contained. Those zombies had been fresh, if a bit pale. If I had gotten a closer look, I'm pretty sure they'd have even been a bit blue as well. This was how the necromancer was churning out so many zombies. A lot of local deaths would warrant some notice, but if there were shipments of bodies from across the city and slums, they'd just be excused as the average attrition of a magical and monstrous society. If I was one to operate during the day, I'm sure I could have spotted the bodies being brought in by trucks and vans. It was an abandoned residential area. Lugging human-sized bags would have gone unnoticed.

I resisted clicking my tongue in disgust.

"To strike in anger is one thing," Treth said. "But to conduct evil so coldly, over such a long time, takes true evil."

I nodded in agreement. Sometimes, I wasn't sure if Treth was meant to be a medieval knight or far eastern sage.

The fridges formed a long icy hall, stretching out to a dark wall at the end. I advanced, rubbing my arms through their sleeves with my swords still in hand. It was quiet. Just the hum and buzz of the cold coffins. Despite being unable to see the corpses within the fridges, I felt their gazes.

But they were dead. Truly dead, I mean. Not undead, yet. They weren't really staring at me. And would I care if they were? I fought zombies as an appetizer. I glanced uneasily at a fogged-up freezer door. Something about these truly dead people, being preserved in such a manner, had me on edge. I wanted to speak to Treth, to get my mind off it, but couldn't. Needed to keep quiet.

I was shocked from my reverie by tapping. I stopped and listened. I didn't need to turn around. Treth would be watching behind me.

No sound. Just the hum.

Did Treth hear it?

I shrugged and proceeded.

Tap. Tap. Tap.

Stopped.

I turned my head, scratching my neck on my scarf. Just the freezers. Just their frozen, fogged up glass facades. I looked closer at the glass door. Normal. Like all the others. I squinted and saw a dark amorphous shape just behind the glass. I'm sure if I had stopped to examine the others, I would have seen something similar. These were, after all, temporary coffins.

The tapping had stopped. Perhaps, just my imagination? I wish I could ask Treth.

"Kat…" he said. I opened my mouth to reply and then felt something. A stare. A predatory gaze. I look down the hall, the way I had come. Illuminated by the glow of the freezers and the faint bulb above, was a naked man without genitalia. Crude stitches adjoined the spot where his manhood once lay. His sickly yellow-brown skin was pockmarked with needle pricks and incision scars. I could not see if he was adequately built, or underweight as the undead often were. Black pipes protruded from his naked chest, snaking like worms in and out of soil made of flesh. A long pipe wormed out of his bellybutton and found itself planted in the gaping hole that should have been his bottom jaw.

Even at this distance, I could see the eyes of the abhorrent. Not the milky white eyes of zombies. Human eyes. White with a dark pupil, watching me. Staring at me. The abhorrent twitched every few seconds. Convulsed. It reached an arm my way, shivering like a rat dying of poison. It pointed at me, with an arm beset with quake-like shaking.

"What is it doing?" I finally asked Treth.

"I don't know. Kill it before it continues."

I went into a combat stance. Knees slightly bent, ready to pounce. Right blade ahead as a pointy barrier, left blade charged behind my back, to slash. I edged towards the creature, its arm still outstretched towards me, still twitching, eyes unblinking and accusatory.

A single tap, and glass exploded behind me. I turned on my heels as a writhing figure burst out of the freezer, roaring in that guttural, clicking undead fashion. The figure landed on its hands, long hair draped across its face and glass shards digging into its flesh. The hum of the freezers stopped, and it looked at me. Human eyes filled with hate. Three teeth as long as my hand. Three pipes protruding from where its bottom jaw should be.

"Kat!" Treth shouted. I ducked. A club, the leg of a wooden chair, passed over my head from behind me. The original abhorrent had closed the gap, suddenly. Shit, they were fast! The abhorrent on the floor hissed and crawled my way, also twitching. It picked up more glass shards in its hands as it approached.

I stabbed behind me, simultaneously kicking out towards the crawler and breaking one of its hand-span teeth. My sword squelched as it found its mark.

A tap and another crash. Another, and another. All the freezers were being broken open, writhing abhorrent pouring like fish out of water. Fish soon finding their bearings and tearing towards me.

Did I say "shit" already?

I jumped back from the standing abhorrent and sank my sword into the one on the ground. It writhed on my blade but didn't stop. A new arrival took a swipe at me and I quickly withdrew my blade while bringing up my other to block the blow. My blade cut into the abhorrent, but the blow rang through my arm.

Too many.

"More coming from behind you."

Way too many. Needed to get out. Now!

Two abhorrent charged at me simultaneously. I cut wide, being rewarded with a stream of black blood and the hissing of pipes as they expelled what seemed to be compressed air.

"Duck!" Treth ordered again. I did so, just as another abhorrent charged over me. I used its momentum against it and threw it into one of its comrades. I rose, sweeping my blades like a windmill and finding marks, glancing off bone.

I saw an opening through the sickly, pock-marked and scarred legs. Arced my blades and ducked through, hamstringing the creatures.

I made it. And then felt a searing pain in my head, heart and then…everything.

***

I awoke to a hard rock surface with lumps digging into my back. My wrists chafed in their plastic-tie bands. It felt familiar. I'm sure you know by now what I'm referring to. Being a lot younger, on such a table, with similar binds and a similar irritating rock poking my tailbone.

I heard clattering to my side and I turned my head. The back of a black robed figure. Typical necromancer getup. A stereotype. All black robes. Probably had a bird-skull pendant. Sick bastard. Looked like a man from the stature. Broad shouldered. No curves. Tall.

He turned and validated my guess. He had a chiselled jawline. Light stubble. Short hair with greying tips. The late end of middle-age. In his day, he must have been attractive. I didn't contemplate that thought then. I only wanted to rip his throat out. With my teeth, if necessary.

"Awake, I see," the necromancer grinned. Toothy. Overly familiar. "I hope your accommodation isn't too uncomfortable. You hurt, even murdered, three of my friends already. Can't have you hurting any more of them."

He shook his head and limped towards me. "No, no. Can't have that."

This was definitely not the cloaked figure. He was too tall. Too masculine. And the cloaked figure had no limp. It was faster than even me.

But if this wasn't the cloaked figure...who was the cloaked figure?

"You don't seem surprised..." the necromancer said, a hint of disappointment in his voice.

"I know the gig. You going to sacrifice me? Got the uniform and the sacrificial stone table right. Summoners keeping up with the 21st century but necromancers still gotta keep up the traditions, right?"

The necromancer let out a haughty, deep laugh.

"Sacrifice? Oh no, my dear girl. You are not a sacrifice."

He turned back to his table and tinkered with something out of my view. He then turned, the object of his interest hidden behind his back.

"But I have been rude. You don't know my name..."

"Let me guess. The Purity?"

The necromancer's grin split his face in two.

"Yes, dear girl. But we're about to become friends, so you can call me Jeremiah Cox."

"Gonna need to do a lot to become friends with me. Hey! I've got a good idea. Cut these binds and we can have tea."

Jeremiah shook his head, smile unwavering.

"You will be my friend, dear girl. A very good friend."

Suddenly, he grabbed my jaw. I considered trying to bite him, but the thought of his flesh in my mouth made me sick. He examined me as one did meat at a supermarket.

"Angry eyes. You will make a fine friend."

"What if I didn't have angry eyes?" I asked, genuinely curious.

"You would still be a friend, but I'd send you across the swamp to hide in the concrete jungle. You'd wait there, feeding, until you were needed."

"You're hiding zombies in the slums?"

"They need to eat," Jeremiah shrugged. "And I can't have them ruining my project here. So, I let them play and feed over the swamp. People don't seem to mind as much there."

"Why?"

"Are you asking because you're interested or because you're trying to delay?"

"Both."

Jeremiah let out another deep chuckle. It sounded truly mirthful. Innocent even. As if he was laughing at the antics of a comedian. That made it even more deplorable.

"I will humour you, dear girl. We have all night, anyway. My project is nearing completion. Tonight, I can have some fun. And what is more fun than speaking of my vision for a better world?"

I didn't reply. How could I? A better world. Total Rift-damned unicorn shite. Jeremiah continued.

"Have you ever dreamed of a world without disease? Without inequality? Without the need for medicine?"

"We don't need medicine. We've got healing magic."

"For the highest bidder. Those without continue to go without. They get sick, and then what can they do?"

"Hire a healer?" I suggested.

"Were you even listening? They don't have anything. How can they pay for healing?"

"By getting a job?"

I heard the slap before I felt it. My cheek stung and Jeremiah's face was red with anger. He was no longer smiling.

"Shut up and let me speak, girl."

I bit down on a retort.

"My vision is a world where no one will be sick. Because when some become ill, they cannot get cured. So, I work to fashion a new humanity. A sickless humanity of the future, crafted in a perfect image of equality and health. My friends. I create my friends. And they do not cough, or wheeze. They only gurgle in anticipation. With a zest for life."

"The zombies?" I risked asking.

He scowled at the term. "*Zombie* is so derogatory. They are human. Like you or me. But they have found a sickless, deathless existence. Well, I'm being unfair on myself there. I helped them. Guided them. Shepherded them to an immortal state. And now, I continue to shepherd them, to ensure they remain and to spread their boon to others."

Rifts and Vortex, this guy was insane!

"And you want me to become like that?"

Jeremiah nodded.

"What if I don't want to?"

"Geniuses are often not appreciated in their time. Prophets are shunned among their own people. This is my lot. The lot of a true martyr."

He drew a black knife seemingly out of nowhere.

"You'll be free of disease, of all types, in just a little bit. You've got angry eyes. You'll make a very good friend..."

Before he could notice that my foot had wriggled out of its binding, I kicked him in the side. He dropped the knife, right into my bound hand, and I hastily worked it across my binds. Jeremiah lunged but I kicked him again. My one hand was free, and I turned to cut free my other.

"I won't let you!" Jeremiah roared, almost incomprehensible. I cut my other hand loose just in time to catch Jeremiah's hands around my throat. I sunk the knife into his wrist and slashed it. He cried out and recoiled, ripping his wrist and hand open. Red blood sprayed, and he tried to staunch the bleeding with his robe.

"Kill her!" he shouted.

Abhorrent, who I now noticed had been lined up around the room, charged at me. The knife wasn't enough…

"Sword, by his desk," Treth said.

I looked and saw my bag and twin swords laid against Jeremiah's desk. Abhorrent closing in. I dove and retrieved a sword just in time to bring it up to block the bladed hand of an abhorrent. It had eyes almost as angry as mine. Almost. With my free hand, I drew my other sword and sliced the abhorrent across its neck. The blade stopped at a bone and I quickly withdrew it, the abhorrent collapsing in a heap.

Abhorrent charged me, but I only had one interest. Jeremiah. The necromancer. He couldn't be allowed to live. Nobody tied me down and lived! Red mist covered my vision and I saw only the impending blood that would spray from Jeremiah's throat.

Just past the charging abhorrent, he stood clutching his bleeding wrist and hand. I made a beeline for him, cutting abhorrent and dodging their gratuitously modified limbs. Closer. Just another layer of abhorrent, then another. Yellowed flesh surrounded me, cutting the air, battering me, bruising. Figures filled the gaps and I slashed and slashed. Cut, stabbed, bludgeoned. They didn't abate. I could no longer see Jeremiah.

Gunshots rang out. A bang and then the light of a fireball.

"No fire! You'll roast her alive," a voice shouted.

Submachine gun fire strafed across my head. Abhorrent fell, black blood spraying. I didn't stop slashing. Slashing. Slashing. Slashing.

"Kat?"

I cut the air, and then stopped. My blade was a centimetre from Brett's neck. He didn't look shocked. I pulled back the blade. My eyes wide. Like an animal's during a hunt. But I no longer knew if I was the hunter or the hunted. I looked around. Looked at all the corpses. All naked. All grotesque and mutated. No black robes. No Jeremiah. No necromancer.

I fell to my knees and shouted my anger wordlessly as Drakenbane agents eliminated the surviving abhorrent, one by one.

Chapter 19.   Debrief

"You not only risked your life," Conrad hissed through gritted teeth. "You failed to get a payday."

His fingers were steepled, covering his lips while he held himself up on his elbows. His hair, usually a greased black, showed hints of grey. He hadn't dyed it or greased it back. He looked oddly vulnerable, and very angry. He had just gotten off the plane from his, I presume, business trip to the Mauritian Sovereignty. Well, I hope it was business. If it was just a random holiday, then I'd be really, really, pissed off. And what would make it worse, is that I had no real room to be pissed off myself. I had screwed up, and now I was paying for it.

"The Purity, or Jeremiah Cox as you say his name is, is gone. Probably out of Hope City or nestled so far into the slums that it will take an elder dragon or an ogre horde to dislodge him."

I opened my mouth to speak, he raised his hand to stop me. His face was red.

"You're good at what you do, Kat, but there are many hunters out there. You're special because you're a novelty. A part-time student, part-time monster hunter. It is a gimmick. But gimmicks can only go so far. You risked your reputation and mine last night."

I wanted to argue. I wanted to shout that I had no choice. That he shouldn't have gone away if he didn't want me rushing into things. I had a deadline. A life or death deadline to put that necromancer down…

But I knew I was wrong.

I rushed in there. Stupidly. I tried to take down a necromancer and his horde by myself, like a fool. The fact that he needed to be put down soon is irrelevant. What I did was impulsive. Foolhardy. Unforgivable. I could have died! I very almost did. But that didn't stop me from getting angry at what Conrad was saying.

Gimmick? I'll show him a rift-damned gimmick! Well, not sure how. But it sounded like a good internal retort.

Conrad didn't fire me. He let me off with a one-strike warning. Asked me nicely to not give him reason for two more strikes. Before I left his office, I asked him.

"How did you know where to send Drakenbane?"

He looked at me sceptically, squinting. The question threw him off-guard and he replied civilly.

"I didn't. They got an anonymous tip-off. Probably some local who heard the ruckus."

I closed Conrad's door behind me and was faced with the dirty service halls of the Gravekeeper pub. There torn flyers from decades ago still stuck to the walls. Decaying. Sun-faded even in a semi-sunless room.

A local? I doubted it. The locals didn't even notice a zombie horde walking past their houses. Nobody was in earshot of the ice cream factory. No neighbour to hear my shouts. But someone had called Drakenbane and told them my location. But the only person who knew the location of the necromancer lair was Jeremiah himself and me. And…the cloaked figure.

What the hell was going on?

I was pretty sure the cloaked figure was also a necromancer. They'd been near that motel zombie and used dark magic on me. Fair enough – they may not be a necromancer. Plenty of dark mages specialised in corruption magic without straying into the even darker necromantic practices. But my gut told me that they were a necromancer. Nothing concrete, but their proximity to that zombie in the motel sparked my intuition. But regardless, if a necromancer or not, they were a dark mage. And they helped me.

Why?

Perhaps, a rivalry between necromancers? Necromancers, when they weren't working together in cabals, didn't like each other that much. I had read about full-on street wars between zombie hordes belonging to rival necromancers post-Cataclysm. It could be a gang thing like that. Would make sense. And if it was like that, it meant I had been played from the start. The cloaked figure wanted to be tailed. It had led me to its rival's lair and expected me to do the dirty work.

But it had also attacked me.

Maybe, I was meant to die in Cox's ice cream factory? But if that was the case, then why did they tip Drakenbane off?

I just didn't know. But I needed to know. Something way more sinister and complex than my usual fare of slaying monsters was afoot. Would I be up to the task?

I hoped so.

I needed to find the cloaked figure. But I didn't know who it was. Or even what it was. But I did know someone. A Jeremiah Cox. The potential target of the cloaked figure and someone I still needed to destroy.

Question was: would Conrad still let me on the case? And even more pertinent: would that stop me?

"Kat?"

I was shaken out of my reverie by Treth's disembodied voice. I was still standing outside Conrad's door. I hadn't moved. I took a step forward. It was hard. I didn't feel like moving. I felt like thinking. Thinking a lot. About everything. About what it all meant and about how I had almost died last night.

Treth didn't say another word. My feet echoed in an almost melancholy fashion across the grey linoleum. Even the pub was eerily quiet. It was raining, and my exit from the pub was greeted by a spray of cold water on my face.

The bus was late. Of course, it was!

Treth was still silent as we waited underneath the cover of the bus stop, rain pelting the translucent plastic roof like pebbles.

"What is it, Treth?" I finally asked. We were alone under the downpour. No need to worry about someone hearing me.

No immediate reply. A long awkward silence. A small part of me wondered if Treth was asleep, or had left, somehow. Then his voice came, quiet, hushed to emphasise the importance of what he was saying.

"Why did you do it, Kat?"

"Do what?" I already knew what he meant. Why did I risk my life? Why did I go charging in? Why am I doing all of this? Rich question coming from him. He was dead. Dead from risking his own life. And it wasn't like he hadn't encouraged me. He was the one who put me on this quest in the first place.

Treth sighed. He knew that I knew he knew the answer.

"I'm not one to talk," he said. "I cheered you on, taught you, encouraged you to risk your life for this undertaking. Would be hypocritical for me to warn you off it."

"Then why are you only now trying to stop me? We've known each other for a long time now, Treth. Why only now do you try to stop me from doing what I've been doing all this time?"

He hesitated. He thought I hadn't noticed. The growing hesitation in his voice. His questioning. It was never blatant. But I noticed. He was no longer as excited about the quest as I was.

"I am scared, Kat," he finally said. The response shocked me.

"Why? We've handled stuff like this before. We've only had two, maybe three, scrapes worth being frightened about lately. Why be scared now and not earlier? Could have just as easily died back then than now."

"It's not that. I resigned myself to die, and I don't think I can unhypocritically take that right away from you. We are both undead in our own way. We teeter on the edge of death. Every breath we take, could be our last. Has been my last. We are the bridge between darkness and light, the hunters and the hunted. And that is not what worries me. I have accepted this for me and you."

"Then what is worrying you?"

More hesitation. A long pause. "Why are you doing this, Kat?"

"To slay monsters."

"Why?"

Why? Stupid question! It was obvious. Of course, it would be obvious. I had dedicated my life to this. Of course, the reason I did it was obvious.

But then: why was I struggling to answer?

"A quest is nothing without a reason, Kat. Why do you fight?"

Why?

A stone table. An obsidian dagger. A horde of slobbering undead. A black robed man and my parents who were no longer with me.

"Because I hate them, Treth. Because they are monsters and they need to die."

"So, you charge, once more unto the breach, again and again and again – blinded by red. Motivated by hatred."

A car rushed past and almost splashed water on me. I didn't pay any mind to the swells of water washed up onto the pavement. I replied with gritted teeth.

"If I don't kill them, nobody else will. If that means risking my life, charging into death, then so be it."

"But why?"

"Because they need to die."

"But why?" it was almost a shout. A plea. I heard the onset of Treth's voice almost breaking there. His knightly façade, crumbling. I didn't reply. Treth did for me.

"Because you hate them?"

I nodded.

Treth shook his head. I felt an intense disappointment coming from his disembodied self. It made me feel ashamed and with that shame, I felt anger. Who was he to judge me? Who was he to judge my hatred for those who had taken everything from me? Did it matter why I killed monsters? Did it matter why I wanted to eliminate the darkness and all it held?

"Why should I slay monsters if not for hate, Treth?"

"For love," he replied, simply.

I scoffed. Clenched my fists and looked at the flooding pavement at my feet. A newspaper was pressed to the floor, rain tearing at the fragile paper. I could just make out the headline. Something about the northern ogre herds.

"Everybody I love is dead," I finally responded. The bus arrived and that was that.

Chapter 20.   Consequences

Conrad hadn't put me back on the Jeremiah case. In fact, the Council had taken him off the case completely. Jeopardising the safety of Hope City and all that crap. As if I had actually threatened anyone. If anything, I had prevented an undead attack! Regardless, Conrad was pissed. The Purity Incident had a huge reward for its completion. But even Drakenbane only received a minimal bounty for trashing his lab. No necromancer, no proper payday. So not only was Conrad iffy with me, so were my contacts in Drakenbane. Even Brett wasn't talking to me.

Things had been quiet after my meeting with Conrad and hard talk with Treth. My savings were dwindling as Conrad sent me on only one call-out. Was a prankster dressed up as a wight. Did beat him with the flat-side of my blade, so I don't think he'll be taking dress-up so lightly next time. Still didn't get paid.

I had to downgrade from the premium cup of noodles to my old brand. The supply of fizzy drinks was also dwindling. Back to my even more frugal ways. Duer didn't like me staying at home all the time. He had grown used to having the place to himself at night. Could hear him muttering irritably in what sounded like Gaelic. I struggled to sleep. My days were returning to what most people would consider normal, but my body rebelled. Night time was when I was meant to be out and about. Fighting. Hunting. Slaying. But without any jobs to go on, I spent the nights studying and trying to sleep. At least, I spent more time with Trudie and Pranish, sometimes Andy. Went to see the new *Silver Strider* movie. Trudie enjoyed it until the end, when the disclaimer that no real unicorns were harmed in the making of the film was shown. I was restless throughout the entire thing. Tapping my feet and fingers, shifting side to side, criticising the actions of the protagonists as unrealistic or incompetent. I don't think Trudie noticed. She was just happy to be hanging out. But even the sight of my friend's pleasure, and the cessation of her nagging, was not enough to stop my anxiety. I needed to get out there. Back to slaying.

But why didn't I? I had functioned as a hunter long before working for Conrad. I didn't need him. Could just go on the MonsterSlayer app and find a job. Plenty of landlords and old ladies didn't care about my rep with the agencies and Council.

But I didn't. And I didn't know why. I chose to rather stay idle, for the first time in a long time. I concerned myself more with the student part of my life. I re-wrote the test I had failed, after the lecturer could see I had not been in any position to write it properly the first time and passed satisfactorily. I also got all my assignments in on time. In a way, this funk was good for me. But it didn't feel that way. It felt like, well, a funk. And nobody likes to be in a funk.

It didn't help that Treth hadn't spoken to me in days. Since our conversation at the bus stop, we stopped talking. I didn't try to speak to him and he didn't try to speak back. Just a long silence. I still felt his presence, but it felt distant. It was as if his attention was elsewhere. As if he was standing far way, with his back turned. I could call to him, but I didn't. It was here that I realised how much the spirit, or whatever he was, meant to me. He had become a part of me. Not an inconvenience, but a constant. I would never admit this to him but, in this space of silence, I missed him.

"Thanks for doing this," Trudie said, suddenly, knocking me out of my reverie. I was tailing her down a dust-filled hallway with grey linoleum flooring, carrying a load of boxes. Some had the Uhurutech branding, others were from other computer manufacturers.

I grunted in reply. She didn't need to thank me! She had done much more for me in the past. I almost reddened.

We arrived at a door somewhere in the arse-end of campus. It was an old building. Like many of the neoclassical-style buildings on campus, its interior had been decimated by generations of architects and designers, creating a labyrinth of shoddily marked classrooms, offices and study centres. Trudie and I were headed to one such hidden room, carrying a load of computer parts that she was setting up for a class she was tutoring. Despite her age (Trudie was the same age as me), Trudie was a natural, and had already been hired to teach classes of first year students. The class she had been given didn't have any computers, however, so she had asked me to help her set it up. I was more than happy to help. I may not be a tech-head, but I had been friends with Trudie long enough to have picked up on some things.

We were approaching the end of semester and I had written all my tests and assignments. So, there was not much else to do but help my friend out. And besides, I enjoyed these semi-silent walks through the bowels of my campus. As I said before, it is an old campus. Plenty of nooks and crannies. Plenty of pre-Cataclysm gems. When I walked through these dusty, ill-repaired halls, I felt like I was breathing in history.

Trudie negotiated the key into the lock of the door, still holding a load of boxes of her own. The act was difficult, and the shifting of boxes to-and-fro as Trudie tried to withdraw the keys and then aim them into the keyhole sent her hair aflutter, bangs covering and uncovering her eyes constantly. The white frills on her black dress were shaking. I always felt that Trudie overdressed for campus. I felt like I was making an effort if I had time to shower before coming up, but Trudie always went all out. Always the vampiric make-up, expertly styled hair and bubble-goth getup. The effort, while I couldn't understand how she did it every day, was impressive. Even calming. It was a constant. And while Trudie's unwanted nurturing may put me off, this more gothic style and dark humour always brought me back and reminded me why we were friends. Eccentricity attracts.

Finally, Trudie's efforts were rewarded by a click and creak as the old wooden door opened.

"I hope there's a network port here," Trudie muttered, entering the room with me in tow.

"I'd be surprised if it even has a power port."

Trudie bent down to look under a desk – a thick, dark wooden antique.

"Has a power port…but it is ancient. Nobody uses these types of plugs anymore."

I put down my baggage and cricked my back, relieved to be done with the heavy lifting. My fighting gimmick was agility. While, not to brag, I am strong, nobody likes lugging multiple computers across campus and up Athena knows how many stairs.

"So, what you gonna do? Contact ICTS?"

ICTS, or Information and Communication Technology Service, was the on-campus support department. They handled everything technological. Setting up computers, handling network ports, repairing and upgrading plug-points…everything. At least in theory. In reality, they were so bound up in self-imposed red-tape that they did nothing. If Trudie had to go through them, then her class would need to be taught how to code using a blackboard.

"No need to make a deal with demons," Trudie said, taking out what looked to be scrap-metal out of her toolbox. "I came prepared."

The scrap-metal was, in fact, a semi-ancient three-prong plug. Trudie had troves of old computer parts. Her grandfather had been a big tech-head too pre-Cataclysm.

"Get some of the cables out. We'll replace the heads. Just like old times."

I smiled. In high school, we did a lot of plug replacements and tinkering with old consoles, so they could work with new magi-tech plug points and paraphernalia. Spent many nights playing old pre-Cataclysm games. Sure, the new games were good, but there was always something about returning to the classics. I hadn't had much time for video games in the last few years. I'm not sure I'd enjoy them quite as much. May seem dull compared to my usual daily activities.

Doing this with Trudie was nostalgic nonetheless. I opened the box full of power cords and tossed some to Trudie, who caught them and then sat cross legged on the floor. I joined her with my own cables. Trudie drew a blade out of her toolbox and began cutting at the rubber wire coating by the plug.

"Knives aren't allowed on campus," I said with a grin. No weapons were. Strictly a weapon-free campus. Decades ago, they'd even tried to ban mages from attending due to them being human weapons and all. The Mages Union threw a fit and alumni funding of and donations to the university plummeted. So, while us husks couldn't carry around even a sachet of demanzite (I did anyway), sorcerers were more than capable of wrecking the place with fireballs, arc-lightning and anything else their narcissistic little minds could conjure. Well, I'm being unfair. Pranish is a sorcerer and one of my best friends. But he's different. More a wizard than a sorcerer. Says wizardry is more earnest, more respectable. It isn't just some arbitrary acquisition of power. It requires study. Hard work. Despite that, his family still saw him as a disappointment. I didn't like Pranish's family.

Trudie passed the knife to me and I began cutting the cables, careful to avoid my fingers. I had enough calluses and scars from my early hunting days already. Trudie opened the ancient three-prong plug and started connecting the internal wires of the power-cables to the plug. I kept on cutting, much more adept with a knife than allocating wires to their conductors.

Trudie and I were silent. Not an awkward silence. A silence because there was nothing that needed to be said. A comfortable, homely silence. But it did allow me to sink once more into reverie and I felt Treth's presence, distant, as if a shadow behind a wall of fog. If I focused hard enough, I could swear I could hear him breathing. Did he have to breathe, wherever he was? Or was it a habit? An artefact of when he was human and when he was alive…

"How you been doing, Kat?" Trudie asked, finished with one plug and moving onto the next.

"Fine," I lied, or was it a lie? I was fine-ish. Had my health and I'm sure that Conrad will have some jobs for me soon. Else, I'll force myself out of this funk and back to finding work for myself. And Treth may stop giving me the silent treatment then – or at least I'll cave and speak to him first.

Trudie nodded. Seemed she believed me, or at least chose to believe me.

There was silence again. This time, it was awkward. I finished stripping another cable and passed it to Trudie. She accepted it but paused.

"I'm sorry about how I've been acting these past months."

I raised my eyebrow and opened my mouth to reply. Trudie continued.

"Shouldn't have tried to hook you up with Andy – especially on the spot like that."

Oh, so that's what this is about.

"It's fine," I said. "Andy's cool. He was pretty chill about the whole thing."

"He is cool but doesn't excuse what I did. Was inappropriate."

I put my arm around my friend and squeezed her shoulder.

"It's fine, Trudie. Really."

She opened her mouth, and then closed it. I let go and we got back to work. One more cable to go, I cut off its plug and stripped the end. Passed it to Trudie, who started connecting it.

"Despite my behaviour," Trudie said, a mischievous grin spreading across her face. "Andy actually is interested in you."

I felt my face heat up. Didn't know why. Trudie burst out laughing. Still embarrassed, I joined her and we laughed together.

Ding. Ding. Ding. Ding. A shrill siren. The fire alarm.

"Prank or drill?" Trudie rolled her eyes.

I grinned, but then my expression straightened. As the alarm blared, I felt a rising unease in my gut. Trudie stood up and stretched, ready to evacuate the building. Before I knew it, I was blocking the doorway. My chest was tight. Stomach doing jumping jacks. Something was up. I'd never felt this way about the usual pranks and drills before.

"Kat?" Trudie asked. My expression must have been an open book, as her grin turned to a frown. "What is it?"

"I'll take a look. Wait here."

I turned and stopped as I felt her hand on my shoulder.

"Don't do anything stupid."

I gave her a weak grin but didn't reply.

The classroom didn't have any useful windows. Just a useless one overlooking a tiny dark atrium filled with bird droppings and ventilation systems. The window across the hall, however, had a clear sight of the campus. I couldn't hear anything from the outside due to the fire alarm. The clanging of the old metal bell and the incessant screech of the newer siren blocked out the usual ambient chatter one could normally hear rising from outside the campus buildings.

White light flooded into the building from the window. It was cloudy. Approaching winter in earnest. I still couldn't hear anything or see anything but the building opposite this one. I hesitantly walked forward, keeping myself low. I grasped for a sword that wasn't there but felt that Trudie's knife was still in my hand. It was a short, stubby thing. It was designed for stripping wiring, not cutting undead. But its hard handle within my grip granted me a bit of comfort.

I finally brought myself to the window and gazed at the footpaths and campus road below.

Empty.

"Kat," Treth finally spoke. "Look to the right."

I did so, and my heart skipped a beat.

Zombies. Tens, no, hundreds of them. A mosh pit of discoloured flesh and bloodied clothes tearing across the campus. They covered Jammie plaza, where they were pouring out of several trucks. One of the trucks had been overturned as the zombies within became too eager in transit, and tipped it off balance, then spilling out like rotting carcasses with teeth and a huge appetite.

"Shit!"

How could this happen? What were they doing here? Where was Puretide? Drakenbane? Campus security for Rifts-sake?

I saw a shambling man wearing the white and red of campus security and got my answer. They wouldn't have been any help anyway. This was a weapon-free campus, after all. Security didn't even have batons. Useless.

"What is it?" Trudie asked, still in the classroom.

"Undead."

Trudie gasped. "How?"

"I don't…"

I looked closer at the horde. Bespeckled within the motley crowd of rotting zombies were yellow-brown skinned creatures, with pipes leading in and out of their stomachs and up where their jaw used to be.

I recognised these creatures, and I knew their creators.

Jeremiah Cox and his damn *friends*. His abhorrent. He had reappeared and brought with him the army he had hid in the slums. But why here?

I felt that Treth knew the answer as I figured it out for myself. I felt a pang. Guilt? Maybe. Fear? Maybe. What I did know, was that I felt sick.

There were consequences for every action. You become a hero, and you attract villains. You destroy a man's work and he comes to destroy you. Tit-for-tat. Every good thing is repaid in kind, with something much more sinister. I bit down on my bottom lip. Trudie was speaking to me but I couldn't hear her. All I knew was that I had brought this upon my campus. I had threatened my friends. Why?

I clenched my fists, my one hand still on the knife. Trudie noticed and stepped back a bit.

Jeremiah would be on campus. This was a coordinated attack. He would need to be near his troops to direct them. And I got the feeling that Jeremiah wanted me alive. He would want to speak to me. He was the type. The typical villain, obsessed with the poetry of outlining his strategy to the hero. But he'd be more careful this time. He wouldn't give me the chance to escape. He'd be quicker if he caught me. He would gloat a bit, and then slit my throat.

I wouldn't give him the chance!

"Please…" Trudie said, almost a whimper. Unbecoming of a girl I respected. I turned. She recoiled at my expression. I had no way of knowing what she saw, but I guessed that she saw rage. Unbridled hatred. I no longer felt the fear. Jeremiah had come to my domain! I'd make him pay.

Trudie was crying, covering her mouth. Her mascara was running, creating black streaks across her face and proper skin coloured streaks through her white makeup.

I turned to walk away but stopped. I looked at my friend. Why was I doing this? It hurt her. It hurt my friend to see me go, and possibly never come back. Why then did I do it? Was it the hate that I had told Treth about? Was it an impulsive arrogance that led me to believe that I couldn't truly die? Was it simple thrill-seeking? Or was it, as Treth had told me, love?

"Please...don't go..." Trudie said, quietly, her voice breaking.

I looked out the window. The horde was spreading, chasing down students. Tearing them apart. Consuming them like the tide consumes the beach. Rage boiled up, but then stilled. Cooled. I looked again at Trudie, and I knew why.

"I'm sorry, Trudie. I have to."

I heard her sobs as I rounded the corner and descended the stairs. I felt a pang of guilt, but an even stronger feeling overwhelmed it. I understood now. It wasn't just hate. There were people I needed to protect. Not just Pranish and Andy, somewhere on this now besieged campus, but

Trudie, who would eventually be found by the zombies if I didn't eliminate their master. I couldn't protect Trudie if the zombies stormed the building, but I could eliminate the source of the danger. I could kill Jeremiah Cox.

The decision lifted a weight off my soul. I knew what I had to do, and why.

"Treth," I said.

"Yes?"

"Welcome back."

He nodded.

"Tough fight ahead. Under-armed. Civilians everywhere. Abhorrent right ahead of you."

I skidded to a halt. The jawless creature stared at me with its eyes of hate, arms twitching uncontrollably, held up like a raptor's. It blocked the exit, a glass door.

"Tips?" I asked, gripping Trudie's knife as if it was my sword. The abhorrent trudged forward, hesitant. They were smarter than zombies. It was sizing me up. Probably trying to figure out if I was the target meant to be brought back alive.

My eyes scanned the hall. Needed a better weapon. Something longer, heavier. Or something red and heavy that shot out foam…

The abhorrent roared forward just as I darted to the side. I smelt its rot as it passed me. Without his freezers, Jeremiah's army had taken on the usual stench. In a way, it made me feel alive. I said that you shouldn't grow used to the stench of rotting corpses. I hope you heed it, despite my hypocrisy. It really is good advice – even if I don't follow it myself.

I grabbed the fire extinguisher on the wall. Much heavier than my usual weapons. The abhorrent skidded and swiped a clawed hand towards me, fingers as long and as sharp as steak knives. I ducked just in time, dropping the extinguisher. The abhorrent pounced and I responded by pushing my back into it, using its momentum to drive it into the wall behind me. I used the respite of it being dazed to pick up the fire extinguisher and drove it into the creature's head. Again, and again, and again. With every blow, the resistance of its skull against my bludgeoning lessened. Until, only a bloody pulp remained. Black blood stained the wall. Cleaning staff, if any were still alive, weren't going to have a nice time.

I dropped the extinguisher and panted. I had dropped Trudie's knife and picked it up. It was a folding blade and I put it in my pocket. It wouldn't be the best, but any knife was better than no knife.

"How do we proceed?" Treth asked.

"Find Jeremiah…" I panted a bit more. "And put him down."

"I advise a stealthy approach. Even if you were fully armed, this many undead is too much for even us to handle."

I nodded.

"Keep to the shadows, keep quiet, engage only when necessary and…find Jeremiah Cox."

I felt some satisfaction emanate from Treth. A feeling of pride. Did he sense my epiphany? Was he speaking to me now not because of the situation but because he sensed that I had realised the real reason why I fought? There was still much I needed to learn about our connection.

"Let's get going," I said, and proceeded towards the door.

Fortunately, the zombie horde were still a way off. This abhorrent was an outlier. A wanderer or scout. I sniffed. Smelled burning. Some mages were firing streams of flames at the zombies, roasting them. Despite my disdain for sorcerers, I felt an intense gratitude for them now.

Hopefully, Pranish and Andy would be with some powerful mages. Maybe, Pranish wouldn't need it. He was a weak sorcerer, but an adept wizard. If given enough warning, he may be able to craft some totems and scrolls just in time to use them. He may even have some memorised combat incantations on hand, but I doubted that. Memorising combat spells was bad for the psyche. Pranish would need to rely on the thick walls of the library and hastily created wards. That left Andy, but I had a feeling that he would be safe. Nothing concrete. Just a hunch. He seemed capable.

The cacophony outside was unlike any of my normal hunts. The roars, growls, gurgles and groans of the writhing horde were deafening and what I could hear over them were the shrill and gut-wrenching screams of living people. I hoped it wasn't anyone I knew.

"Where would Jeremiah be?"

"Necromancers, wizards and sorcerer varieties, prefer central locations to direct their armies. Let's them channel equally to the entire horde."

"So, Jammie Hall?" I was referring to the Greco-Roman style main hall on campus, at the top of the stairs leading up from the plaza. The plaza now covered in zombies.

"Probably," Treth replied. "But best take an indirect route."

A good idea. A horde of zombies was still shambling around the plaza and up the stairs to Jammie Hall. They were idling. Not usual zombie behaviour. There was a reason they were there. It further confirmed my suspicions. Jeremiah was in the hall.

I looked both ways for zombies. None too close. Then I bolted across the road to an alley on the other side. Then through the alley, over ventilation boxes and garbage containers. I used ivy-covered metal service stairs that I had always seen during my time at UCT, but never used. They brought me to the upper levels of the campus, where I saw zombies and abhorrent killing my fellow students.

I gritted my teeth and went past them.

"There's nothing we could have done." Treth told me. I didn't truly believe him, and I doubted he believed it himself. We went past all the same, using the students as decoys. I couldn't help but think about it that way. Was there anything I could have done? Anything at all? I had to tell myself, "No, they're dead already."

I snuck forward, gritting my teeth and clenching my fists. I may have established that rage was not the reason I fought, but I was angry anyway. And perhaps it was good that I was angry. If I wasn't angry, I may have keeled over and wept.

Suddenly, gunshots rang out. The zombies heads snapped up, their maws covered in red and their hands clutching mounds of flesh. I didn't hesitate and dove for cover behind some bins. I didn't hear the zombies stand or rustle towards me. Food was more important than loud noises, after all.

"Agencies must have arrived," Treth said. I nodded. He was probably right. Only agencies were armed and would be coming into this quagmire. Best rendezvous with them. Could get reinforcements. Hopefully, they'd listen to me.

More gunshots rang out. Some heavy shotgun fire and the ratatat of machine pistols. They were coming from the next level. Made sense. There was a parking lot there. If the agencies were coming in to collect bounties and security contract work, they'd need to park there. Otherwise, they'd have to run up the hill, lugging equipment and facing a mob of undead on higher ground.

I found a service ladder and ascended it to the next level. I peeked my head over the lip and saw a mosh pit of zombies surrounding the familiar figures of Brett, Guy and an unknown Drakenbane mage bearing a caduceus crest on a white and blue robe, indicating that she was a healer. They were ringed by zombies, charging mindlessly into their gunfire. Rank by rank fell, but there were too many, from too many angles. The three were being pressed into a corner. They wouldn't be able to last much longer.

I lifted myself up over the edge and scanned my surroundings. A discarded rod of wrought iron was shoved into the soil near some dead flowers. Good enough.

I picked up the metal as I ran, drawing Trudie's knife and flicking it open. One zombie fell, my knife skewering its forehead as I pulled it back and plunged the blade into its head. Blackened blood spilled out of the wound like jelly. I caught another zombie, attempting to bite me, with the iron rod. It bit down and shattered its mutated sharp teeth. I stabbed it in the eye and it stopped writhing, falling limply off its would-be metal meal.

The gunfire was deafening. I'd need to check in to a healer to repair my ears. Didn't want to get tinnitus. More zombies were coming. I dashed back to the edge of the parking lot, with the steep drop beside it, and then dodged at the last moment. Three zombies went barrelling over the edge. The sound of their groans lessened in volume but didn't change. Zombies didn't have any sense of self-preservation. They wouldn't even register the ground rushing up towards them.

One zombie corrected its footing and lunged at me. I smacked it across the cheek with the rod and then kicked it over the edge to join its friends.

More zombies still surrounded the Drakenbane agents. They had their backs to a black SUV. An SUV with one zombie on top of it, which they hadn't noticed.

I charged, rounding around the mob and avoiding their grasps. Jumped onto a car, and then leapt to another. The zombie was just about to pounce when I collided into it, knocking it to the ground. Brett recoiled as I drove the rod into the zombie's head.

"Katty! I owe you one."

I grunted and unsheathed the rod from the corpse, then driving it down the throat of another assailant. The healer mage was chanting, eyes closed and stroking her arm. It was covered in scars the shape of ancient runes. Memorising spells was a strain. Like a boil trying to pop in your brain. To avoid that strain, mages kept spells on hand, so they could incant without the need for memorisation. Very important spells were written as more permanent reminders. I felt a power rising in her voice as she chanted, and then, with a crescendo, she finished the incantation and opened her eyes. A wave of golden light was let forth and the zombies in the immediate vicinity slumped. Truly dead.

Repel undead. A powerful purification spell. It tore the dark talon of necromancy away from an animated corpse. Unfortunately, the corpses could be reanimated again. One needed to destroy the corpse to give it a respectful send-off, free from corruption.

"Katty, didn't expect to see you up here," Brett said, trying not to pant.

"This is my campus."

"Oh right. Sorry."

Guy lit a cigarette and checked over his machine pistols. "We've got our work cut out for us. Kat, how many are there deeper in?"

"Hundreds. Maybe thousands. Jeremiah has been hiding zombies in the slums for months."

"This is Jeremiah's work? The Purity?" Brett asked, lighting his own cigarette. I noticed his hands shake, just a bit.

I nodded. "I recognised his abhorrent. The piped bastards."

The three nodded. I had seen Brett at the ice cream factory, but the others could have also been there.

"Do you have a plan?" I asked.

They shook their heads. "Thought this was a typical call-out. Didn't know it was this big. Puretide hasn't even arrived yet. We're probably the only agents here."

"Shit." Wasn't good enough. I doubted that even the combined might of Puretide and Drakenbane could stem this tide of undeath.

"Why are they here?" the mage asked.

I hesitated and then replied, "I think it's revenge. Jeremiah, the Purity, wants to punish me for ruining his plans."

"Do you think he's here?" Brett asked. He was serious now. Work mode.

I nodded. "Definitely. Tre…I think he's in Jammie Hall. He'll be directing them. Perhaps even turning the hall into his new lair."

"Dumb shit. He'll be put down when the bulk of our forces get here."

"And how long will that be?"

None of them answered.

"I can't let any more people die. I'm going in and putting him down."

The three, especially the healer, squirmed. They were monster hunters. Seldom were they ever expected to kill a human. Sure, necromancers were basically monsters, but they were still human. I doubted that Guy, Brett or this mage had ever killed a human. Neither had I, but if that's what it took to save people, I'd do it.

"What's your plan?" Guy finally asked.

"Going through the back entrance to Jammie Hall, avoiding undead, and then killing the necromancer."

"You're gonna need this." Brett handed me a bowie knife, 24cm long. The Drakenbane insignia was emblazoned on the blade.

"Thanks." I accepted it and pocketed Trudie's knife.

"We'll help," the mage said.

"Can't let you take the entire bounty," Guy grinned, tossing his cigarette to the ground.

"Okay, Katty. Lead the way."

***

With the Drakenbane firepower alongside me, I was able to take a more direct route to Jammie Hall. There was so much noise on campus, that a few extra gunshots didn't attract undue attention. Countless undead out of the way, we arrived within sight of the hall.

"So many abhorrent…" Guy commented.

"There were more at his old lair. These are the dregs," I replied.

Abhorrent, naked, castrated, mutilated and carrying blades and clubs, surrounded the back entrance to the hall. They were twitching, shaking as if having a seizure. I got the brief thought that they must be in excruciating pain. Another, even worse, thought arose. Were the living victims trapped in these flesh puppet bodies? Were they conscious slaves to Jeremiah's whims? I shook the thought away. It was too unpleasant to bear. Regardless, it wouldn't change my actions. If the abhorrent were sentient, then putting them down was a mercy.

The four of us returned to our cover, a car parked twenty meters from the back entrance of the hall.

"We can't go in guns blazing. Too many zoms out front and it'll tip Jeremiah off," I said.

"How else we going to get in, then?"

"I'll go. Silent. You create a distraction."

"Kat…"

I put up my hand to silence Brett. "None of you know how to fight undead silently. Only I do."

They couldn't argue. It was true. Drakenbane was loud. Guns blazing. Even the mage had to incant out loud and it was obvious that her magic reserves were running low. She had dark marks underneath her eyes. She had even puked a little when she thought we weren't looking.

"Set up in a nearby building. Open fire when you're ready and draw the horde away. I'll find a way to sneak in unnoticed. Then…I'll put a stop to this."

They hesitated, but then nodded. Brett looked reluctant. He must have known what I was going to do. They all did. None of them liked it. But they knew it had to be done. Finally, he stood up and went with the crew. I was alone, again. Well, not alone.

"You ready for this, Kat?" Treth asked.

I gulped and nodded.

"He's a person," Treth reminded me. Why? This was hard enough as is.

"Barely." I said, stoically. I believed it, but why then did I still feel bile rising in my stomach?

Treth nodded. Hard to argue. He agreed with me.

"Don't hesitate when you're in there. Not for a second. End him, and this all ends."

"I know." No hesitation. Couldn't even risk asking about the cloaked figure. Couldn't give him time to speak. A speaking mage was a dangerous mage. I covered my mouth with my fist just in case the bile rose any further. I hoped Treth thought I was just in thought.

I scaled a ladder to the next level, overlooking the back-entrance. Didn't need a door to get in. I may be taller than Trudie, but I'm still small enough to fit through a window. I found such a window, clouded with dust and grime, and then waited for the Drakenbane gunfire.

Bangs. Again, and again. The horde roared, and I heard a stampede of feet. I hoped that they held up. They'd only need to for just a bit. Jeremiah was maintaining strict control over his zombies. Once he was dead, they'd all de-animate. That was the cost of control over the undead. If you wanted them to do as you willed, then you had to reanimate them as slaves feeding constantly off your power. It was costly business. It drove men insane. Even if the dark magic didn't corrupt the necromancer's soul, the strain of maintaining such an army would surely drive him mad. Not even the strongest, finest men could remain so after using necromancy. It was impossible.

I opened the window and was relieved that it didn't screech. The other side looked clear. Brett's knife in my hand, I negotiated my way through the window, falling with a thud on the other side.

It was quieter inside, among the dust and abandoned spare chairs of the storeroom behind the hall proper. The gunshots and stampede were muffled. Deeper in, I heard the twisted sound of dark incantation. The words sounded as close to pure evil as one could get. It made me want to scream at my post-modernist lecturers who rejected that evil was a thing. They hadn't seen darkness, until today, and they hadn't heard its incomprehensible and undeniably malevolent sound. Those who doubt the existence of evil should only listen to the ancient words of power of the darkest magics. It was no wonder that dark magic could only corrupt. Even without its use, how could anyone studying such a discipline remain pure?

Jeremiah lay further into the building. Probably in the main hall itself. Probably surrounded by his abhorrent.

No hesitation, I reminded myself. Not even stopping to fight his guards. No point stopping to fight them. He was the target. End him, end them all.

I took a deep but quiet breath. I looked at my hands. Brett's knife in the one, Trudie's knife in the other. They were shaking.

"You can leave, Kat. You can climb through that window and run."

I shook my head and whispered. "No, I can't."

I felt a wave of pride wash over me. I had given the correct answer.

The back room of the hall was dark, besides the little bit of lighting coming through the fogged-up windows. I wished I had my face-mask to keep the dust out. Thinking about that, I wished I had my face-mask to keep the necro-blood out. Would definitely need to seek medical attention after this. If there was an after this.

The wood creaked underneath my sneakers. It was an old building. Everything in it creaked. The incantations didn't stop. Jeremiah was focused on his spells. I wish I knew what he was trying to cast. But then again, I didn't. Knowing what he was casting would expose me to the dark magic itself. Couldn't learn about evil without becoming at least a little bit evil.

The incanting became louder as I went further and further into the building. My skin started to crawl, and I wanted to be sick. The words were of malice. Of sick arrogance. They were the words of a man who thought himself God. And yet how could I know this? To me, it sounded like mindless gibberish and retching. But there was an essence of lore hidden in the speech. A power that overcomes language and comprehension. A natural language that spoke to the soul. If smoke meant fire, then these incantations meant pure and utter evil.

And then, I saw him.

He was as I had seen him before. Cloaked in black. He had a black dagger clipped to his belt. His hands were held towards the roof. His words were growing in volume, approaching a crescendo. He stood in the centre of a runic circle, drawn onto the wood with red, fresh blood. Corpses of students and staff lay to one side. Encircling him were abhorrent, wearing metal breastplates of dark, crude iron. Their hands had been replaced with all manner of blades, straight from a kitchen. Steak knife blades, cleavers, serrated bread knives and even a hand filled with crudely sharpened butter knives. None had noticed me.

"No openings," Treth said.

He was right. An abhorrent was watching every angle. Their angry eyes, with black pupils darting back and forth in milky white seas. Their bodies twitching. If only I could free them and have them fight alongside me. But I was no mage. I only had my blades. My blades and the will to use them.

20 metres.

I went forward. There was only one way. The gunfire outside was abating. Zombies may even be by Trudie's building by now. I was running out of time. No more prudence. It wasn't my style.

15 metres.

An abhorrent noticed me, and then I ran forward. Full blast, blades forward. I ducked as a scythe cut the space above my head. Abhorrent charged me and I kept running. Faster, faster, ducking under blades, rolling from stabs and charges. My ribbon was cut out and my hair fell loosely. I could still see as my momentum kept the hair out of my eyes.

10 metres.

Jeremiah noticed me and shouted incomprehensibly. Zombies tore into the room. I didn't stop. An abhorrent nicked me with its blade. I didn't stop.

5 metres.

Brett's blade in front of me, ready to stab. Jeremiah held up a totem and it disintegrated as he activated it. Sheer power knocked Brett's knife out of my hands.

I barrelled into Jeremiah, knocking the wind out of him. The undead surrounded us. I had Trudie's knife in my hand.

No hesitation.

The blade didn't sink in easily. It took one blow, and then another, and then another. With both hands, I pushed the little blade into Jeremiah's head, until it squelched, and then I brought it up, and plunged it again. Again. Again. Again…

I didn't notice that I was crying as I lifted the now dulled blade in and out of the necromancer's skull. I barely noted that all the walking corpses had slumped over. They were free.

At the back of my head, I also kicked myself. I hadn't interrogated him about the cloaked figure. It was still a mystery. But I knew I wouldn't be able to. Still, it was a pity. But in my conscious thoughts, none of this mattered. I finally let go of the blade, letting it clatter onto the floor next to the lifeless, black-robed man. Blood. Human blood, covered my hands, my knees, his face.

He was human. Jeremiah. A human with a dark soul, but a human all the same.

And I had killed him.

I turned away, and I heaved. Vomit followed, and I expelled everything I could. And I realised then that I was always heading down this path. Not after meeting Treth, but before. I had been heading down this road after, by some sick twist of fate, an evil man abducted me and my parents. And I swore revenge. Was this the destiny that Treth had alluded to? Blood covering my hands, vomit pooling on the floor? Was this my fate, to slay more than the undead, but those like me?

"You understand now, don't you?" Treth said.

I looked at the man I had killed and retched again.

"It isn't enough that they are monsters as well as men. It doesn't matter how much we hate them. It hurts."

"Does it ever stop hurting?" I sobbed, retched again. Only a bit of bile came out.

I felt Treth shake his head.

"I once fought for hate, Kat. Like you. I fought for vengeance. For rage. For simple revenge. It ultimately destroyed me."

I tried to stand, but my body didn't obey. I couldn't move.

Treth sighed. "Perhaps, I was drawn to you because we are so alike. Earnest. Angry. Tied together through macabre accidents. Maybe, my purpose in being fettered to you is to warn you off my fatal path. But maybe not. I think I cannot take you off this path. Your destiny. It is both of our natures to destroy everything. Our enemies, our friends and ourselves. Maybe, we were put together because misery loves company. Or maybe: there is no reason at all."

My vision blurred through my tears and exhaustion. I felt vomit coating my mouth and chin. My stomach stung.

"Perhaps, we are meant to walk this path of destruction. We are meant to doom ourselves for something greater. A chance at redemption and absolution from the darkness. Perhaps, we are meant to hurt ourselves – because it is the only way."

Treth shook his head again.

"I don't know. But what I do know, is that we are together in this. One body, two souls, staring down the abyss of chaos. And if we continue to walk the same path together, we may save more than just the light. We may save each other."

I blinked the tears out of my eyes and wiped my mouth, then stood. My body shook. Trudie's knife was still on the ground, covered with blood. I don't think she'd want it back.

"Let's go, Treth," I said, and then turned my back on the scene I knew I'd have to see many times again before the end.

Chapter 21.   Beginnings

Only twenty-two students were killed. Ten security guards. Three academic staff members. Nobody I knew personally. The campus had been mercifully empty. Study break before exams. Late time of day. Most of the people still on campus had managed to barricade themselves inside their offices and study rooms, until surviving security and clean-up crews dug them out.

As I had predicted, Jeremiah had been maintaining total control over his entire horde. When he died, all the zombies and abhorrent de-animated, crumpling to the floor like unattended puppets. I wonder if Jeremiah would have noticed the irony if he was alive? If he had not been so obsessed with power and control, he could have manifested an independent spirit into his undead and let them loose upon the living. Thankfully, his need to control won out. But, perhaps that didn't matter to him. Now that he was dead, why should he care about the fate of his horde?

Campus was closed, and exams moved to an external venue while Sanitation cleaned up all the corpses, bloodstains, and necromantic ritual sites. Only then could the more mundane cleaners pick up all the shattered glass, splintered doors, broken furniture and other assorted debris from the siege of UCT.

No one openly blamed me for the attack. Neither did anyone thank me for putting a stop to it. Best I got was a nod of approval from the Drakenbane bunch. The cops who picked me up for murder weren't that impressed. Just shocked and a bit revolted. I'm not sure if by the undead, by the blood and vomit, or the state of Jeremiah's face. But that's a story for another time.

For now, it's just important to know that I wasn't openly blamed for aggravating Jeremiah and causing the attack, but a lot of people thought it. I couldn't blame them. I was one of them. I had kicked a hornet's nest, and those hornets had killed thirty-five people.

I would live with that knowledge forever.

After Jeremiah's death, the rise of lesser undead stopped. North-Road no longer reported any zombie sightings and the slums were back down to their usual level of undead related incidents. That at least solved one mystery. Jeremiah had been hiding his zombie hordes in the slums, letting them feed to sustain themselves. Didn't count on anyone caring about the poor. So much for equality.

But there was still one mystery that was unsolved: the cloaked figure.

Who were they? What were they? And what did they want?

Perhaps, Jeremiah had the answer. Perhaps not. It didn't matter. His face looked like cherry sorbet roundabout now. In no position to give me an answer.

Even without Jeremiah, I still had a feeling I hadn't seen the last of the cloaked figure. I stayed away from the North-Road when I could help it. While I wanted to know more about this shadowy character, I also still had nightmares about them. I still saw them standing underneath the dim streetlight, and still felt the coal in my veins.

I needed to know more about them, but I also didn't want to face them ever again. But I somehow knew that wasn't my choice.

Treth speaks about destiny. I scoff at it. But it's not purely because of my disdain for superstition. The reason I disliked the notion of destiny was also why I still studied. I didn't like the idea that I couldn't change. I didn't like the idea of the set path. Of fate. If I kept on studying, I at least believed I could change. I could step off the path to darkness. I could be happy living a life of peace.

But I know that's not possible. It's a vain effort holding onto a life of normalcy when one lives a life of paranormality. And it is impossible to be innocent ever again when you've taken the life of another, and been stained with as much blood as I.

But, I'm still studying. And, I'm still monster hunting (much to the public prosecutor's displeasure, you'll soon learn). I keep doing both, fighting against destiny while rushing towards it. Towards another slain zombie, another impaled vampire and another necromancer, lying in a puddle of his own blood, with my knife in his face.

Afterword

When I first decided to write about Kat Drummond, I had a simple idea. I wanted a straightforward storyline about a university student turned monster hunter. It was meant to be a short project to provide some variety to my fledgeling writing career.

Oh boy, was I wrong.

In the last year of writing this series, Kat has become an inseparable part of my life. I live and breathe Hope City and Post-Cataclysm Earth, even developing a tabletop RPG to run games set in the world. And, in many ways, Kat has become a very good friend (which makes me a terrible friend for what I do to her).

Spending the end of 2018 and the vast majority of 2019 writing Kat Drummond has been an amazing experience. I'm in love with my characters and my universe, and I hope you fall in love with them just as much as I did.

Acknowledgements

While books are (often) the work of a single person, they take a veritable organisation to produce. I'm an independent author because I value my freedom and am sceptical of the traditional publishing industry. While this makes some aspects of my business easier, it also means that I lack a certain connection to an institution. Succinctly: this is a lonely career.

But there are people in my life who have helped me along and have been integral to the creation of this book and series.

It takes a lot of patience to write six books before releasing a single one, and without the feedback and conversation of my beta readers, Tyler Sudweeks and Chelsea Murphy, I would have gone insane a long time ago. Thank you!

I would also like to thank my mother for providing her editing skills to get these books into a condition fit for human consumption, and for being someone I can always natter to about Kat, Hope City and necromancy.

Thank you to Deranged Doctor Design for the wonderful cover art. I advise them to any author looking for a professional design.

And finally: thank you. Without you, this book would not be read and enjoyed. Without you, these words are just the scribblings of a half-mad author.

So, thank you!

And until next time.

Nicholas Woode-Smith is a full-time fantasy and science fiction author from Cape Town, South Africa. He has a degree in philosophy and economic history from the University of Cape Town. In his off-time, he plays PC strategy games, Magic: The Gathering, and Dungeons & Dragons.

Follow him on Facebook:

https://www.facebook.com/nickwoodesmith/